Praise fo
Gretch

T0030761

"[*The Book Haters' Book Club* ...
Once again, Anthony has created a cast of lovable characters and
set them loose in a propulsive, humorous, and heartwarming story.
This is her best novel yet."
—**J. Ryan Stradal**, *New York Times* bestselling author
of *Saturday Night at the Lakeside Supper Club*

"This sparkling novel starts with high energy and unique characters
that move from one surprise to another all the way to the final pages."
—**Ann Garvin**, *USA TODAY* bestselling author
of *There's No Coming Back from This*

"*Evergreen Tidings from the Baumgartners* hits all the right notes;
you'll double over with laughter, but you'll also find yourself at times
misty-eyed and introspective."
—**Kristin Harmel**, #1 internationally bestselling author
of *The Book of Lost Names*

"Sparkling... Anthony includes a slew of real recommendations
sourced from her own friends, bookstore employees, and librarians,
giving readers a chance to head off on their own paths."
—**Booklist**

"*The Kids Are Gonna Ask* is a touching, wonderful novel
about the discoveries we make when the simplest questions
spark the most complicated answers."
—**Abbi Waxman**, *USA TODAY* bestselling author
of *The Bookish Life of Nina Hill*

"Anthony's debut successfully mixes realistic emotional responses
to big life events with a sense of humor, preventing any single
character from becoming a victim or villain."
—**Library Journal**, starred review

"*The Kids Are Gonna Ask* is a smart, engaging send-up of our
modern age wrapped up in a story too delicious to put down."
—**Kelly Harms**, *USA TODAY* bestselling author
of *The Overdue Life of Amy Byler*

TIRED LADIES TAKE A STAND

GRETCHEN ANTHONY

PARK
ROW
BOOKS

PARK
ROW
BOOKS™

Recycling programs
for this product may
not exist in your area.

ISBN-13: 978-0-7783-0796-9

Tired Ladies Take a Stand

Park Row Books
22 Adelaide St. West, 41st Floor
Toronto, Ontario M5H 4E3, Canada
ParkRowBooks.com
BookClubbish.com

Printed in U.S.A.

To Chad

Thanks for that ride to the airport.
What a trip.

All Aboard the Yes Train

From *Smart Girls Say Yes*
by Fern McAllister

The first bed I ever bought myself belonged to a dead person. I don't know if they died on it. What I do know is that I paid thirty dollars for the mattress and box spring set at an estate sale in Davis, California. The springs groaned, and the quilted cover was purple, except for a faded ghostly patch shaped like a body in the middle.

Convincing myself that was the comfy spot, I stuffed my cash into the estate agent's hand.

This was fall 1995, and I was a first-year graduate student living on $1,000 a month. My single secretarial-salaried mother believed in the power of education, but she'd already contributed all that she could financially by buying my plane ticket from Milwaukee to Sacramento.

Of my monthly teaching assistant stipend, I paid $350 rent and put $50 toward the interest on my undergraduate loans. I didn't eat much, since "skeletal" was the '90s woman's ideal body shape. But weekends equaled beer, and cheap beer was for undergraduates. We drank craft. When it all added up, I could either snag this "grandma died, let's sell her stuff" garage sale bargain, or sleep on the floor.

A year later, I began to sleep at my boyfriend's apartment, where I luxuriated in his warehouse-brand double. I liked him for other things, but the fact that his mattress didn't screech every time we did the thumpity-bumpit made "your place or mine?" a nonissue. Always his place.

We moved to San Francisco together after graduation and rented what became "our place." Until two years later when I discovered he didn't restrict his definition of "ours" to simply "me and you." There was also "mistake" and "it won't happen again." Which is how in 1999 I found myself at the Mattress Train on Market Street with my three closest friends, Andi, Emma, and Carolina.

A week earlier, I'd called Andi, who'd recently signed a new lease after breaking up with her law school boyfriend. I told her about the extra people in my bed.

She said, "Oh, my God, Fern, please come keep me company so neither one of us has to face this alone."

The apartment was on Filbert Street near Buchanan in the Marina District. I had urged her to avoid the Marina because that's where all the buildings collapsed during the 1989 earthquake. She promised me she wouldn't move to the "falling-down part," and I felt much better when she produced a US Geological map that showed nothing but bedrock beneath her house.

Soon, it was my bedrock, too.

Though the apartment was technically a one-bedroom, we made a second by converting the dining room. We permanently closed off a set of pocket doors and ordered a wire-frame garment rack from the Ikea catalog. This forced us to eat in front of the living room TV, but we ate out most days, anyhow.

As luck would have it, our friends Emma and Carolina soon moved to the Marina together following their own breakups.

Their apartment was closer to the falling-down part, though still above Divisadero. Still on bedrock.

What all this bedrock lease-signing meant was that the four of us were single, heading into what would become the summer of "Buy Me a Drink BINGO;" of joining 896 other women running up Grant Street in bridal gowns; that the actions of one man would change the lives of four women.

But those are stories for other chapters.

First, let me tell you about these friends of mine. We met each other via the usual channels—Andi and I in graduate school, Emma and Carolina and I at work. Our origin stories are boring, but these three women are anything but.

Carolina and Emma are planners and doers. The apartment they shared had real furniture and matching towels.

Besides our apartment, Andi and I shared one other thing: our antianxiety prescription. Pot and Kettle had just moved in together. Some nights, there was enough vexation ricocheting through the one-bedroom on Filbert Street to rattle its walls.

But here's where we differed. Andi suffered from what-if angst, forever expecting the world to bring the worst to bear on her life.

What if her clients lied to her?

What if MUNI derailed and made her late to court?

What if it rained, and she'd forgotten her umbrella and missed the bus, and the flooded sewers released the sprites of hell to terrorize her so thoroughly that she arrived at work looking worse than when she'd woken up?

I, on the other hand, preferred a more self-centered form of worry, an angst of the "I'm not, I can't, I'll never" variety.

I'm not as smart as the other people in the room.

I can't compete with that idea.

I'll never be as [insert adjective here] as her.

As the Anxiety Twins, Andi and I gravitated to Carolina and Emma. Carolina made us feel protected. She was all planning and action. She knew street-names and intersections. Not once did she get into a cab and tell the driver to drop her off "next to that nail salon that gave me a toenail fungus."

Emma was so empathetic it made you feel ridiculous for worrying. Nothing cures anxiety better than hearing your friend ask, "How did that presentation go? Were you able to remember the acronym for Inter-Departmental Cyclical Change Dynamics?"

So, back to that day in March 1999. I had a new address, a new neighborhood, and a new roommate. All I lacked was a mattress. And this time, I hoped to buy one dressed in its factory-original plastic.

The Mattress Train is a chain of stores, most of them overgrown warehouses with ivory walls and gray carpet. We were at the location on Market Street, empty that afternoon except for the four of us and a sales guy wearing a pair of polyester dress pants screaming "I'd rather be anywhere but here."

Whoever did the company's advertising blanketed local radio with spots featuring a wooden train whistle, the kind you find in toy stores and novelty shops. And they were always having a sale. Today was the "Spring Fling." *Toot! Toot! to savings!*

We walked in just before closing.

"If we buy a mattress, will you blow your whistle?" Carolina bounced on the display bed next to mine.

Sales Guy avoided the question by picking up the phone.

She flopped onto her side to pout. "I think he's faking that call."

"Can you blame him?" I toed the price tag at my foot. The mattress on which I lounged with my dirty Doc Martens cost $899, though a gold "Spring Fling!" applique shouted at me to Act Now and Save $200!

The thought of putting $699 on my credit card had me suddenly so frightened I wanted to cry. "I make more money than my mom ever did, and I still can't buy myself a bed."

Carolina said, "This isn't like debating whether you need another pair of shoes."

"Yesterday you told me I need a pair of strappy sandals to wear with my new wrap dress."

"You do. But you know what I'm saying."

Beautiful Emma, who was too polite to do anything but stand by quietly while we debated, planted herself next to my feet. "Find something?"

"A hole in my wallet." The fear tears crept up my throat again.

I'd just turned twenty-nine. I had a master's degree and a professional job and a corporate credit card but couldn't buy myself a place to lay my head.

No, scratch that. I could afford the pillow. On layaway.

No matter how strong your friendships are, money panic is not a communal experience, especially when you're young and single. Everyone comes to a friendship with different financial histories, hang-ups, and hookups. Yet, we tend to assume that the people with whom we laugh, play, and eat can put cash toward all the same things we do. And we make this assumption because it's only when a friend has the nerve to ask, "Can you afford this?" that the shit goes down.

Carolina said, "Ferny-bear is having a hard time convincing herself that she deserves a decent night's sleep."

"That's not true. I'm just wondering what, exactly, is inside of this thing that costs nine hundred dollars?"

Emma being Emma leaned over to examine the stitches.

Carolina being Carolina catapulted herself to standing. "Let's see what else they got. Where's Andi?"

We found her beneath a sign reading Warehouse Buys! And, of course, there was an exclamation point. Everything at the Mattress Train had one.

"Clearance section!" Carolina made for the first available display and belly flopped.

Emma planted herself carefully at the foot of a nearby bed and bounced like Tinker Bell landing on a flower petal.

I looked at Andi's face for a sign. Salary-wise, she made a lot more money than any of us. But she was also carrying about a hundred thousand in law school loans, which she'd be paying off into her forties.

Andi said, "Okay, count of three, everyone find a decent, mid-price mattress and pitch Fern on why she should buy it."

Then she looked at me and said, "You're a grown-up. You have a job. People rely on you. You need a place to sleep." Because Andi is the sort of woman who recognizes the difference between necessity and indulgence.

The three of them each found a mattress and tried to convince me why it was the *toot! toot! toot-able* best deal. I chose the one I was already sitting on. Queen-size, far less jiggly than Jell-O, and at an affordable $399.

Andi lay down next to me. "Maybe I should upgrade, too. The mattress I have is the same one I had in high school."

"That's old. We're old."

"Old enough to buy ourselves our own damn beds." This was Carolina, who launched herself onto the end. "Oooh, I like the firmness of this one."

That grabbed Emma's attention, and she migrated to the corner opposite Carolina, testing the bounce. "Yep, this is it. This one."

Carolina called toward the front of the store. "Garçon? Some help for the ladies with cash over here?"

Sales Guy wilted with every step in our direction.

Carolina said, "If we buy four of this same mattress here, how much of a discount can you give us?"

"We can't really do that. It's sticker-pricing." The guy wasn't speaking with exclamation points. Very un–Mattress Train.

"Only, I bet you can," said Carolina. "Because it's almost closing time, and you have four guaranteed sales in front of you, and everything is negotiable."

That made the already uncomfortable looking twenty-something begin to sweat.

She continued, "Three hundred each. Times four. That's a twelve-hundred-dollar sales day and it's almost closing time."

He must have known there was wiggle room in the pricing because he hadn't walked away.

"Call your manager if you need permission to deal. We'll wait."

When he turned, the rest of us let out a collective breath.

Andi said, "You're a genius."

Carolina accepted the compliment. "Why shouldn't we get a deal? Worst-case scenario, he comes back and says no."

I, however, hoped she remembered that I was currently sleeping on the couch. "What if he does say no?" To which Emma clucked sympathetically, the way she does when there's nothing particular to say but doesn't want you to feel alone.

But Carolina remained undeterred. "One step at a time, ladies."

Sales Guy hung up the phone. "I can do three-seventy-five each."

My fingertips were about to pop from the anxiety pooled in my clenched fists. Twenty-five dollars was twenty-five dollars. Especially in 1999. I willed Carolina to take it.

"I know your manager said that you can go as low as three-twenty-five." Carolina started to laugh, and I was about to wee my pants when Sales Guy did the strangest thing I'd ever seen.

He laughed back.

This may be hyperbole, but if memory serves, Carolina was by this point glowing gold she exuded so much confidence. "I'm right, aren't I? Your manager totally said, 'Stay as close to sticker price as you can but don't take anything less than three-and-a-quarter.'"

Sales Guy tried to wipe his face back to serious. "Shit. You know you're breaking me here."

"No, I'm not." She got to her knees, bouncing slightly and making the plastic crinkle. She extended a palm. "I'll say yes if you say yes."

And the next thing we knew, all four of us were handing over credit cards.

More than a decade later, that mattress resides in my guest room. No one has died on it, nor do the springs squeak. It remains my favorite spot to nap. Had my friends not surrounded me that afternoon in March, I doubt I'd have had the courage to buy it. Certainly not through negotiation.

But I said yes. Because Carolina said yes and got Sales Guy to say yes and Andi and Emma followed, each of us baptized in the power of unity. Where one could go, so could we all.

I learned several lessons that day. One of them being that grown women with grown-ass jobs need to accept their fate and prioritize bedding over beer. The other was that whether you're the president of the Menudo fan club or a sales guy at the Mattress Train, you're just as likely to end up in someone's book wearing unfortunate pants.

But the most important lesson was this: no journey is undertaken alone.

Onward, friends…

Say "yes" and turn the page.

March

Fern

Fern McAllister's pocket is vibrating again, so she pulls her phone from her pocket and peeks at it beneath the tablecloth, hoping the move looks as if she's simply fidgeting with her skirt. She's ignored the buzzing several times, presuming it's the doorbell app Mack installed that now shouts at her all day long. Because how could they possibly have survived all these years without the knowledge that the neighbor was walking her dog, or that the middle-school bus had just dropped off the kids it had been dropping off every afternoon at 3:25 p.m. since forever?

Bzzzzt.

Either the Huns have invaded the block, or someone actually needs to get ahold of her. She unlocks her screen.

"Don't even!" Carolina clocks the move and flicks her head toward the neighboring table. "You'll look like those Vitbags over there."

"Ensuring that my children haven't been horribly disfigured in a car accident isn't Vitbagging, it's parenting."

Vitbag is Carolina shorthand for Valley *shitbags*, or the six men sitting nearby, downing absinthe and digitally insulting each other.

They're on the back patio of a wine bar in San Francisco celebrating the engagement of their friend Emma's daughter, Portia. Portia is an elementary schoolteacher like her mother. Her fiancé, Lyle, does something in tech like everyone else in the Bay Area. They met as students at Cal State Sacramento and graduated last year.

The notion that Portia and Lyle are twenty-three and already signing up to spend the rest of their lives together makes Fern itch. She and her friends—Carolina, Emma, Andi, and Chandler— hadn't even met each other by that age.

Her screen lights to reveal a series of texts from her literary agent. **Got a sec?**

Fern has been a writer for twenty years. In the early 2000s, she traded corporate life for publishing hot takes in gossip magazines until she woke up one morning and looked at her husband. "If I have to write one more piece on a pseudo-celebrity sex tape, I'm going to drive an ice pick through my eyeball."

Mack didn't want her to do that. So, she got pregnant instead.

Three babies and four years later, she was twice as restless.

"There has got to be more to life than poop and *Don't Let the Pigeon Drive the Bus*." She was also in bed when she said this, only she hadn't just woken up and she wasn't talking to Mack. She had a baby attached to her boob, her husband was out of town for work, and Fern had picked up the phone to cry with the first person who answered.

It happened to be Andi.

"Why don't you go back to work, then? You never planned to stay out forever."

"Because the whole journalism industry decided to pack its bags and leave while I was busy with morning sickness and diaper changes. Nobody's hiring."

At which point Andi probably suggested Fern write a mommy blog.

But Fern didn't want to spend time reading about other people's lives. She wanted to go out and live her own.

Damn her and Mack for being so fertile.

"If you don't want to write a blog, then pitch an article."
Andi was nothing if not a solution suggester. At the time, however, she was also childless. "Find something you can do with
the kids in tow. I read an article about this woman who signed
her whole family up to manage a community garden for a summer. They spent every day out there together, helping people
manage their plots, and whatever else, I can't remember. Apparently, it was transformative."

Fern briefly tried to picture her life chasing three children
across open fields and decided Andi had lost her mind. "Let's
do this, instead. You have a baby. Then try to give me the
same advice."

Thing was, though, Andi was onto something. Because the
idea of pitching a story that she could research while also being
a mother had her head spinning most of that night.

That summer, she wrote a series of articles about entertain-
ing her children with zero-dollar activities, and it gained her a
following with *SFGate* readers. The pieces were popular mostly
because she skipped the no-brainer ideas—every parent knows
to take their kids to the beach and watch for the free days at
local museums. Fern and her kids instead spent that summer
gathering rocks with the Northern California Geological So-
ciety. They attended open rehearsals for both the San Francisco
Symphony and Opera. They learned to scrape barnacles from
the piers of Sausalito. They watched veterinarians care for injured sea lions at the Marine Mammal Center and, by pure
stroke of luck, were in the right place at the right time to witness the birth of elephant seal pups. That one generated a mixed
reaction. Her daughter was riveted. The boys were grossed out
into speechless silence.

Flash forward two decades, and she had three books under
her belt. Her first two were essay collections about parenting—
Aim at the Water! and Other Things I Tell My Boys followed by

Dress Shoe, or Dead Turtle? Both were very popular—with the tidy group of people who read them.

Her third, *Smart Girls Say Yes*, came out eight years ago.

This book, like her others, was a series of essays. But it focused on the spring and summer of 1999, when Fern, Carolina, Andi, and Emma decided they'd had enough of needy bosses and cheating boyfriends. They were twenty-nine years old with professional careers and naturally perky boobs. If there was any time to live their best lives, this was it. And it all started with a commitment to one powerful sentence, "I'll say yes if you say yes."

The book did fine, on par with the others. But after having cried, sweat, and plodded her way to achieving a hat trick of underwhelming books, she lost her mojo.

"Maybe I'm not a writer, after all." Fern remembers clearly the night she suggested to Mack that she might be ready to raise the white flag, though their now college-bound daughter was still requesting bedtime stories when the conversation took place. "I know I can write, but should I? Should I devote my life to something that pays me back in nickels?"

Mack responded by radiating the same calm that she'd married him for. "Money and attention aren't the only worthwhile measures of success."

"Just ask van Gogh, right?"

"If writing makes you happy, you should keep doing it."

Therein lay the problem. "But I like things that like me back. Our children may drive me wild from the minute they wake up until the minute we chase them to bed at night. And yet, I know they need me and love me. I know my time with them is of value. I used to be able to rationalize the work of writing the same way—difficult, but worthwhile. Increasingly, though, it feels like a job for which I'm not getting paid."

Fern has barely written a word in six years. Every once in a while, she teases her agent with the promise of a book proposal, but a tease is called a tease for a reason. Frankly, it is a miracle she still has an agent at all.

Now her phone is buzzing so much in her pocket that it's beginning to feel sexually explicit. Given Carolina's sudden distaste for cell phones, she looks to Andi for guidance. "My agent has texted me three times since I got here."

"What?" Andi yawns, then blushes. "Sorry."

Fern notices the dark circles under her eyes. "You sure you're okay?"

Andi is a woman driven by so much loyalty and passion she'll land herself in the hospital for fear of letting someone down. She once called Fern on the way to the prison, where she was headed to drop off a set of long underwear for a defendant who couldn't sleep at night for the cold.

"I'm dead tired, to tell the truth. But it's fine."

"Is there any way you can cut back on how much travel you're doing?" Fern suspects she knows the answer but it's worth a shot.

"Someday. Just as soon as there's world peace." This level of cynicism is unusual, even for a woman who sees as much as Andi does. She catches herself and sighs. "Sorry, *again*. What were you saying?"

"My thing feels ridiculous now."

"Better than tragic."

Fern stands and pats her friend on the back. "Really, it's nothing. I'm a big girl. I can figure it out."

Then like a high schooler jonesing for a cigarette, she makes a beeline to the restroom to hide.

Andi

On a scale of one to ten, Andi Abdallah wonders, how offensive is it to slide off her heels and go barefoot for the rest of the engagement party?

Problem: she hasn't had a pedicure in months.

Advantage: her feet never stink, plus she showered this morning before getting on the plane.

Or wait. Was that this morning? She remembers waking before dawn, wanting to throw the alarm clock at the wall. Though whether she left Panama within the last twenty-four hours… God, she was tired. There was a missed connection in Miami. A layover in Chicago. Or St. Louis? If the throbbing in her feet or her head would stop, she might be able to remember.

Her husband, Dominick, had picked her up at SFO and driven straight here. She changed in the bathroom. He'd brought her a dress, the pair of three-inch Louboutin's he loved, and forgotten to throw in SPANX.

Men have no concept.

"Andi, have you seen the circles under your eyes?" Emma comes in for a hug and stops, holding her at arm's length. "When was the last time you slept?"

I'd crawl under the table right now if I could. "Gee, Emma. Way to make me feel at my best." The response is more cutting than intended, and the subsequent guilt is too sticky to swallow. "Sorry. Long flight. My words aren't working."

Emma squeezes her shoulder. "I worry about you. Running all over the globe. Burning the candle at both ends."

"I'm fine." Say something often enough and it might come true.

"Well, I'm just glad you're here." Emma scans the room until she finds her daughter. "Portia looks lovely tonight, doesn't she?"

She does. Andi has always enjoyed Portia, a bright pretty young woman with an easy laugh and the ability to get along with practically anyone. Andi and Dom have one son, Cameron. He's a sixteen-year-old hormonal mess in possession of a brain powerful enough to change the world. Right now, he's supposed to be at home writing a paper three weeks overdue. She was out of town when the teacher's email came, so Dom exploded at Cam with anger enough for them both. He threatened to take his cell phone, his computer, and even his car keys.

The discipline resulted in a tear-filled late-night call to Andi's hotel room. "Mom, where are you? Dad's being a total asshole!"

Thankfully, she'd had the wherewithal to back Dom up before chastising Cam for using that kind of language about his father. Now Cam's grounded until the paper is turned in. But neither she nor Dom are holding their breath that he'll use this time to get his act together.

Plus, she's here now. Celebrating Emma's kid.

"We like Portia's fiancé, right? Lyle?"

Emma lights up. "Love him."

A crash near the kitchen steals her friend's attention. "I better go check on that. But, Andi, let's have lunch. I want to hear all the latest. You're my favorite superhero."

"I'd love that." The sentiment is sincere. The likelihood of making it happen, doubtful.

Eighteen months ago, Andi's law firm got a call from The

International Council for the Safety of Women, a well-respected nongovernmental organization tied to the UN and NATO. With immigration from Central and South America rising at staggering rates, women and children are being victimized and exploited in equally horrifying numbers. Civil and human rights attorneys are in short supply. ICSW had the funding if the firm had bodies and brains to spare.

Andi hasn't slept easily since. Could anyone, seeing what she does?

Many days, the mission feels big enough to swallow her whole. But Andi has never been one to stand on the sidelines. She can't quit, no matter the stakes, because people like her are wired to either fret or fight. In twenty-plus years of practicing law, she's yet to meet a civil rights attorney like herself whose motto is "Don't worry. Everything will work out." In their line of work, things rarely do.

Today's party is a happy distraction, however, and she's glad she practically turned herself inside out to get here. Her friendship with Emma, Fern, and Carolina is a keystone to her survival. She might fall asleep, drool down her chin, and otherwise make a fool of herself, but at least she'll be doing it in the presence of three people prepared to forgive her, no matter what.

Fern

Fern returns from the bathroom just in time to hear Carolina say, "Sure, sex is great. But have you tried salmon?"

This is the moment, fifty-four-year-old Fern thinks. She's officially old. "Did you just say 'sex is great, but have you tried salmon?' Or do I need to succumb to hearing aids?"

Carolina, who's also fifty-four but looks fresh off forty, gives her a look that tells Fern she's finding an audiologist Monday.

"Flax!" Carolina shouts. She looks at Fern's husband, Mack, and together they fall into humiliating hysterics. "Your husband was talking about boosting his omega-3s. He said he'd been putting flax in his smoothies." Nutrition and a borderline obsession with fitness are precisely why Carolina looks a decade younger than the rest of them.

Fern bats her eyelashes at Mack. "I thought she was trying to convince you to quit having sex with me."

He buries a chuckle in his drink. "I'm still trying to process the idea of a salmon smoothie."

"Gross." Carolina raises her glass and takes a long sip. "But a red-wine smoothie? I'd try that."

Andi stifles a yawn, her neck looking for a few seconds like a bleating frog. Dominick, Andi's husband, pounds the table. "Wakey-wakey, darling."

"Sorry." These days, Andi always seems to be somewhere on the exhausted spectrum. She's a civil rights attorney who sees very dark things in her professional life but does her best to mask them with a fantastic wardrobe and expensive concealer. Today, it's not working as well as usual.

"I picked her up at the airport an hour ago." Dominick is also an attorney, but the icky corporate kind. He's not a terrible person. He just earns the kind of salary that makes you assume he ought to be. "Handed her a garment bag and a fresh pair of underwear."

Andi nods toward the corner. "I changed in the bathroom over there."

The same bathroom in which Fern just read a text that very well could change her life. She's desperate to share the news, but it's not time yet. More details are coming.

Queenie, Carolina's partner of twenty years, appears carrying a serving tray loaded with a plate of appetizers and three bottles of wine. He places it at the center of the table. "Got enough for everyone."

Carolina eyes the goods. "Who'd you have to bribe into handing that over?"

"Nobody." Queenie wags his eyebrows. "I'm charming and witty. No need for cash."

Fern picks up a piece of prosciutto-wrapped asparagus and wonders if Italian ham is high in cholesterol. Her last checkup had included a stern talking-to about triglycerides. "Is anyone else's doctor threatening statins?"

Dom nods. Carolina says, "Chandler's already on them."

Andi drops her face back into her palm. "I'm so tired I wonder if my heart's even pumping anymore."

Mack hands Dom an empty water glass. "Put this against her chest and listen."

The music shifts to up-tempo jazz as Emma, shimmering

in a champagne-gold jumpsuit, appears table-side. "Can you believe it? Two weeks ago, I was changing Portia's diapers and here she is, already engaged. I don't have any idea how I'm going to get this wedding organized by Labor Day."

Fern mumbles an absent-minded offer to help, though she's still hung up on Portia's age. Had Fern married the man she'd been dating at twenty-three, she'd own a house in suburban Fargo and be wed to a development manager—though what he developed, she had no idea; the Christmas cards never said.

"Don't go anywhere." Emma swings a manicured nail, stopping pointedly at Fern, Carolina, and Andi. "We're making toasts soon and I'm determined not to let Devin steal all the glory." Her ex-husband, Devin, made his fortune as a silver-tongued attorney. So many lawyers in their circle. It makes the head spin.

"Are you nervous?" Fern asks, finally surfacing from her thoughts. "Want me to wordsmith something quick?"

"Nope." Emma's teeth shine especially white against her burgundy lipstick. "For once, I'm prepared."

Fern snickers. Emma is nothing if not the most organized, perpetually prepared person she's ever known. She could disassemble her house, board by board, and have it thoroughly cleaned and reassembled again before bedtime.

"Don't worry," Fern assures her. "Everything will be fine."

Emma

An hour into her daughter's engagement party, and Emma May is still fussing with the hem of her blouse. It won't lie flat and pops inside out every time she moves. If she could, she'd glue her arm to her side to keep it in place, but there's too much for the mother of the bride to do. Too many hands to shake, waiters to direct, small details to fix.

One of the hydrangea blooms in the arrangement on the front table has begun to droop. She tucks it behind a lily and wills it to stay.

"Are you sure they have the right address?" Portia asks. They're waiting for Lyle's parents, and her daughter's worry lines are going to crease her makeup if they don't arrive soon.

Lyle kisses his fiancée gently. "I guarantee you this is what's happening: my parents got into town twenty minutes ago, but my dad refuses to pay for parking. Mom is grousing about having to walk too far in heels, and at the same time refuses to let Dad drop her off at the door because it'll make her look like—" he makes finger quotes "—a call girl in a cab."

Good grief. Emma smooths her shirt. *Don't they sound like a pair.*

She has not yet met her daughter's future in-laws. She's ex-

tended several invitations, but Mr. and Mrs. Fluke live in suburban Sacramento, two hours away from Emma in Petaluma.

"Is there anything I can do to help your parents fully enjoy
the evening? Do they know many of your friends?"

She glances around the patio, expecting to recognize more
of Portia's friends than she does.

Lyle doesn't have time to answer. "Dad! Mom! Over here."

A man with Lyle's angular chin plus forty years of sun damage scans the courtyard. He's no more than six feet away, but
the look on his face says he'd just exited customs and can't lo-
cate his passport.

The woman beside him reaches for his elbow and pulls it
close, a guarded tourist clutching her possessions tight.

"Mr. and Mrs. Fluke?" Portia waves her fingers in the air
and her diamond catches the sun, throwing glitter.

The in-laws remain frozen in place.

"I'll get them." Emma squeezes between a cocktail table and
a man wearing a three-piece suit with flip-flops. Lyle has been
interrupted briefly by a round of congratulatory backslaps, and
Portia shouldn't have to be responsible for rescuing her fiancé's
parents at her own engagement party.

Come to think of it, where has Portia's father, Devin, disappeared to?

"Sylvester? Doris? I'm Emma May, Portia's mother." She extends her hand.

Sylvester ignores it. "Where did you park? I couldn't find
any lots charging less than twenty-five dollars." The man is
dressed as if he'd just stepped out of the State Farm Insurance
office he's reportedly owned for thirty-some years.

Emma withdraws her unshaken palm and uses it to straighten
her hem. "I used the valet, actually." Her cheeks flush with em-
barrassment, though why, she cannot imagine. How she spends
her money is her business.

At least she arrived on time.

Doris Fluke hugs her husband's elbow ever more tightly to her side, adding nothing.

"You look lovely, Doris. That color is—" Emma has blanked. *Lovely* is the only word coming to mind, but she's already said that. "Lovely. It's just lovely."

Tasteful. The word comes too late. Doris's pantsuit is a *tasteful* shade of lilac. Not too-polyester purple nor nursing-home lavender. Lyle obviously gets his height from his mother, who stands a half of a head taller than her husband. She's at least six feet tall. And imposing. Broad. Not fat, so much as, well, Emma can't put her finger on it. Just that she can't be an easy woman to dress. There's the height, plus a certain lack of curves.

But the pantsuit really is lovely. Ruching circles Doris's waist and the jacket lapels meet at a single mother-of-pearl button. The pants do tug a bit at the thighs, which causes the line to flare wider than intended, though Emma can see the outline of swelling around her knees.

She's suddenly aware that there has been no conversation for several seconds.

"Mom. Dad. Thanks for coming." Lyle pecks his mom on the cheek and extends a hand to his father. Which the man takes, unlike Emma's.

"How did you get here? What did the cab cost?"

Lyle shakes his head. "My place is close enough to walk. One of the reasons we chose to hold the party here."

The venue, Giardino Blanco, is less than two blocks away from Lyle's Hayes Valley apartment. Emma knows because she and Portia have walked here several times, even though neither of them live in the city. Portia lives in Napa, where she teaches second grade. But Emma isn't afraid of the city; she likes it.

Portia beams at her soon-to-be family. "We're so pleased you decided to join us."

Emma's ears perk at the word *decided.*

"And you're certain you don't want to stay at my place overnight?" Lyle's generosity of spirit was one of the first things

Emma liked about him. "I'll take the couch so you can have my bedroom."

Sylvester grimaces. "I have a 7:00 a.m. tee time with Bernie Rundgren."

Doris lifts her foot ever so imperceptibly, wiggling her toes inside her shoe.

"Let's get you seated." Emma takes her by the hand, not giving the woman the option to refuse. "I saved you a table near my friends." She catches Portia's eye as they pass. *You were right about these two.*

With the Flukes seated at a table with a few of Lyle's childhood friends, Emma reviews the to-do list in her head. She'd been on her way to greet Portia's bridesmaids before getting distracted.

"Emma?" She feels a hand on her shoulder and turns.

The face she sees is one she'd have recognized anywhere. "Benjamin." She throws her arms around him.

Emma and Ben went to high school together. A good-looking kid loaded with multiple talents, he played goalie on the soccer team and went to the state debate team championships. In other words, he was way out of quiet Emma Johnson's league.

Thirty-five years later, his hair gray and his muscular build softened, he looked just as good as he had back then.

"You're even more beautiful than you were in high school," he told her.

Emma blushed. Then reminded herself that he'd been captain of the debate team in high school. The compliment wasn't anything more than skilled flattery.

"It's astonishing." Ben beamed. "You really haven't changed a bit."

If only you knew, she wanted to reply. Instead, she tossed her hair and laughed. "I've had a good life. I'm very lucky." She tried not to look for a ring, keeping her eyes glued to his face. Could she help it that he used his left hand to scratch his chin?

Carolina

Carolina Kahele turns her face to the corner and grabs a tissue from her pocket. A sudden burst of tears seems to have sprung up from nowhere and for no purpose except to smudge her mascara.

What else is new?

She's in a constant state of emotional flux these days. Her fifty-four-year-old self has gone soft on the inside. Most nights she cries after work. Yesterday, she cried through her morning shower. This afternoon, she cried in the car all the way to the party.

Right now, she might be crying tears of joy, her love for Emma and Portia so overwhelming she can't hold back. But it's equally plausible that she's crying because the sandals she's wearing pinch her toes.

There's just no telling.

Her friends have long described her as one part Hawaiian aloha, and one part Portuguese man-of-war. As Fern says, "She'll give you her last bite of bread if you're hungry, but step on her tail and she'll put you in the hospital." To Carolina, that's just bluster. She's intense, yes. Loves her family and friends deeply. Is maybe a bit of a workaholic. Has been told by both her trainer and her doctor she needs to learn how to listen to her body.

She doesn't abuse people; she runs, exercising until the anger and stress dissipate. Every year, she completes a dozen or more marathons, trains seven days a week, and keeps a physical therapist in her text app. Physiological Prozac, she calls it. Homeopathic Xanax.

And yet, she can't find a mascara capable of withstanding her recent mood swings.

This soft inner part, she tries not to show anyone except Queenie, her partner of twenty years. He's six feet of doughy data analyst nerd, and Carolina adores him. Born Theodore, his cut cheekbones and sandy hair make him a dead ringer for Steve McQueen, the '60s screen star who raced his Ford Mustang up and down the hills of San Francisco in *Bullitt*. Queenie is all anyone has called him since high school.

"I'm heading to the bar," he says, hand at the small of her back. "Want another glass of wine?"

She swipes at her eyes and stuffs the tissue away. "No, I'm good, thanks."

"Okay." Queenie plants a kiss on her forehead. Norah Jones sings "Come Away With Me," ghostlike among the guests. Carolina smiles.

She is exhausted.

Happy to be here with her friends.

Celebrating Portia. Celebrating love.

Thankful for the big dopey nerd she'd chosen for herself.

But achingly, disconcertingly tired.

The tears threaten again, but she lacks the energy to boost them up and over her lids. They dry where they sit.

When she no longer feels at risk of melting, Carolina makes her way back to their table. Everyone is gone except for Andi, and she's half-asleep with her face propped on her hand. Carolina quietly pulls out a chair and sits without disturbing her friend. The quiet could do them both good.

A few weeks ago, Carolina's mother caught her tearing up during a family dinner and has talked nonstop ever since about menopause. "You're just like me, Carolina, and I never cry. Except for three times in my life—the six months after you and your sister were born, and the five years it took me to get through the change."

Carolina doesn't believe her. Mainly because her mom does cry—specifically, every time she asks if she and Queenie are ever going to get married. But also, because Carolina doesn't have five years to waste being a wet puddle on the floor.

Especially not at work. Carolina is a VP at a Silicon Valley Fortune 100 tech giant. She's a power performer leading a team of sixty, the biggest team on the corporation's biggest initiative, MAVERIK. There have been some hiccups. Every project has them. But her business stakeholders love her. They trust Carolina. They sing her praises to the higher-ups. One says he'll quit if anything ever happens to her.

As if reading Carolina's mind, Andi opens her eyes and yawns. "So what's up with you these days? How's work?"

"Out of control." It's her standard answer, and always true. "But no busier than your job."

"Ugh. Tell me about it." Andi has a crimson imprint on her cheek where her wedding ring dug into her skin. "How's the new boss? A woman finally, right?"

Carolina reports directly to the CIO, a woman named Sandra whom the CEO personally wooed away from a competitor six months ago. "Yeah, and I don't know whether I like working for her or not. I can't get a read on where I stand."

Since her arrival, Sandra has already overseen one reorganization and is hinting at another.

"I have a hard time trusting anyone whose motto is 'do more with less' but also wears eight-hundred-dollar shoes." Sandra owns the suede buckle pumps Carolina had tried on at Neiman Marcus but refused to let herself buy. "Far be it from me to criticize another woman's style, but it's bad form to call layoffs 'a necessary cost reduction' when you're walking around with a car payment on your feet."

Andi stifles another yawn. "You worried about your job?"

"I don't think so. My stakeholders would throw a fit if anything happened to me. But I would like to know if I'll be expected to achieve the same standards with fewer and fewer resources."

There's a morale hangover that follows every layoff. Employees silently debate whether they want to give so much of their energy and time to a company they can't trust. Productivity slips, sick days rise. Carolina knows this, which is why she did her best to support her team through the last transition, telling them what she knew as soon as she knew it, and treating them with the respect they deserve. She's only just managed to get her numbers back on track.

No wonder she's emotional.

Andi says, "I need to find myself some caffeine. You want anything?"

There are so many things Carolina desires. Some work stability. A new attitude. The ability to make like a duck and shake off whatever keeps sending up tears. "No, I'm great, thanks." She straightens her back and fails to find something witty to say. "Just be back in time for the toasts or Emma will kill us."

Fern

"Oh, my God, it's happening!" Fern has no sooner checked her texts again than she hears a knock on the restroom stall door.

"Everything all right in there, dear? Can I do anything to help?"

"No, Mrs. Johnson, I'm fine, thank you." She's snuck off a second time to check her phone, but now Emma's mother thinks she's having some sort of bathroom emergency.

"Is that Fern?" Mrs. Johnson's shrinking eighty-year-old voice echoes strangely against the pressed tin ceiling.

Fern's screen lights.

Holly: Are you aware of the SmartGirls on TikTok? Call me.

Fern swallows hard. She'd be dialing her agent right this second if she didn't have company.

"Yep, it's me, Mrs. D."

Trying to find a quiet spot. Will call asap. Can you send more details in the meantime?

Unlike her children, Fern has resisted the TikTok phenomenon. Why download and learn a new app when another cooler, more fascinating one was surely just behind?

"Have I ever told you that I had my book club read your last novel? They were so impressed that I knew the author."

Fern resists the temptation to correct the old woman. She doesn't write novels, she's an essayist. And yes, Mrs. Johnson did tell her that story—years ago.

Three delicious dots dance on her screen.

Emma's mom hums to herself, and Fern has to actively scroll to keep herself from imagining the scene on the other side of the stall wall.

"I have a few stories that would make for a great book. I'll have to share them with you."

Fern's eyelid twitches reflexively, as it always does when force-fed book suggestions. She rubs at it, waiting for the dots to become words.

Holly: Bit complex. Better to chat live.

"Oh, listen to that." Mrs. Johnson swipes at the toilet paper. "I hear glasses clinking for the toasts. Best get out there."

What did Holly mean, *a bit complex*? Her stomach drops.

"And you're sure you're okay? Nothing you need before I go?" Mrs. Johnson flips the latch on her door and runs the sink. The hand dryer whirrs with the force of a jet.

"No, thank you, Mrs. D."

Cocktail music and laughter briefly fill the room, then go muted again as the door clicks shut.

Fern piles out of the stall. The restroom is hers. Does she dare? She can hear the crowd beginning to quiet as the toasts begin.

Just one call. She'll make it quick. Tell Holly she only has a few seconds.

She pulls off a shoe and shoves it under the jamb, a makeshift doorstop, then leans her full weight against the wood and dials.

"Who are the SmartGirls and what do they have to do with me?"

Andi

Apparently, wine bars don't serve coffee. Or so says the waiter who Andi asks—the one who looks at her bare feet and scowls.

Dom offers to go get coffee for her, but he and Queenie are half in the bag and partway through a cigar. Nor does Andi begrudge him the night off. Dom picks up the parental slack without complaint. Plus, the party is making her claustrophobic; mixing with the über-privileged becomes more difficult with every trip. She was in Panama for a conference, slept in a hotel room with luxury Egyptian cotton sheets, and delivered a presentation filled with images of battered women.

There was the mother beaten with the branch of a tree until she could no longer shield her nine-year-old daughter from the men who would callously trade her for water and food.

Anjelo, the boy who'd left Nicaragua with his mother, grandmother, and sister, but now traveled alone, the women, one by one, *desaparecida* in the night.

She closes her eyes. Breathes. Blows the memories out of her brain.

"Ma'am?"

Oh, for fuck's sake. "Sorry." She's at Peet's Coffee, not the Grand Hilton, Panama City.

The barista raises an eyebrow. "Did you order on the app?"

"No, I—" In this kid's mind, she's a hundred years old. "Just a small double-shot Americano, please." Or, no. That will have her prowling the house all night like an amphetamine addict. "Make that a single shot." No, that's too disappointing. "Hang on. How about— Can you make it a double but with half decaf?"

The barista blinks, fantastically unperturbed. "I can make fairies fly out of your ass if you ask nicely enough."

She takes that as a yes and moves aside to wait. Her phone buzzes in her pocket. It's Carolina.

W r you? Toasts starting

Emma

Emma isn't sure if she's going to happy cry or ugly cry, but the tears are going to come. Lyle just toasted Portia with a couplet from Shakespeare's *The Merchant of Venice*, the scene between Portia and her secret love, Bassanio.

"One half of me is yours, the other half yours,
Mine own, I would say; but if mine, then yours,
And so all yours."

It's the classic equivalent to "you had me at hello" from *Jerry Maguire*, only Shakespeare did it first and so, so much better. Devin would've quoted the movie, which becomes reason 13,421 of how she knows she was right to divorce him. That, and his habit of fucking his legal assistant on the Xerox machine.

Was it worse that he'd had sex with another woman, or that he'd done it in front of a security camera? She doesn't have time to debate that right now because she is going to cry. The tears are already dropping, pulling her makeup with them.

"To the happy couple!" Devin raises his glass and the guests drink, then begin dispersing, returning to their conversations and cocktails. Emma's friends, however, are nowhere to be seen. Except Carolina.

"Where is everyone?" The tears are streaming now. "I asked you all to stay close."

Carolina hesitates. "We did wait. It's just—"

Queenie appears and gives Emma a hug and she can't hear whether Carolina finished explaining or not. "Lovely toast, Ems. Lovely party, lovely daughter, lovely everything."

She pulls free of his grasp and finds Carolina's eyes. "Ten minutes! You all had to stick around for ten minutes!" She feels suddenly aware that even at her own party, her friends consider her the least important among them, or the least intimidating, or whatever the hell it is that makes people stick around when they say they will.

Carolina opens her mouth to argue but burbles her lips like a child instead. "I don't know. What can I say? Fern went to the restroom. Andi needed coffee." She quits apologizing and beams. "But your toast was great! We told you it would be!"

Emma doesn't know what hurts more, the disappearance of her friends or her one loyal friend's patronizing tone. "Nobody laughed."

"Were we supposed to?"

"Devin had the room practically doubled over."

"Yeah, but that's not you."

"I'm funny!"

"Of course. With us. But 'stand-up comedian' isn't a phrase most people would use to describe you."

"I didn't say I wanted to be a stand-up comedian. I said I wanted to give a better toast than Devin and you all said you'd be here to listen."

Carolina closes the gap and hugs her. "I was here. And you were great."

"I said, better than Devin."

"Emma, you are better than Devin in so many ways I couldn't even begin to count."

A rush of excitement sounds from across the room, and

Emma turns to see Fern's husband, Mack, pull her into a bear hug, spinning her while she laughs.

"Where did she come from?"

Carolina doesn't know.

Fern spots the two of them, and parts the crowd like Charlton Heston at the Red Sea. "Get ready to be famous!"

She's holding one of her shoes in her hand. Emma wants to knock her over the head with it. "Where were you?"

"In the bathroom taking a call from my agent. A couple of comedians started reenacting scenes from *Smart Girls Say Yes* on TikTok and now Dakota Winters wants to option the screen rights."

"What?"

"I know, right? I can't even imagine where they found the book in the first place."

Emma bursts into tears. "No." It's the only word she can muster. Between the adrenaline of the party and meeting Portia's future family and trying to breathe under three layers of SPANX, it's a wonder she's still upright.

She needs a hug. Needs the clock to rewind fifteen minutes. To have her best friends cheering her on, celebrating with Portia, who's like a goddaughter to them all. Not scoring deals in the ladies' room.

Emma looks up, tilting her face to the sky to keep her streaming makeup from staining her outfit. And then she sees her. Greta Magnussen, six full feet of nothing but ice-blue eyes and killer boobs. The woman who ended her marriage.

"That sly motherfucker." Carolina has spotted her, too, recognizing Greta from the hours the friends had spent studying her social media after the fallout. "Did you know he invited his pollywog?"

Emma's so taken aback she snort-laughs a stream of snot directly into her champagne. "Oh, my God, I forgot you called her that." Normally, she didn't condone the cruelty of name-calling, especially when done to women. Only, the image of her ex-husband's mistress as a not-yet fully developed tongue-flicker was too good. "And no, I did not. I think Portia tried to warn me, but I probably ignored her."

Fern, still unreliable for more than a few seconds of attention at a time, begins thumbing away at her phone.

"Fern!"

"I know. The pollywog. Hang on." She doesn't raise her eyes, even in apologizing. "Just let me finish this text and I'm all yours."

She isn't exactly sure why, but Emma finds herself saying, "Just go home, Fern."

At this, Fern finally looks up. "What? No. I just need to answer this and I'm done."

Emma isn't buying it. She knows Fern well enough to sense she'll be glued to her phone for the rest of the night. And right now, her brain is telling her that she can't handle being within slapping distance of Greta Magnussen without the full and undivided backup of her girlfriends.

"I mean it. You are preoccupied and I'm about to lose my shit right here in front of my daughter's closest friends. In front of her strangely unreadable in-laws. And in front of the walking, talking representation of how much my ex-husband hated my middle-aged hips and lady parts."

"Emma!" She doesn't know who says it—Carolina or Fern or even Andi, who's finally just shown up holding a Peet's cup in her hand.

"Is THAT where you were?" Emma stomps her foot, thinking somehow that's what this moment needs. "All I wanted was my friends around me, but no! Fern's playing Cecil B. DeMille in the bathroom and you're out for coffee!" The screeching draws the attention of several strangers, but Emma's too far gone to rein it in.

"I honestly thought I'd be gone for five minutes." Andi's expression, unlike Fern's, is at least remorseful. "I feel awful. I'm so sorry."

Emma knows she means it but she can't help herself. "Look. I know I don't have the big careers you all have. But this party meant something to me."

God, listen to her, all self-pity and *don't treat me as lesser than even though I probably am*. It's making her sick even as she hears herself.

Andi tries to placate her with platitudes, but they only make Emma want to scream. "Don't!" She raises a palm. "A phone call can wait five minutes, Fern. And, Andi, you seriously missed my speech to go to Peet's Coffee? It's gonna take a lot more than caffeine to cover up the fact that you look like you haven't slept in years."

"That's cold," Andi snaps.

Emma snaps back, "No, it's called honesty. More people ought to try it."

Fern says, "Calm down, Emma. You're upset because of the whole Devin situation. We get it. Don't take your frustration out on Andi."

"Oh, my God!" Is anyone listening to her? "I'm not *frustrated* because my ex-husband showed up at our daughter's engagement party with the woman he's screwing. No, I'm *pissed* because two of my closest friends chose phone calls and coffee over supporting me."

Andi has morphed from remorseful to looking as if she can't decide between exploding in anger or hysterics. "I didn't choose coffee. I had to get coffee because they don't serve it here!"

"You should have waited!" She spins from Andi to Fern. "And you should have waited to make your phone call!"

"Emma!" This time she knows it's Carolina speaking. "You're understandably frustrated and tired but take it easy."

She obviously thinks she's innocent, and she is absolutely not. "Who are you to tell me to take it easy, Carolina? You're such a workaholic we have to advise Queenie on how to keep you from falling over dead with the stress."

"EMMA!" Now it's all of them yelling.

Except for Carolina, whose mouth is gaping open. "What do you mean, you're all helping Queenie? Do you talk about me?"

"NO—" say Andi and Fern, while Emma says, "Of course, we do!"

"EMMMMMAAA!"

Now they've definitely drawn the attention of the crowd, which Emma knows because even Greta, who's so tall her head pokes above the crowd like a nipple, smirks at her from across the patio.

"You run a thousand marathons a year, Carolina, and who takes care of Mrs. Roper when you're gone? Me. I do. Because she pees on Queenie's side of the bed every time you leave." Carolina's six-year-old Japanese Chin, Mrs. Roper, has scrawny toothpick legs that poke out of her long silky coat the way Mrs. Roper from *Three's Company* looked in her kitten heels and caftans. She wears an enormous faux-pearl collar in honor of her namesake.

"I thought you liked taking care of Mrs. Roper."

"I do! That's not my point." She spins now, aiming her ire at Fern. "And you wrote a whole book about our sexy single San Francisco days and didn't change our names! For years, I've had to deal with acquaintances thinking they have the right to ask me if I really gave a blow job to a banana!"

Fern appears less than adequately concerned. "Oh, come on. You have never once complained to me about anything in that book."

Emma doesn't have time to argue because Portia has caught wind of the upset and is making her way over. Emma turns to Andi before intervention arrives. "Andi, you think you're Mother Teresa in a power suit. But seriously. Is it worth killing yourself over a problem that's never going to be fixed?"

"Take a breath, girlfriend." Andi is sharp and stone-faced.

Portia appears, trying to hide her concern behind a toothy grin and reassuring coos. "Everything okay here? How can I help?"

Emma hears *elementary schoolteacher* in every syllable of her daughter's voice. "My friends need a lesson in learning how to say no."

"I'm sure that's not true."

Carolina ignores Portia and keeps her eyes on Emma. "I can't decide if you need another glass of wine to calm down, or if you've already had too much."

Andi stiffens.

Fern glances at her phone.

Emma slaps it to the floor.

"HEY!"

"EMMA!"

"MOM!"

Emma has gone full-blown maniacal. She knows this the way a dead person hovers above their body and realizes, *Wow. So, I guess that's that.*

A year ago, life went off the rails and every day since has been a twenty-four-hour exercise in trying to focus on what remains good. She lost her husband but kept her house. Her daughter is moving away but she's gaining a son-in-law. Her schoolteacher salary is less than she'd make slinging burgers but at least she's doing what she loves.

Emma has exhausted herself with optimism.

"Well, I'm saying no!"

"To what?" Carolina cocks an eyebrow.

Fern crosses her arms.

Andi remains silent but confounded.

Emma is confused, herself. She doesn't know what she means, just that for once, she refuses to be the "happy, charming, keeping-it-all-together" person people expect her to be.

"I'm saying no to us." She sweeps her hand, encircling the four friends. "You're too busy to stick around for a five-minute toast. But I'm busy, too. And now I have a wedding to help plan. I don't need to put up with your drama on top of it all."

The more the words come, the more she understands them.

All those hours in her therapist's office coming to light, coming to fruition.

"I'm no longer afraid of being alone. I know that I am a perfectly capable human being. I do not need to earn people's love by trying to please them."

These are her daily affirmations, the things she says aloud to the mirror every morning hoping that, someday, she'll start to believe it. Well, now she does. Even though Andi, Carolina, Fern, and even Portia all stare at her, mouths agape.

"Andi, you need to slow down, and you know it. Carolina, you're too thin, which means you're running too much. You say it's for stress management, but it's actually because you don't have any work-life balance. And, Fern—" Oh, her heart is thumping now. She's been holding this in for way too long. "When you put that day in your book, you destroyed my trust. And now you have the nerve to get excited about putting it on-screen?"

Fern's face is stark white. For once, she's speechless.

"Do not make that movie, Fern. It's our lives you're messing with."

Four Camels and a Thermos of Booze

From *Smart Girls Say Yes*
by Fern McAllister

Emma had us at "Federal Withholdings."

Carolina and I met sitting side by side in a conference room while filling out new-hire paperwork—a merry-go-round of letters and numbers from W-4 to the 401(k). Emma was our guide.

Our employer was a global consulting mega-firm whose logo faintly resembled a giant penis pointing skyward. All men wore dark suits. Women, skirts and pantyhose. Every seat was full, and in a room full of Young Republicans, there were only two people I wanted to meet: the gal on my right with the wild curly hair and an ankle tattoo of the sun peeking through her nylons, and the one standing at the front of the room in a white-bibbed blouse and brown Mary Janes looking like a lost librarian.

"You can always change your withholdings later," she said,

walking us through the W-4. "Nothing in life is permanent, folks. Not your rent, not your pant size, and not your taxes."

Afterward, I asked Wild Curls about her tattoo. "Oh, that? It's a somewhat regrettable spring break decision. I never liked it much until the executive who offered me this job strongly recommended that I cover it with a Band-Aid. I told him, 'You want me to squeeze myself into pantyhose *and* wrap my ankle? Forget it.'"

When you meet a woman that confident, you make her your best friend.

Two years prior, Andi and I fell in bestie love in line at a coffee cart on campus at the University of California, Davis. When she got to the window and asked for a can of "pop," I knew we'd spend the rest of our lives together.

"You must be from the Midwest," I said.

"Minneapolis," she answered.

"Milwaukee for me. Technically, most people there say 'soda,' but my mom was a transplant."

It's scintillating topics like this one that earn Midwesterners a reputation for being boring. We're not. We simply appreciate clarity.

I soon learned that Andi was in her second year of law school. When not in class, she studied. When not studying, she helped her law-student boyfriend study.

"You're probably thinking I need a social life but when would I squeeze it in?"

From that day on, stealing Andi away from the books became my favorite hobby.

Not that I had much time for such tomfoolery. I was in the first year of my master's program and I taught three times a week. My department, however, offered slim pickings by way of interesting colleagues. The only woman who showed any social potential at all did so by inviting me to a place called Apple Hill to "fart around for the day."

The Midwesterner in me balked, the invitation appealing neither in its ambiguity nor its clarity.

Fast-forward two years, and Andi and I both landed in San Francisco, ready to grab our slice of the silicon pie. Several months later, over drinks, Andi said, "I thought after law school I'd finally get a life. But now all I do is go to work and then come home and study for the bar."

I wasn't faring much better. Only, my pattern was work, minor anxiety attack, crawl under the covers, try again tomorrow. The obvious solution to our social woes was to start a book club. And that is how the four of us—Andi, Carolina, Emma, and Fern—became a We.

As a founding mother, I chose the first book, a memoir about a woefully unprepared twenty-something woman who rode camels across the Australian outback. For what reason, none of us could figure out, and when each of us hated the story with colorful abandon, I knew there was no stopping this new venture of ours.

Emma, God bless her, selected the *Divine Secrets of the Ya-Ya Sisterhood* next and showed up to the meeting wearing a thermos full of cosmopolitans.

"I was on BART last weekend, and I saw a group of girlfriends pouring cocktails out of a thermos. It looked so fun I had to buy my own." Hers was pink plaid and hung from her shoulder on a pink leather strap.

The Ya-Yas were fierce in every way our little group longed to be—in their pursuit of fun, in their cocktails, and in their devotion to each other. Perhaps we didn't recognize it at the time, but we were four women desperate to love and be loved. None of us were getting it from the men in our lives. And none of the men in our lives deserved the love we surrendered to them.

Andi's law school, now-attorney boyfriend seemed to get needier by the hour. Couldn't press a shirt but refused to pay for dry cleaning. Pouted when she went out but lay on the couch when she stayed home. He was a man with a bright future, if only he'd bother to stand up and turn on the light.

Carolina's boyfriend at the time was a head-scratcher of a love interest. Where she was driven, he couldn't keep a job. He agreed to pay half the rent on their Japantown apartment, but half the time he borrowed his share from her. She was never home, and he never left. Later, she'd admit, "He was a little bit dense. I took advantage of the fact that it never occurred to him to wonder about where I went and who I was with."

And Emma, the bright, cheerful young woman with the playful heart we'd grown to love, was busy planning her wedding to a perpetually grouchy financial analyst. By the time he asked for her hand, she had her sights set on a home in Marin and private school for the two daughters they'd have two years apart. Their thermoses would hold ice-cold organic milk.

And what was I up to? I was dating the emotionally clogged cheater I met in graduate school. He was just charming and persuasive enough that I decided every problem in our relationship must be due to my shortcomings. If I only exercised more, I wouldn't hate my body in the bikinis he loved. If I could just relax, I wouldn't nag him to talk when he wanted to be left alone. I'd fallen in love because he made me feel as if I could accomplish anything. But somewhere, gradually, I'd lost my magic.

By the afternoon we four friends lay atop the merchandise at the Mattress Train daring each other to say "yes!", the self-confident girls inside us were primed to claw back the years, tears, and fears we'd wasted on such unfortunate boys. Andi caught her boyfriend trying to cheat on the bar exam. Carolina was out of money and out of love. Emma broke off the engagement when her fiancé broke into her underwear drawer. And I forced myself to admit that the woman who routinely called our apartment late at night did not have the wrong number.

Shortly after our breakups, someone suggested we read Jon Krakauer's account of the disastrous Mount Everest expedition that claimed five lives, *Into Thin Air*. I don't recall the evening's cocktail, but I do remember looking around the room at Emma, Carolina, and Andi knowing that they'd never leave me in the midst of my trauma. Not one of them would step over my decaying oxygen-deprived body in pursuit of their own ambitions. We were in this thing called life all the way to the top.

Because when we finally reach the summit, none of us wants to reach it alone. Who would we celebrate with when we got there?

April

Fern

Fern is sitting on a bench in the neighborhood park, watching two girls dare each other ever higher on the swings. She has one daughter, Maisy, who's a senior in high school, too busy for her parents, and about to leave the nest altogether. Her sons, Owen and Jackson, are twenty-one and twenty, respectively. Both are away at school. One calls her regularly to check in, the other texts when he's short on money.

She doesn't begrudge her independent kids. She and Mack raised them that way. They told them to go take on the world, and to know their parents were around if they ever got too far over their skis. It's that "go get 'em" spirit that brought her to the park today. She needs to remind herself that she's succeeded in the midst of more trying times than what she's going through now.

They'd had three kids quickly. One with off-the-charts ADHD, a second who insisted on doing everything himself, and a third who demanded she never be left behind, ever. When writing, Fern described their household as *chaotic, competitive, and loud*. Later, Mack would read the words and gently add, "And wonderful."

He was right. It had been wonderful.

But also unpredictable and grueling. So here she sits at the park, not so much watching the girls swing, but rather stealing glances at their mothers as they dig through their bags for water bottles and hand sanitizer while also calling "two-minute warning" at least ten times before dragging the whining girls away from their fun.

Fern gives the women a sympathetic "been there" look while secretly delighting that those days are done for her.

At least until the grandkids arrive.

For now, she has some thinking to do. There's an offer on the table to option the book. There'd been a few interested parties, and the screen rights agent had been hoping for a bidding war. It didn't materialize. "More of a quibble," her literary agent, Holly, told her. "But we're pleased with the terms. Definitely worth considering."

Which is what Fern tells herself she's doing now. Considering.

Really, though, she knows she's stewing. The engagement party happened nearly three weeks ago, and Emma still isn't responding to her texts or calls.

"Give her time," Carolina advised.

Andi promised, "She'll cool down."

Maybe they're right. But the more time passes, the more Fern loses track of Emma's primary grievance. Missing a toast is unfortunate, but hardly a betrayal. A betrayal is asking Fern to give up on her dream of seeing one of her books brought to life on-screen.

"You have to admit, you didn't warn us about *everything* you planned to include in *Smart Girls Say Yes*." Andi, who is still speaking to Fern—though just barely, with everything happening in her own life—called last night. "You're talented and I love you, but I wish you would have asked my permission to write about some of that stuff. My law school relationship, for example. I was in therapy for years on account of him, and now you want to put it all in a movie?"

Fern hadn't referred to her friends by their full names in the book, but within their network of friends and acquaintances, it wasn't difficult to put faces to the real women behind the caricatures.

"It's bad enough that one of my colleagues still asks if I really threw up all over the inside of a new BMW."

Fern couldn't help but laugh.

"It's not funny!" Andi's voice pitched into dog whistle, then dropped as she, too, began to giggle. "Okay, maybe it is. That poor guy. He had to have the interior detailed three times to get the smell out."

"Oh, believe me, I know." Fern had included the story in a chapter titled, "Buy Me a Drink BINGO." His name was Matthew and he was old money, one of the many liveried Brooks Brothers, East Coast men who'd gone west to claim their stake of the dot-com boom. Their type, which the friends nicknamed the Brooks Bros, were almost too easy to spot.

They paid for valet parking and slipped the tickets into their money clips.

Their belts were new leather, never frayed at the notches.

They rarely had roommates or, if they did, one of them owned the condo they shared.

Fern and friends practically made a game of targeting them. Okay, not practically. Carolina really did make BINGO cards one night and they sat at a table at the City Tavern marking off squares. Fern had written about it, and now thanks to the SmartGirls on TikTok, Gen Zers were playing the game again for real.

"The nineties are hot right now." Maisy, their in-house social media expert, deigned to sit down one evening and explain this SmartGirls phenomenon to her Luddite mother. "The trend is boyfriend jeans, crop tops, SJP, flannel, plaid—a general 'end of the world' vibe counterbalanced by 'in your face' fun."

"SJP as in Sarah Jessica Parker?"

"Right, but the original *Sex and the City* version, not including the movies. And definitely not *And Just Like That* SJP. That version is too much."

Sarah Jessica Parker had versions? "Since when can a person be in and out at the same time? It makes no sense."

"Don't blame me, Mom. You're a child of the eighties. You practically invented the commoditization of personality."

"*I* didn't invent—" Fern stopped herself. She was a stranger in a strange land, and she didn't intend to go to war with her daughter over Sarah Jessica Parker. "Never mind. Do these SmartGirls say how they found out about my book?"

"Goodwill," said Maisy. "Thrifting is also hot these days, but not nearly as hot as it was two years ago."

This, at least, Fern knew, as she'd spent a full year driving Maisy and her friends to every thrift store in the East Bay. She still couldn't imagine specifically why her book attracted the attention of these two young comedians.

"I don't know, Mom. You did some weird stuff. The wedding dresses?"

In one of the essays, Fern, Andi, Carolina, and Emma hold a tea party while wearing wedding dresses, a celebration of sorts for Emma, who'd just ended her engagement.

The SmartGirls spoof of that day was the first video Fern saw—the two comedians, billowing in ridiculous amounts of white tulle, burning effigies of past loves, and maintaining stuffy conversation with a life-size cardboard cutout of Princess Diana. "Charles is ever the dull cad, isn't he? It's a wonder Camilla doesn't string him up by those satellites he passes for ears."

The reenactment was hardly exact. Princess Diana wasn't at the original party. But the comedic brilliance lay in the fact that these women had taken a moment from Fern's book, blown it ridiculously out of proportion, and still managed to drive home the whole point of that day.

"Like I've always told you, Maisy. Don't get married just to wear the dress. Other options can be cheaper and a lot more fun."

"Whatever." Maisy raised her hands, surrendering the point. "You asked about the SmartGirls, so I told you."

"Thank you."

Now Fern sits on the same park bench where she used to watch her children hold pine cone fights, grappling with the two versions of her own self. She is a writer who may have an opportunity to see one of her books brought to life. But she's also a loyal friend to the women on its pages, and they're not prepared to give her their blessing.

She wonders what Faust would do.

It is possible she's overblowing this dilemma. A tiny fraction of the books optioned make it into development, and a tinier fraction still make it all the way to the screen. The odds are infinitely higher that the *Smart Girls Say Yes* project will get shoved in a drawer and forgotten. Nothing is guaranteed except for a paycheck that, who is she kidding, could go a long way in paying her three children's college bills. Owen and Jackson are at public state schools, but Maisy has her heart set on leaving home and heading east. That means private school tuition plus plane fare.

But here's what really makes the hair on Fern's arms puff: if she says yes, she'll finally be able to say that one of her books had been optioned for screen.

During the pandemic, she'd sat on Twitter watching one author after another announce screen deals, every one of them scream-tweeting, Pinch me! I can't believe it. Fern couldn't believe it, either. What did their work offer that hers didn't? An article titled "Lockdown Ushers in a Gold Rush for Authors and Producers" detailed the inordinate number of books that had been sold for rights in 2020. Apparently, producers had nothing but time to read and then buy up their favorites. Only, none of them must have read Fern's stuff.

She pinches herself on the thigh. *Stop it.* No more beating herself up over things beyond her control. Anyway, the correct way to look at her current situation is to think of it as a multi-

tude of blessings. She had a career while also raising a family.
She's happily married and maintains a group of close friends.
And yet none of that justifies giving up on her dreams.

There's one other thing, too. The producer who wants the
rights to *Smart Girls Say Yes* is a Lady Boss named Dakota Winters, a woman who made a name for herself as a teen star on
the Disney Channel and who shockingly didn't go on to blow
her millions on drugs and rehab. Fern never watched her show
Double-Twos, but she's been told that for Millennials it's what *The
Facts of Life* was for Gen X. A touchstone for millions of women.

After making a name for herself in television, Dakota went
on to earn her business degree, and has since produced a string
of well-respected, top-earning limited-run series for Netflix
and Hulu. In other words, she's the personification of a smart
girl, a woman who doesn't wait for opportunity, but makes it.
When Dakota Winters says yes, she means it.

"I am a certified mess," Fern says aloud. The pigeon picking
Cheerios from among the wood chips looks at her and nods.

All this navel-gazing and self-doubt…she doesn't understand
what's gotten into her. If anything, the defining characteristic
of Fern's life has been her decisiveness. Don't stand in the paint
store diddling over the colors; pick one that's close enough and
put it on the wall. She once redecorated the living room while
Mack was out of town for a week. She wandered by a shop
window, saw a furniture set she liked on sale, hired a truck,
got the old junk out, and put the new pieces in.

Mack barely batted an eye. "Is this your way of telling me
I'm on the road too much?"

"Maybe. And it's easier to clean baby barf off leather than
velour."

Had Fern tried to talk him into buying new furniture while
he was home, it would have taken forever—comparing prices
and hunting for coupons and debating how to maximize the
credit card points on a purchase of that size. By the time Mack
was ready to buy, Fern would've been spinning in frustration

and CDC agents in biohazard suits would be hauling their old couches away for study.

And, dammit, isn't Fern the woman who wrote a whole book about stepping up, saying yes, and taking control of your life?

"Why, yes, I am."

The pigeon drops the Cheerios and walks away.

She picks up her phone and dials Holly.

Emma

It's past four o'clock, and Emma is still in her classroom writing an email to the parents of one of her second-grade students. Henry is a bright, happy boy who won't pull his nose out of his books during class. In math, she'd had to pry away a copy of Percy Jackson to get him to finish his multiplication worksheet. Later, while students were at tables labeling the earth's continents, he pulled an Alan Gratz book from his backpack and crawled under the desk with it.

It goes against a teacher's every instinct to advise a family their child is reading too much. In fact, she can only remember a handful of occasions on which she's had to do so. She sends a far greater number of notes encouraging parents to push the books at home and consider limiting the time their child spends in front of a screen.

She also suspects that this particular set of parents may not consider Henry's reading problematic. On the contrary, they'll likely blame her for it. Could this be an indication of boredom? they'll write, implying that if she challenged their son properly, he wouldn't be forced to engage his mind elsewhere.

Even the anticipation is draining, and Emma slumps in her chair, the cursor blinking against a blank screen.

Bzzzt. She knows without looking that Andi has just texted her, as she's been doing every afternoon for the past week, trying to draw her out after the debacle at the engagement party. Even though Emma isn't ready.

Checking in. I'm sure you're busy. Chat soon?

Andi is a great checker-in-er, Emma will grant her that. She usually welcomes it. But not recently, when she's been so hurt that the pain and shock of their argument walks with her constantly, clouding her memories of what was supposed to be a wonderful day. Part of Emma wants to believe the whole thing was an unfortunate mishap. Carelessness and poor timing. And that might be true if the hurt hadn't run so deep. An emotionally intelligent woman knows who she's safe with, and she'd never had reason to question that with Carolina, Andi, or Fern.

A year ago, she'd never questioned it with Devin, either. Then Ginny Milton called.

It was the night of the gala at Devin's firm. The event began in an hour, and Emma had forgone a professional blowout at the salon. Last time, getting her hair done cost more than a hundred dollars. Financially, she could afford it. Ethically, however, it was an extravagance she couldn't stomach when the beneficiary of the night's charity auction was the Anti-Human Trafficking Fund. It would have felt obscene sitting in the chair, sipping wine and answering the obvious, "So what's this event raising money for?"

When the phone rang, her caller ID announced it was Ginny on the line, the wife of another of the firm's senior partners. Emma hesitated before pressing the speakerphone button with her pinkie. Even if the sky were raining fire, Ginny would find a way to have her hair done, and Emma was just superstitious enough to suspect that somehow Ginny could tell that she hadn't.

"Emma? I know I'm calling at a bad time. You're probably mid-zip, slipping into heels, and nearly out the door."

Emma puffer-fished at a strand of hair that refused to curl.

"Believe me, I've spent all day debating whether or not to call. This isn't the type of thing you just drop on a friend. Not without cocktails ready."

Were they friends? Emma supposed so. Friendly, at least. She and Ginny differed in their priorities, but she was good for a chat over a glass of wine at dinner.

"But I decided that if the roles were reversed, I would want to know. I would want you to tell me if my life were about to fall apart."

Emma heard their corgis, Kanga and Roo, barking downstairs at the door. Devin was pulling into the garage. He'd be anxious to leave as soon as he changed into his tuxedo.

"I can't let you walk into the event tonight the last one to know."

As it turned out, Emma wouldn't be going to the event at all.

That evening, Devin had come straight up to the bedroom swaddling the smaller of their corgis, Roo, in his arms like a baby. Thanks to Emma's speakerphone, Ginny heard him enter, and she did the decent thing by hanging up.

"You look lovely, Ems." Devin patted her on the hip, not even flinching at the layers of body slimmer under which it was swaddled. Roo yipped, jealous of his attention. "Oh, what? You think you're not my favorite girl just 'cuz I pat another woman's butt?"

Emma considered staying silent, wary of confronting him with his mind already on the gala. Until she burned her finger on the hot curling iron. "Dammit, Devin." The shock tangled the nerves from her fingers to her brain. "Did you really fuck Greta Magnussen?"

She saw his face in the mirror. It flashed with the quickest temptation to lie.

"I'm giving you one chance to be honest. Which you better damn well take because I already know the truth."

What boggles Emma perhaps more than anything about that night was the fact that Devin cried, but she didn't. Eventually, of course, she'd cried herself through every box of tissues in the house. But that night, she'd only watched. Her life a scene, their bedroom the stage.

"I don't know why I did it. Honest, Ems. I never saw it coming."

Devin had tried to sit beside her on the love seat beneath the window, but she stood and left him, taking the antique rocking chair in the corner instead.

"It's like I was possessed or something. Like I was powerless to resist."

Emma watched as a bulbous tear clung to his eyelash and refused to fall.

"I mean, you're everything to me. You and Portia are my everything."

"We're individuals, Devin. Not plural entities." It's all she had to give him. A correction of his grammar.

"I know. What I'm saying is—"

"Do you remember what you used to say to Portia's boyfriends in high school?" She didn't want to listen to anything from Devin right now. Everything she needed to know about her husband she'd already heard. "You'd say, 'Hurt them and I hurt you.'" She pictured him as he laughed and flexed his unimpressive biceps while simultaneously flicking his business card at the young man from between his fingers. *Devin May, Attorney at Law.*

"I know. *I know.*"

Now, however many days, nights, and weeks later, Emma sits in her empty classroom, wondering why everyone seems to already know everything she has to say.

Everything, except the ache that comes with the realization she—a fifty-four-year-old divorcée whose daughter has officially flown the nest—hardly occupies enough space in this world to make an impression.

A spark of defiance shoots up her spine. She picks up her phone and opens Andi's text.

Thank you for checking in. I am too busy to connect these days. My answer is no.

Channeling the energy generated from that action, she composes a precise and pointed email to Henry's parents, inviting them in for a conference and suggesting three available times over the next week from which to choose.

That finished, she opens her email and clicks on a request from the school principal that she serve as their school's faculty representative on a newly formed district committee responsible for evaluating current curriculum against the new literary standards enacted by the state legislature. The email arrived two days ago, and she's spent two days agonizing over how to weasel out of the job without having to look like she was weaseling. She ought to say no. She's on a roll, no coffee with Andi and no excuses for Henry's parents. Now, however, she realizes the curriculum committee is an opportunity to do precisely what she always regretted not being able to do—have a say in what she teaches. If she has become inconsequential in every other area of her life, she can at least matter professionally.

"I am honored to be asked and will be pleased to serve," she writes. Then presses Send and powers down the computer, her tasks accomplished for the day.

Of course, there is one more question awaiting her response. She wakes her phone and scrolls until she finds it.

What a great surprise to bump into you at Lyle and Portia's engagement party. I really would love to catch up more in person. Can I take you to dinner?

Who could have anticipated that Lyle would turn out to be Benjamin Guy's nephew?

Frankly, she wasn't surprised when they exchanged numbers. It was only polite. But the text that came a few days later made her gulp. The more she thinks about it, though, the invitation is a smart move on his part, politically. They were about to be family. However loosely connected they were, Benjamin owed it to Lyle's family to act as the good ambassador. He owed it to Emma to assure her that Portia was making a safe landing. There isn't any romantic intention in the outreach. Nothing more than serendipity, two former classmates brought together by a younger generation.

Staring at the screen, she knows she's searching for subtext where there isn't any, and kicks herself for it. They're not in high school anymore. If he wanted the reunion to be anything more than a friendly dinner between soon-to-be family, he would have said so. He's a debate champion; that sort of thing comes naturally to a person with his skills.

Anyway, she's planning a wedding and has just accepted the principal's invitation to do more (unpaid) work. There's virtually no time for dinner out. The realization washes over her with relief.

Benjamin, I, too, look forward to reconnecting. Hopefully we'll share a glass of champagne and a nice chat at the reception in September!

It's a shock to realize how liberating that feels. She said no without being rude. Now she's free from the anxiety surrounding all of it—what to wear and what to say at dinner. And afterward, the hours she'd have spent second-guessing every reaction, hers and his. Did she laugh hard enough at his joke, or too hard? Did she seem too eager to impress? Even now, she feels herself beginning to sweat at the prospect of having said yes. She'd have had to shove Kleenex under her armpits just to keep from perspiring through her shirt at the table.

Then again. She looks back at the text she's written. Was the exclamation point too juvenile? She decides it's okay as is. She's just turned down his dinner invitation. An exclamation point is the least she can do.

Andi

Andi is sitting at a Southwest Airlines gate in Oakland waiting for a flight to Bakersfield. Her day is back-to-back visits with detainee clients at the ICE Processing Center.

The Venezuelan mother of two who woke up with a fellow detainee's hand down her pants.

The twenty-year-old Haitian woman who's pregnant and claiming the child is the result of having been raped by one of the guards.

The group of young women mysteriously subjected to monthly vaginal swabs.

It's enough work to justify a two- or three-day stay in Bakersfield, but she's doing it in one, booked on the last flight home tonight. Ever since the episode with Cam's long-overdue English paper, she's vowed to be more present in her son's life. The paper earned a C, but the teacher's final comments set Andi's maternal flares aflame. *This could have been an A paper, Cameron. Next time, take the assignment seriously. And don't forget— deadlines are deadlines!*

Andi was failing her son. Or, maybe not failing yet, but at risk of failing him. All her time on the road dropped the lion's share of parenting on Dominick's shoulders, and though he was a good father, he wasn't superhuman.

This perspective of hers was newly found, of course. Born of an argument that began less than five minutes after walking in the door from a four-day trip to San Ysidro, a town just north of the Mexican border. Dom was in the kitchen hollering at Cam, who'd locked himself in his bedroom.

"No more excuses, Cameron! I'm sick of this shit!"

It was the swearing that triggered her. "What are you doing? Don't speak to him like that!"

"Oh, yeah? What language would you use after telling the kid more than a thousand times to write that damn paper?"

"I don't know. But clearly swearing at him isn't the answer!"

And just like that, they were all yelling. Dominick at the end of his rope. Andi, bleary-eyed. And Cameron too angry to come out of his room.

That night in bed, she and Dom had their sixty-fourth discussion about her ICSW work.

"This is a new level of stress, Andi. The tragedy associated with these cases drains you until you've got nothing left, and we're the ones paying the price. You're hardly ever home, but when you are, you're either falling asleep or picking a fight."

The accusation came hot as an iron rod straight from the fire. "*Me?* What do you think it's been like to live with you? The year you were gunning to make partner was like trying to avoid a bear in the forest. There was no telling when you'd show up or what kind of mood you'd be in."

The fact that she'd made countless concessions to Dom's career was seemingly all too convenient for her privileged, well-educated white male husband to forget, and her body seized on the rage it provoked, back stiffening, the muscles in her neck and jaw twisting and knotting.

Dom reached for her, hand on her arm. "But making partner was a goal with an end point. What's the timeline here, Andi?

When do we get you back?" He softened his voice, slid his fingers from her arm to her middle. "When do I get you back?"

His hand may as well have been a snake.

"Are you *effing* kidding me right now? You go from 'Hey, Andi, why are you always in such a shitty mood?' to 'Wanna have sex?'"

He winced, clearly stung, though not badly enough to satisfy her.

"Can't I miss you for multiple reasons?" He had not, she noticed, moved his fingers off her belly.

"You're unbelievable."

"Thank you. I'll take that as a compliment."

"I'm not having sex with you. I'm too mad. And I'm bloated from the plane."

He smiled, saying nothing.

She still wasn't in the mood. But something about him being such a fool calmed her. Cooled the fire inside. "Cam's lucky his teacher didn't give him an F on that paper. You know, I offered to help him with it. Said I'd read and edit it, even if I had to do it on the plane."

"I offered, too," said Dom.

"What is happening with him?"

"He misses you." The words weren't meant to hurt, but they did. "At his age, I could hardly stand to be in the same room with my mom, but the minute she wasn't available, I didn't know what to do. She could be at the grocery store shopping for my favorites, and I'd still get pissed that she wasn't right by my side the second I needed her."

Cameron still needed his mom. It was as simple as that. If only the solution to this dilemma was as easy to come by as the insight.

Andi's flight boards in ten minutes. Just enough time for a call with her legal assistant, Issah, to distribute a stack of new cases that came in over the weekend.

"ICSW wanted to give us thirty cases," Issah reports. "I talked them down to a dozen."

"Where does that bring the numbers?" Andi's phone is pinging. A text from Fern.

Has Emma returned any of your calls or is it just me?

Issah clicks her tongue while doing the math. "Rivera settled two cases last week. O'Neill had her summary judgment come through...so with these new ones, we've got ninety-eight cases in the pipeline."

The cases are divided among Andi and the three lawyers she snagged for her dedicated ICSW team. They share three legal assistants, including Issah. By Sanders and Wiggs standards, the workload is ridiculous. Compared to the average public defender, though, it's nothing. In the two years Andi spent in the Federal Public Defender's Office following law school, she regularly juggled a hundred or more cases at a time. Constitutionally, everyone in the United States is entitled to legal representation. The constitution does not say anything about preventing such representative from being hideously overworked and woefully underpaid.

Issah reviews the new batch of cases. There's a woman suffering debilitating third-degree burns after fellow detainees at the Ciudad Juárez detention center started a fire in their unit to protest the poor conditions. The tragedy has been all over the news, several detainees died, and the Mexican government is facing responsibility. The woman named in this case, however, wasn't meant to be in Ciudad Juárez at all. She'd mistakenly been denied amnesty by US officials who misidentified her in the California facility where she was housed. They were supposed to deport Madelena Torre-Flores. The woman in this case is named Madelena Flores.

"Give that one to O'Neill," Andi says. "What's next?"

"Four rape cases," Issah reports.

The twenty-nine-year-old mother of four.

The fifty-nine-year-old grandmother.

The sixteen-year-old girl.

The nine-year-old boy.

Those go to Rivera.

Andi assigns herself the case involving a ring of contract ICE officials accused of taking and trading naked photos of detainees. Victim complaints would likely have continued to go unaddressed had the guards not been brazen enough to transfer the images onto a deck of playing cards.

The details are so familiarly enraging that Andi goes numb upon hearing them. Every one of these people is real, their lives inexorably changed by violence and vulnerability. And yet, seen as cases, they're reduced to numbers.

A lawyer is never supposed to flatline emotionally. Nearly every lawyer eventually does.

Andi tosses her bagel in the trash. She no longer has the stomach for it.

"Anything else?" The gate attendants begin their pre-boarding instructions. Andi has flown to the backwaters of California, Arizona, and New Mexico so often recently she's got top-priority status. A privilege perverse enough that she sometimes feels like a hooker.

"Just that I was finally able to line up an interpreter for your court appearance on the thirteenth. I'll get the details to your assistant."

"Thanks, Issah. You're a rock star."

"Not a problem. Text me when you get to the facility if you need anything."

Andi's phone buzzes as she enters the Jetway. This time it's Dom.

Heading home. Cameron overslept. Driving him to school myself.

On a scale of one to ten, Andi wonders, *how likely is it that ordering a Bloody Mary on a 9:00 a.m. flight qualifies me as a problem drinker?*

Carolina

The CIO's assistant puts a meeting on Carolina's calendar for nine o'clock. It overrides two other meetings scheduled in the same slot, but C-level execs don't look for openings in your calendar, they create them.

When Carolina walks in, she sees that Sandra is wearing her signature eight-hundred-dollar buckle pumps. "This won't take long," she begins.

Carolina scans her face for clues. Good news, or bad?

"As you're aware, the Board and the CEO have tasked me with reinventing the way we devise and utilize our information systems. I've been instructed to disrupt. Reinvent. Define the future."

A gas bubble climbs Carolina's throat. She wishes Sandra would skip the word salad and deliver the main course.

Sandra stands and picks up her laptop, returning to the table with it. "The Board has approved a second phase of employee cost reductions. This time, however, we're offering voluntary severance packages."

"Voluntary?"

"Yes. Wall Street usually loves a layoff but if we announce a second round so soon on the heels of the last, we risk the appearance of financial instability. By making them voluntary, we can spin the reductions as a continuation of our previous efforts."

"So, you're going to offer layoff packages and see who takes them."

"Voluntarily, yes. They'll further reduce costs while weeding out employees who are less committed to our mission. Research always shows that highly committed teams are able to do more with less."

There's that phrase again. Carolina glances at Sandra's luxury-clad feet. "You need to exclude my team."

"Excuse me?"

Carolina knows she should hold her tongue but chooses not to. "My team is responsible for one of the company's most important initiatives and we're stretched thin. Everyone has been working overtime since the last round of layoffs. We've managed to reassign and streamline the work as much as possible, but if I lose any more of my resources, something is going to give. That's the bare truth of it."

"Believe me, I hear you." Sandra's sympathy appears strangely authentic. "But leadership believes we have transferable internal resources to help you fill the gap."

"No, you don't." Again, Carolina knows she's crossing a line by being so blunt, but if she doesn't speak up now, this pie-in-the-sky idea will gain credence and momentum. "First of all, the skill set required for members of the MAVERIK project is highly specialized. Most were external hires to begin with, specifically because we didn't have the skills in-house."

Sandra doesn't interrupt, which Carolina takes as a green light.

"Second of all, how do you know who's going to leave? My team leads are working fifty and sixty hours a week. What if they decide they've had enough and take the package?"

"Then that becomes an issue we'll have to deal with."

"Exactly. A big issue." Carolina can no longer sit in her chair. She stands up and begins to pace. "And an avoidable one. I mean, what you're proposing is like leaving the front door open and then wondering why your TV disappeared."

Sandra does not stand. "I understand your concerns, but on balance, the Board believes this is the best approach." Her voice is so calm Carolina suddenly sees the truth behind this meeting—Sandra intends to strangle her objections now so that by the time Carolina walks out the door, she has no option but to support the layoffs.

"So that's it, then?" she says. "We just wait to see who decides to grab the money and run, then deal with the consequences?"

Sandra nods. "And I'm sure I don't need to remind you that this information is to be kept confidential until the official announcement early next month."

"No, thank you." Contrary to Emma's accusations, Carolina doesn't have a problem saying no. The real problem is that people don't listen when she says it. "I don't need a reminder."

Her hand is already on the doorknob when Sandra says, "Oh, by the way. Your name came up in a meeting with Mark's team yesterday."

Shit. "Oh, yeah?" Only a rookie assumes that when you get name-dropped in the CEO's office, it's good news.

"Carlton Willis stopped by and sang your praises."

"Oh, nice. I thought that was Carlton I saw in the lobby." Her tone is light despite the conversational boulder Sandra just dropped on her foot. Carlton Willis is a tech billionaire who behaves as if his money affords him the right to inject his bizarro-world political views into the national debate. Carolina knows better than to believe a single word that escapes the man's mouth, and not just because he made his fortune selling tax software but now espouses eliminating the IRS.

And while there's a lot to hate about Carlton Willis as a public figure, Carolina's disgust of the man is all personal. What he did to Emma is something no one in her friend group likes to talk about.

What she told Sandra was true, however—Carolina had seen

Carlton in the lobby yesterday, flanked by a beefy security guard and a female colleague in heels so high they ought to be redlined by the World Health Organization. They made eye contact. He smiled. She walked away.

So why had he name-checked her to the company's top brass?

Carolina says, "Is there some sort of partnership or development project in the works?"

Sandra replies, "Something like that." Her "Cheshire cat" grin tells Carolina it's not like that at all.

This day just keeps getting curiouser and curiouser...

Buy Me a Drink
BINGO

From *Smart Girls Say Yes*
by Fern McAllister

Henry Sands Brooks founded his retail empire, Brooks Brothers, in Manhattan in 1818. An offshoot of Henry's legacy, the category of men who my friends and I referred to as the Brooks Bros, began arriving in San Francisco around the mid-1990s.

In the late '90s, the Brooks Bros formed one of the largest populations migrating to San Francisco, second only to "Fraternity Brothers from Chico State." Like the marginally less populous migrant group, "Women with Last Names for First Names" (McKenzie, McKinley, McKenna, Piper, and Hollis), the Brooks Bros grew up "back east," attended a school draped in ivy, and decided that Silicon Valley was a more desirable location to seek their fortune than Wall Street.

As far as I can recall, Carolina coined the term Brooks Bro. Everybody knew at least one, as he was easy to spot and proud to display his colors. He used valet parking and slipped his ticket into a monogrammed money clip. His outfits coordinated in a "Garanimals for Grown-ups" sort of way.

Our group of friends didn't seek out a Brook Bros interpreter, but we gained one in a man named Chandler. No, not that Chandler. Little did his parents know what was coming when they registered his birth certificate in 1971.

Unfortunate pop culture mishap aside, our Chandler had all the attributes of a Brooks Bro—he graduated from Cornell and wore a belt with tiny anchors on it; the cash in his money clip always seemed in inverse proportion to his job (when he had one). Unlike typical members of his species, however, when none of us four ladies agreed to go out with Chandler, he stuck around, anyway.

And then, we were five.

Here's the nice thing about having a token Brooks Bro as a friend: he's always available. Late nights don't matter when his job isn't his identity. Nor will he ever tell you he's staying in tonight because his "credit card might combust from overuse."

So, there we were, Emma, Andi, Carolina, Chandler, and me. That night it was the City Tavern in Cow Hollow, all whiskey-colored wood and burgundy leather booths. Carolina pulled a stack of index-sized cards from her pocket and slid one to each of us.

At the top: *Buy Me a Drink BINGO.*

She said, "Chandler, you can play if you want but it might get awkward." Gen Xers may have been more progressive than our Boomer parents, but even in the '90s, boys were expected to pay for more stuff than girls.

Andi said, "WHAT is this?" In her world, human beings didn't turn other human beings into games.

Carolina explained. "None of us has dated in a long time. We have to break out of our shells."

Chandler raised his hand as if asking, *What am I, chopped liver?* Which we ignored.

Because Carolina was right. Having a boyfriend, which we'd

all had until very recently, was demonstratively different than dating. Having a boyfriend meant never having to panic about spending the weekend alone. Having a boyfriend meant people introduced you by saying, "She's Toby's girlfriend."

In contrast, dating was the young adult version of a ball pit. It can be wickedly fun for the first minute. Then it strikes you that maybe you should wonder why everything is so sticky; the girl at the center of the crowd gets an elbow to the face; and the kid you thought was your new friend suddenly vomits all over your shoes.

I've since come to believe that Buy Me a Drink BINGO was a sign of its times, a tool born of contextual necessity. By the late '90s, our generation, known as X, had mostly come of age and most of us were making full attempts to partner up. We weren't, however, looking to settle down. Women born in the '70s had been taught by our Eisenhower-era mothers that, unlike them, we weren't to consider ourselves old maids until well into our thirties. We had careers to build and adventures to seek. Husbands and babies could wait, but sex no longer had to.

No wonder Tammy Faye was crying.

Gen Xers left the nest believing we could fly, only to discover that our Boomer forebears had turned the adult world into a hall of mirrors nearly impossible to navigate. Boomers promised us a thing called "The Pill" and then sandwiched it with a thing called "AIDS." They fueled their all night, every night Disco craze with cocaine, then set our hometowns on fire with crack. Everything good was theirs. Anything left was deadly enough to kill.

By the late '90s, Gen Xers were so confused we both spawned the boy band and sent Woodstock to its grave. But we also invented Buy Me a Drink BINGO.

Here's how it was played. Each square contained a challenge. A player's goal was to complete five challenges in a row.

Things like:

"Ask a stranger to buy you a drink."

"Learn a guy's middle name."

"Meet a boy from Connecticut."

In explaining her creation, Carolina said, "It's not like you have to go home with someone. You're just initiating conversation. A square is a square is a square."

I asked, "What do we win if we get a BINGO?"

Carolina hadn't actually thought that part through. "Huh. I guess I didn't expect anyone to get that far."

"You probably won't." Chandler never liked it when our attentions fell anywhere other than on him. "In fact, just to make it interesting, I'll bet each of you a drink that you quit playing before any of you get five in a row."

"Deal," Carolina said.

Emma said, "This will be fun!"

Andi held her card as if doused in poison.

As for me, I was still hoping I'd meet someone the same way I met every other man I'd dated—without trying. BINGO was going to require me to act as if I cared, when experience had taught me that caring was dangerous.

At twenty-nine, I was just getting used to the idea that I might not be hideous. I'd had boobs and height and decent cheekbones since the age of fourteen, but they'd been masked by plaque psoriasis and eczema deep into my twenties. Scales aren't on many boys' lists of what they look for in a girl. Nor was crippling teen anxiety, a barking laugh, and the need to play the clown. I wasn't everyone's cup of tea.

I'd had relationships. But I shouldered the belief that all those boys had dated me "despite." I rationalized their imperfections with imperfections of my own.

Eric may not have been cute, but I had a face that shed like a snake.

Patrick was boring, but I laughed enough for the two of us.

Steve turned into an intellectual snob when he was high, but I quit dating him as soon as I met Jason.

Toby may have cheated but… Actually, I had enough self-respect to draw the line at cheaters.

Finally, by 1999, I looked like a different person. Thanks to a series of medical advances, decent insurance coverage, and the ability to manage my own health care, I was a girl with a fresh face and a new attitude. Carolina had me running regularly, too, so my waist, hips, and thighs smoothed into more natural proportions. I was a long, lean auburn-haired beauty who didn't know what to do with herself.

And yet, the last time I'd tried to talk to a guy at City Tavern, he mocked my Wisconsin accent and asked me if I'd ever heard of a cheese called Brie. That, however, was before the afternoon at the mattress store. Now, I was riding the Yes Train.

I said, "How do we do this?"

Carolina said, "However you want."

Emma suggested, "I'm going to pretend I'm someone else. Like I'm performing a role in a play."

Andi gasped. "What? That's terrible advice." She existed in a state of perpetual moral shock. "You have to be yourself."

"Trust me, it works," said Emma. "It'll get you out of your head and out of your own way."

When we'd met, I could never have imagined Emma having roadblocks of any kind, mental or otherwise. She was pretty but unassuming, well-dressed without looking snooty. Shiny hair, white smile, a man perpetually on her tail. She even smelled good.

It was only after *the incident* that I recognized not all was well in her "Pleasant Valley Sunday" world. Pretty girls had problems, too. But again, that's a story for another chapter.

Emma said, "Just go up to the bar, stand next to a guy, and pretend you're trying to get the bartender's attention. When you fail, ask if he's able to do it for you. It'll play to his ego." Her superpower was playing to people's egos.

I don't recall how long we debated my approach. I do remember walking to the bar, taking the seat next to my mark and saying, "Buy me a drink."

And he goddamn well did it.

"What are you having?"

"A cosmopolitan." Because in 1999, thanks to *Sex and the City*, there was no other drink. If it wasn't pink and didn't come in a martini glass, it may as well have been water.

Here's the other thing I remember about my first BINGO encounter: it lasted just long enough to realize that a free drink was all I wanted from my Brooks Bro. It arrived, we tried small talk, I thanked him, and left. He laughed as I walked away, and I heard him tell his Bro friends that I told him to buy me a drink, so he did.

My dating life was never the same. I talked to well-dressed men I didn't know on BART and collected their phone numbers. I flirted with bartenders who floated me drinks. I had my first one-night stand with an Australian tourist wearing a FILA sweatshirt. (I didn't like it, but I only discovered that after I'd had the tenacity to land in the sack with an exotic sweet-tongued stranger.)

Some weeks or months later, a Brooks Bro named Matthew walked into our apartment. He, too, had been one of our BINGO marks. It's only with modern hindsight and a penchant for British television that I recognize how much our Matthew resembled the actor who played Matthew Crawley on *Downton Abbey*. Tall, moneyed, and to the manor born. Our Matthew even wore brogues.

One afternoon, there he was in my kitchen, sharing a laugh with Andi and Carolina. I was in my room trying on a dress I'd purchased for an upcoming work party. The conversation stopped when I walked through the door.

"Wow," Matthew said. It was the most flattering reaction I'd ever received from a man.

Later, when the apartment emptied and I was feeling the re-

sidual high only a once-ugly duckling can feel, Andi told me
I should go for it.

"He obviously likes you."

Matthew had already asked me out for drinks. "Don't you
think he's sort of nerdy, though?" I'd noticed that he didn't so
much laugh at my jokes as stare at me in awe and chuckle at
the fact that I'd made one.

Andi shrugged. "I tilt heavily toward nerds."

"Maybe you should go out with Matthew."

"But he likes *you*," she answered. "And if you don't end up
falling for each other, you can pass him on to me."

I realize our conversation makes him sound like a sandwich.
But remember, I was playing with a BINGO state of mind. A
square, was a square, was a Brooks Bro.

My date with Matthew was mostly forgettable other than his
platinum Amex card and his pinstripes. Pinstripe tie. Pinstripe
shirt. Pinstripe boxer shorts. Yes, we made out. Some clothing
came off. He was down to his Brooks Brothers button-down and
his underwear. We were in my room with the door closed when
the doorbell rang, and Carolina's voice filled the apartment. She
and Chandler had been at a party nearby. They didn't want the
night to end.

I don't remember much else, but I do remember the image
of Matthew, standing beside the sliding doors enclosing my
dining-room-turned-bedroom. Blue-and-white pinstripes on
his billowing dress shirt. Black socks. And boxers. He and I
were no longer kissing, but Carolina, Chandler, and Andi had
an after-after party underway in my living room.

Matthew announced, "Bit late, don't you think, folks?"

He looked to me for affirmation, but all I could think was,
How did I end up with this Father Knows Best *wannabe?*

"Let's join them," I said, suddenly desperate for the escape.
If I had been confident enough to accept his dinner invitation,
I could be confident enough to end our evening together.

After one beer, I told Matthew I was tired and going to bed. When he tried to follow me, I handed him his pants and shoes.

A few days later, when I hadn't returned his calls, he called Andi to ask if she'd be willing to meet for drinks.

She told me, "He's just going to want to ask me why you're not into him."

I agreed. "Probably."

"And why is that again?"

"Because I never felt as if I was hanging out with him so much as being watched like a zoo animal."

"He wasn't that bad."

I knew how much she needed to believe that. "He might not have been bad, but together, we weren't good."

She met him for drinks. They talked about me. He paid. He also made her laugh.

A few nights later, much to my surprise, Matthew appeared at our door to pick her up for dinner. He walked in wearing a tweed sport coat, black cashmere turtleneck sweater, and slacks—very Professor Plum in the library. Nerd-loving Andi was going to want to eat his face.

"Hiya." I kept it cool, even though I wanted to run into her bedroom screaming, *You seriously want to go out with him again?* "Where ya going tonight?"

He smirked. "I got us a table at Tiburon."

"Ooh. Good score." Tiburon was the hot new restaurant that everyone was talking about but for which few were able to land a reservation. I wanted to go for the chandeliers. Rumor had it they looked like jellyfish. Which I had explicitly told Matthew on our date. "She'll love it. She said she's been dying to go." *Just like me.*

Andi emerged wearing a gorgeous black Donna Karan wrap dress I recognized as Carolina's and a look that said, *I know what you're thinking and that's exactly why I didn't tell you.*

I closed the door behind them and made dinner plans of my own.

Andi called me in tears around midnight. Only, in 1999, cell phone coverage was as spotty as a teenager's beard and neither I, Emma, nor Carolina answered our phones. So, she called Chandler. "I did something bad." When she explained, he came over to pick her up with a roll of paper towels and a garbage bag. He put Andi to bed, and helped Matthew clean the remnants of three lemon drop cocktails and a bottle of champagne off the dashboard of his new BMW. If the folklore is true, Matthew took it in for detailing three times before selling it.

"He'll never call me again," she told me the next morning.

"Oh, well," I said. "But I do need to know…do the chandeliers at Tiburon really look like jellyfish?"

Perhaps our travels with that particular Brooks Bro were over, but Matthew had served as the perfect test case for our Say Yes strategy. I learned I didn't enjoy stuffy Connecticut types, and Andi learned she wasn't ready to date a guy who drove such an expensive car. Insights that came to us thanks to Buy Me a Drink BINGO.

Most of the evenings when we played, Emma won. Her strategy? Pull the card out of her pocket and pass it around a bar full of men. Because not only was Emma talkative and "girl next door" pretty, but entire groups of men also found her endlessly charming.

One bought her a drink.

Another sang his school fight song.

A third told her his mother's maiden name was Pierce.

The fourth guy said his first pet was a hamster named Weasel.

By the time guy number five gave her his phone number, she was a winner. Chandler paid up.

Andi, meanwhile, played reluctantly, never convinced the game didn't cross some sort of ethical or moral line. She'd fill one or two squares and let her anxiety take over. At some point, she'd stomp her feet and say, "You GUYS!" Meaning, she hadn't wanted to play BINGO in the first place. Though, by that time, Emma and I were usually too far in to care.

As for Carolina, she played Buy Me a Drink BINGO merely in the sense that she'd created it. Rarely did she fill the squares. Carolina ran burning hot or Wisconsin cold on dating. Some nights, she was "off men altogether," in which case she and Chandler would huddle and make snarky play-by-play of the action around them. Other nights, she'd break down and dial one of her rotating make-out buddies.

Short Matthew came along a few months after BMW Matthew. That night we were at the Mauna Loa Club on Fillmore. I was trying to fill the square "Take a sip of a stranger's drink," and like a moth, fluttered toward the Day-Glo orange Dreamsicle martini in his hand.

It tasted like an orange Popsicle dipped in vodka.

He was in finance. Because if you lived in San Francisco in 1999 and weren't in high tech, you worked in finance. I let him buy me several drinks. We made out. I told him I was going home because I had to get up in the morning to train for the Bay to Breakers. He whined at me for leaving too soon.

Over the course of the next week or so, I let him buy me dinner. He drove me to the airport for a work trip. When I got home, he came over to my apartment with burritos and beer.

My conscience wants me to believe that I was clear with Short Matthew from the beginning. I'd said, "I just broke off a long-term thing. I'm only having fun." Then we'd make out again. He'd take me to dinner and pay. In other words, he seemed fine with the arrangement.

But one day, he suggested I meet some of his friends.

After that, I'll admit, things changed. I got his voicemails but scrubbed the bathroom tile before returning them. I met him for six o'clock drinks but left for a date at seven. I canceled our arrangements more often than I showed up.

Then, Short Matthew tried to win my love with 49ers tickets at Candlestick Park.

They say that everybody has a kryptonite, and in 1999, mine was 49ers football. I'd never been to a game. Seeing the Niners wasn't like getting tickets for the Raiders. Oakland fans rarely sold out their stadium, and getting there was a short BART ride underneath the San Francisco Bay. But Candlestick Park was a legend on the water, and the Niners of 1999 had Steve Young for a quarterback. Fans still basked in the glow of the Jerry Rice glory days. I watched a man at a charity auction spend five-thousand dollars on one of Joe Montana's jerseys.

Since Short Matthew scalped tickets for the Monday night game at a higher price point than I cared to think about, I postponed a scheduled flight to Chicago until Tuesday morning. Niners tickets were Niners tickets, even if it meant having to put up with Short Matthew. Even if he had become one of those "how come" guys.

"How come you're going home? The night's barely started."

"How come you're staying in? You can't be that tired."

"How come you didn't answer? You said you'd be home."

All day Monday, the skies looked angry. I called Andi.

"It's freezing out. It's going to be even colder on the water. And it's probably going to rain."

"So, bring a rain jacket."

"But what if I don't want to go at all?"

Andi and I had been close friends long enough to understand the dynamic of our relationship. I made plans that I didn't want to keep, and it was Andi's job to tell me why I had to go, anyway.

"That's a shitty thing to do to the guy."

"I didn't ask him to buy the tickets."

"No, but you told him you'd go if he got them. That's as good as asking."

"Legally speaking?"

Andi's moral compass is infallible. It points due north, which in moral compass terms is called "do no harm to others." As a civil rights attorney, Andi sticks up for people and gets paid for it.

Disregarding the advice of my attorney, I changed my plane

ticket and hopped the red-eye that night, anyway. The Niners game was on in the airport bar. I watched it alone with a beer, because I'd finally realized that saying yes to the tickets was saying yes to Short Matthew. I wanted to see the Niners someday, but not badly enough to extend our doomed relationship by even a few hours. I caught the end of the game before boarding. They lost, but I felt like I'd caught a Hail Mary and come to my senses.

Short Matthew never called again. Thank goodness.

None of us ended up with the boys on our BINGO cards. The men we met back then were merely training wheels. The point of playing Buy Me a Drink BINGO was that, for once, it allowed us to define the dating game for ourselves. To Say Yes to possibility without getting tied down by responsibility.

Until then, life's predetermined path had always been defined for us—and poorly, at that. Common wisdom told us to settle down, but not too soon. Date some, but make sure it's only with guys you think might be marriage material. Build your career, but not at the expense of your personal life. Don't wait to have children until you're too old, but don't have them too young, either.

Buy Me a Drink BINGO gave us the chance to take control. To quit waiting. Stop fearing the worst. Was it risky? A little bit. Borderline unethical? Maybe. Life changing? Absolutely.

And let's not forget…memorable. After all, you're reading about it all these years later. I bet you a Dreamsicle martini that you're also wondering, "Why didn't I think of playing that?"

May

Emma

Emma sets a pitcher of water on the patio table and settles into a chair. Portia is sitting with her back to the sun, the sunlight filtering through her hair, turning it shades of caramel and bronze. It's a beautiful morning, an increasingly rare Saturday with her daughter.

"I know this sounds petty, Mom, but I swear to you, it was the most pointless piece of schlock I've ever seen." Portia is re-telling the story of having spent last weekend in Sacramento with Lyle's parents. They'd gone to Macy's to begin their bridal registry and his mother, Doris, is, apparently a woman with strong opinions.

"I mean, what am I supposed to do with a china figurine of two kissing doves?"

"Lladró is quite collectible, Portia. They're handcrafted." Not that Emma knows much more than that. Her style is toss more, collect less.

"Can I drink coffee from it? Entertain with it? No. Which means I don't need my wedding guests to spend four hundred dollars to give me the pleasure of staring at two kissing doves for the rest of my life."

Emma's not about to argue. Portia's always had a good head

on her shoulders. She makes to-do lists and gets things done. Puts a portion of her paycheck directly into savings. Shops vintage. Today, she's wearing a darling Lilly Pulitzer shirt with the white jeans Emma gave her for Christmas, and she looks so adorable Emma could practically eat her up.

"Doris will learn your style eventually. It just takes time." Heaven knows her own mother-in-law had been anything but easy. Lydia May deferred entirely to her husband, Donald. What time should Emma and Devin arrive for dinner? Well, that depended on what time Donald finished his round of golf. What did she plan to serve? Well, that depended on what Donald wanted. Did Lydia wish to join Emma for lunch on Tuesday? Well, that depended on whether Donald's dry cleaning would be ready to pick up.

Soon after learning of Devin's affair, when Emma was feeling especially bitter and very drunk, she'd fought the temptation to call Lydia in the nursing home and ask, "Would you like me to come over and tell you about Devin fucking his legal assistant?" just to hear what Donald—by then long deceased—could have possibly had to say about it.

"I wonder if that's true, though." Portia spoons a helping of fresh-cut fruit onto her plate. The strawberries at the farmer's market this week were the size of walnuts and filled the air with sunshine and sweetness. "Lyle's mom does this thing... I don't know how to describe it."

"Does she criticize you?" Emma feels her spine straighten at the implication.

"No, it's not that. I think she likes me fine. As much as she can like anyone besides herself and her precious son." Portia points her fork for emphasis. "That's the issue."

"Oh. He's a mama's boy." This surprises her, with Lyle being as attentive and generous as he is. Portia drives his new hybrid Honda CR-V after he offered to swap for her gas-fueled 2018 Civic because she drives so many more miles than him.

"He's not a mama's boy so much as... I don't know. Like I

said, she does this thing." Portia picks up her empty water glass and examines it, pinching her lips and scowling. She sighs, then hmms and puts it down again. "Like that."

"She's discerning?"

"No. The *sigh...hmm*. She doesn't give an actual opinion about anything. She just—" Portia does it again. *Sigh. Hmm.*

"Oh." Emma thinks she gets it now and it's worse. "She's passive-aggressive."

"Yes! To the extreme. And it's like a dog whistle to Lyle. As soon as he hears it, he springs into action." She imitates, "'Well, what about this one, Mom? Is this other one better?' I don't even think he's aware of it, honestly."

"Families usually aren't." Emma hadn't been the perfect mother or wife. No one is. That's what it means to be human. But neither did she understand many of her shortcomings until divorce was already barreling full speed toward her heart.

It leads her to a sickening thought. "Does Lyle feel comfortable around me? I hope I don't manipulate our time together. I'm trying to be a good future mother-in-law."

"Mom, you're fine! You're great."

"But do you know that? Have you asked?"

Portia sighs again, this time with exasperation. "Yes. In fact, I don't need to. He tells me regularly how much he appreciates you and Daddy."

You, specifically, Mom, Emma wants her to say.

"Well, if that ever changes, you let me know. I have no interest in being overbearing or difficult to deal with."

"Yes, Mother." Portia smirks and reaches for the mini quiches.

Emma watches. Some of her moments of greatest pleasure as a mom have simply been observing her daughter. The way she moves. Laughs. Chats with friends. Converses with strangers. There's a confidence about Portia. Even now, picking only the spinach quiche, leaving the bacon and cheddar untouched. Of course, it's a small thing, and a woman Portia's age ought to know what she likes to eat. But many wouldn't. Or they'd take them out of politeness, not wanting to offend.

What mini quiche would Donald choose? Emma chuckles and folds an entire slice of bacon into her mouth because, frankly, she doesn't give a damn.

"I have a thought." Lord, who's the passive-aggressive mother now? *I have a thought.* As if it's a miracle. "Hear me out."

Portia's looking at her expectantly.

"Maybe I can help smooth the transition with Doris. We're around the same age. Certainly, we have a few things in common. If nothing else, we both raised an only child. This is the one wedding we get."

Finger crossed, she silently adds.

"It sounds as if she may enjoy playing a role in your decisions. Everybody knows the mother of the groom tends to get short shrift. Why don't you and Lyle include both mothers in your planning excursions?"

"You mean, like registering?"

Emma flashes to the planning app Portia showed her. She'd entered dates and budget and ideas, and it spit out a list of tasks that needed to be accomplished in the order in which they needed to be completed. "We can start with the wedding registry, sure. There's plenty of stuff. Choosing flowers, wedding dress shopping—"

"No." Portia holds up a hand. "I draw the line on dress shopping. I'm not going to have her *sigh-hmm* her way through the showroom."

"Fair enough." Far be it from Emma to disrespect her daughter's boundaries.

"But I don't hate the idea of double-teaming her for other stuff."

"I'm not sure that's what I'm saying."

"Yes, you are." Portia laughs. "I can already see it. You're gonna just butter her up, ask all kinds of questions about what she likes and this and that. And whenever she tries the passive thing, you're going to draw out an opinion before she even realizes you're doing it. 'Oh, Doris,'" she mimics Emma in a remarkably accurate manner, "'I was wondering about that myself, but I didn't want to say anything. What are your hesitations?'"

Emma draws in a deep breath and sighs it out. "*Hmm*. I suppose I could do that."

"Oh, my God." Portia throws a strawberry at her. "That just gave me the shivers."

It's settled. Emma is officially on point with Doris throughout wedding prep. "I just want you to start your marriage off on the right foot. It's stressful to fight over family issues, and I don't wish that on you or anyone."

Time for dessert. Emma pops up and retrieves the brownies from the kitchen.

"Hey." Portia doesn't wait for her to set the plate down before grabbing one. "Lyle told me you know his uncle Ben."

Images of boxed rice dart across Emma's brain. "We graduated from high school together."

"You know he's like this big-time crisis PR guy, right? Lyle says he keeps a go bag packed in his office so he can catch a flight on a moment's notice."

"Sounds awful." Truly. She tries to picture what she'd even keep in a go bag. Would she have to buy doubles of all her cosmetics?

"I think it sounds amazing. He gets calls from companies all over the world. He handled that big pipeline leak in South Dakota or Montana or whatever a few months back. Apparently, there aren't many hotels in the area and all the rooms were booked up by press, so he lived in a trailer for a month."

Emma studies her over the top of her sunglasses. "And that sounds awesome to you?"

"Not the trailer, obviously. But the high stakes, catch the first flight to Geneva or whatever, yeah. Plus, think about all the insider knowledge he has. All the crap these corporations have pulled over the years."

This isn't her daughter at all. "You're watching too much television."

"Nobody watches TV anymore, Mom. And he's interesting. I like him. Lyle thinks we should all get together for a BBQ or something." Then, Portia does something that makes the brownie try to crawl back up Emma's throat. She wiggles an eyebrow and says, "He's single, too, you know."

"Portia Elaine." Of all the things she does not want her daughter thinking about, her love life tops the list.

"I'm just saying. And handsome, too." That wiggling brow again.

Emma stands and throws a napkin over Portia's face. "I'm gonna pluck that eyebrow out of your forehead if you keep wagging it at me."

She needs coffee. Or brain surgery. Anything to get her off this patio.

"It's only a barbecue!" Portia calls after her.

But Emma answers before retreating out of earshot. "No. No thank you. Nope. Nuh-uh. Take your pick. They all work the same."

Later, when they've finished and Portia kisses her mother goodbye, Emma stands in the driveway watching her go, not turning away until she's down the block and out of sight. Emma has always been an attentive mother, but this is a new habit, stealing every last glimpse of her daughter. It never feels like enough.

How can it be that I'm already done? she wonders as she waves. There are no more children to raise, and as soon as the wedding is over, Portia and Lyle will officially be their own family. Which leaves Emma alone.

Technically, she's been *on her own* for over a year now, and she's grown to appreciate the silence of coming home to an empty house. But math is math, as she likes to tell her students.

Take three people, subtract one, and you have two. Take two people, subtract one, and the cheese stands alone.

"I am alone." She speaks the words aloud. Maybe if she says them enough, she'll become desensitized. With repetition, she might even stop needing to choke back the tears that accompany them. "I am—"

Is that what she thinks it is?

Emma steps off the front stoop and walks a few feet into the grass. Sure enough, a dog has pooped on her lawn. This isn't Kanga or Roo's handiwork. Emma's dogs go in the back, and she's quick with the cleanup. The neighbor, however, has a white something about the size of a pig. Black spot on its back. She's seen it sneaking into her yard more than once.

The neighbor, Kent, is a single guy somewhere in his early thirties who lives alone and drives a very un–Northern California gas-powered Land Rover. He parks it in the street because his garage has been full of unpacked boxes for over a year.

Kent moved in shortly after Devin moved out, and Emma was briefly pleased to know that she would have a more capable and sprightlier neighbor than the elderly Mrs. Harrison on the other side. Then she noticed that he had a habit of putting his garbage cans out on the wrong day and instead of correcting his mistake, simply left them at the curb until collection day eventually rolled around—sometimes close to a full week.

And now his dog seems to have defecated on her grass.

She retrieves an empty bread bag from her recycling and scoops up the mess, then walks to the curb and deposits the mess into Kent's cans which are, conveniently and unsurprisingly, still out even though it's Saturday. Next time he's outside, she'll kindly ask him to keep better watch over his pet. She can do that now. Saying "no" may just be her new favorite hobby.

Carolina

Carolina has never loved email, but now it's giving her agita. The CEO announced the voluntary severance program on Monday, and she's spent the last two days replying to her team's questions about it.

Is this going to lead to layoffs if enough people don't volunteer?

Will those layoff packages be better or worse than the voluntary deals?

Is it better for me to take this and start looking for a new job, or take my chances that I'll survive further cuts?

The only answer she's legally permitted to give: Contact Human Resources via the helpline listed in the announcement. She'd have preferred to be physically gagged and bound to her chair. Then answering wouldn't be an option at all.

If she knew who she was going to lose, she'd get to work planning for mitigation. Carolina can plan anything, could pack a thousand hot dogs into a knapsack if that was the challenge. But to do so, she needed specifics. Is she working with cocktail weenies or footlongs?

Three times in the past week, she's scheduled time on Sandra's calendar, only to be edged out by an investor call or a last-minute trip to Shenzhen.

"She knows I want to know if anyone has volunteered yet." Carolina is at home lacing up her running shoes for a quick couple of miles. Queenie is half tuned in to a video conference, camera off, one earbud out. "I'm starting to wonder if she's icing me out."

"No, she's telling you to focus on the work in front of you." Queenie turns suddenly, unmutes himself, and puts on his work voice. "We can cache the feed early, if necessary."

Carolina heads out the door. She has three hours before she needs to be online with her team in Bangalore. One of her leads there is out unexpectedly for a family emergency and the work is suffering. She didn't know how many of the day-to-day headaches Kushal was sparing her from until he disappeared.

This morning, she woke to her phone blowing up over a data migration gone horribly wrong. One of the sales divisions her team supports requested a modification to the level of customer information available. It should have been a small change. Instead, an errant piece of code sent the accounts of fourteen-thousand customers into a loop, billing them repeatedly overnight. One customer reportedly received 360 identical notifications that she owed $19,763.62 for a product she'd already paid for.

This mishap, Sandra heard about, though not from Carolina directly. She would have told her, had Sandra not canceled their previously scheduled 10:00 a.m. meeting. Word of the sudden change came down from her assistant. "Sandra needs to be on a call with overseas folks but would like to be kept updated on the cleanup of last night's data migration."

It's a clear sign that your screwup is getting top management billing when an exec's assistant knows about it. It's also curious that even with fourteen-thousand customers complaining about being electronically buried in bills, Sandra still doesn't have the time to check in with the VP responsible for the mess. Queenie says it's a sign management trusts Carolina to fix it, but she's skeptical. Had this occurred under the previous CIO, Carolina's butt would have been called to his office immediately and her team would have remained under his hot glare until every last record glistened.

Realistically, Carolina knows the most she can do as a leader is to clear the obstacles threatening her team's ability to fix the issue. Which, right now, are none. But there are three people glued to their desks in San Jose who will be scrubbing away errant data until 7:00 p.m., at which point they'll hand the work over to their Bangalore counterparts for the next shift. Thus, Carolina runs. Because she can't fix the data herself and moving feels better than helplessness.

She exits her condo building and turns up Bellevue toward Howard, heading for Coyote Point. The arch of her left foot is aching again. Her trainer is worried about another stress fracture, but Carolina doesn't have the patience to get couched by her orthopedist. If she's not able to exercise, her head will explode, and heads are harder to fix than feet.

She feels her pace pick up as possible scenarios unfold in her head. Maybe no one on MAVERIK will leave. Team morale has dipped with the recent overtime, but employee survey data shows that it's higher than the corporate average. It's also possible she'll lose a few people, but less critical players—a painful, though not fatal, blow to the program.

The horror scenario is, of course, one in which her team leads leave. Each has been there since the program's inception, and that history gives them a skill set that can't be replicated. That sort of loss would qualify as a MAVERIK disaster.

She quickens her pace even more and comes upon a trail of electric and hybrid SUVs lining up several blocks deep outside Washington Elementary, parents and nannies on pickup duty.

She skirts a $100,000 Rivian and has to look twice before seeing the woman behind the wheel. She's barely tall enough to peek over the steering wheel. It's as if someone's toddler has escaped the playpen and driven a tank to school.

In this valley, people will do whatever it takes to get noticed.

Andi

Andi isn't flying to San Diego today as planned. She's at home, working in the tiny bedroom she and Dom converted to a shared office during the pandemic. School is out for two days, and Cameron has a Civics project due next week. He claims he's started it, but given the recent emails from both his English and Biology teachers citing missing work, his word can no longer be trusted. Andi's sixteen-year-old high school sophomore needs a babysitter.

She can hear him playing a video game through the shared wall. He thinks his headphones disguise the sound, but even the most enthusiastic civil servant is unlikely to regularly holler, "Hell yeah!" at regular intervals. If he's still at it after she finishes the brief she's reading, she'll have to crack down.

Last night, Andi and Dom tried to engage Cameron with a talk about the future. He'd never been a studious kid; they knew this by now. They understood that he was wickedly bright but bored by the classroom—an avid reader who only resists the novels assigned to him. The kid who built his own computer in seventh grade but ditched every session of the middle-school electronics club Andi paid for.

Cameron is going to do something with his life. That "something" just won't be the result of anyone else's encouragement or insistence.

The problem they can no longer ignore, however, is that his grades—never equal to his abilities—have slipped. Bs used to be a given, but now they are a pleasant surprise. At this rate, acceptance at a UC school will be a stretch for him. Andi graduated from UC Davis, Dom from UC San Francisco. Their son seems intent on throwing away his chances at either campus.

"I'll just go to San Diego State," he'd said while smearing peanut butter on a banana as if one accomplishment were no more difficult than the other.

Dom said, "That's not a guarantee, you know."

Andi asked, "Do you have any idea what you'd like to study?"

His response to both was a casual shrug. "I'll worry about that later."

Part of her can't blame him. The pressure put on teenagers nowadays is unnerving. Especially boys. The male brain doesn't fully develop until around the age of twenty-one, yet we expect them to make decisions about the rest of their lives several years before they're biologically prepared. Sixteen-year-old Cameron has only recently stopped taking hour-long showers.

And still, he has just two years of high school left. Choices will need to be made.

That is, if he doesn't fail Civics. Feeling a sudden jolt of anxiety, Andi pounds on the office wall. "Get to work, Cameron!"

Last week, Andi's mother called to wonder aloud whether he was acting out because she was working and traveling so much.

"I've already cut my travel down significantly, if that's what you're hinting at. Not to mention that I've worked his whole life, Mom. Kids benefit to see both parents pursue their passions." It's the line she's consoled herself with since leaving him with a nanny at six-weeks old.

Her mother, Geneva, had worked, too, as a leader in the Minnesota movement to adopt the Equal Rights Amendment. On February 8, 1973, the day the state successfully voted to ratify, her mother bundled Andi and her toddler sister into the stroller and buried them beneath a pile of blankets, heading out in eight-degree weather to celebrate with hundreds of other supporters outside the capital in St. Paul.

Sometimes Andi wonders if her commitment to women's civil rights wasn't frozen into her DNA that wintery day, written in ice on her personal constitution.

"I agree," her mother said. "Cameron is lucky to see you as a whole person. What worries me is that he doesn't see enough of you."

The guilt stabs, sharp and quick. "God, Mom. Do you hear yourself?" It's a judo move, to turn the pain aimed at her back onto her accuser. "Would you say that to Dom? He travels, too, you know."

"I do know, and yes, I would say the same to him."

Andi realizes she doesn't doubt it for a second. Geneva is not known for withholding her opinions.

"These years go by quickly, Andi. You can't get them back."

She knows. *She knows.* And yet. "You didn't get to choose the timing of your ERA work. And I don't get to convince those in power to quit causing so much human turmoil. The crisis is happening now. I'm compelled and equipped to help."

More than that, she considers her work a moral imperative. One taught to her by her mother. How many nickels and dimes had she collected in her UNICEF boxes as a kid for the starving children in Africa? This isn't any different. It simply requires more of her.

Geneva wasn't buying it. "As crass as it sounds, this violence will still be happening after Cameron is out of the house. There will always be people who need you, but those people won't always include your son."

"Kids go through phases, Mom. Isn't that what you told me when he quit eating meat? That as soon as he discovered how hard it is to cook for himself, he'd come back to the family table? You said, 'Let him experience the consequences of his choices.'"

Andi had supported her son's short-lived vegetarian pursuits. His rationale was well-intended—reduce carbon emissions, reduce his environmental footprint. But neither she nor Dom had time to cook multiple dinners. They barely managed to sit down together as it was.

"I know you don't like me butting in, but, Andi, look at the signs. His grades are slipping. He's not following through on his promises. Heck, he's brazenly lying to you." The impetus for their phone call that afternoon was a text in which Andi had been silly enough to tell her mom that Cameron had been busted at a house party, even though he'd explicitly told them he was staying overnight at a friend's house.

In the car on the way home, Dom asked why he hadn't tried to run when the police showed up. Cameron said he wasn't drinking and, therefore, didn't have anything to hide. His attorney father nearly drove the car off the road in an explosive lecture on reasonable suspicion.

"We're handling it, Mom." Though whether that was true, Andi was increasingly unsure.

"The signs are blinking yellow, sweetheart. Figure out what's going on with him before they turn red."

She knows. She knows!

Andi's attention returns to Cameron playing video games in the room next door. She hates to hover, but what choice does she have? She hits the wall, pounding her fist against the yellow paint she's hated for years but never taken the time to fix. "Cameron! Civics project! Now!"

She feels his urge to procrastinate the way a mama bird feels the gnawing hunger in her hatchlings' bellies. Obviously, no one wants to put their nose to the grindstone, but that's what living a full and productive life requires. It was supposed to have been enough for Cam to see his parents show a passion for their professions, to see firsthand what hard work looks like.

He wanted her home more often, so she made it happen, delegating more of her work to her already overworked team. And still, this kid of hers sits on the other side of the wall, ignoring her sacrifices, flaunting the privilege she blessed him with. Daring her to do something. Draining her patience. Forcing her hand.

"That's it." She stands so quickly she knocks over a full glass of water on her desk, soaking the briefs she's yet to read.

He hasn't even bothered to close his door. Probably for the better, since she would likely have kicked it in. He's laughing, his gaming headset on, the microphone brushing his chin. "DUDE! *What the hell are you doing?*"

Andi couldn't have said it better herself.

She leans over and grabs the PC tower off the floor. It's heavier than she expected, tweaking her back as she stands. One tug, and the room is aflutter in cords—black, white, and red snakes snapping from the wall, pulling the keyboard and monitor with them.

"MOM!" Cameron's voice breaks, along with his tether to the imaginary world where he has no homework, no responsibility. "WHAT THE ACTUAL FU—"

He's raging. But not nearly as loud as Andi's indignation. She's going to change this kid's attitude no matter how many thousands of dollars in computer hardware it costs her.

The heat from the tower's fan burns her hands as she carries it out the front door and down the porch steps. Cam's hot on her heels, cursing her with words and images she'll fret about later, when she's not busy teaching him a lesson.

Their neighbor Pamela is at the curb checking her mailbox. Pamela has a resale business on eBay. Mostly bras, socks, and underwear she buys on clearance, then lists for a small profit.

"Oh, Pamela!" Andi feels a cord brush against her ankle and prays it doesn't decide to trip her. "I'm wondering if you might be able to find a purpose for this—maybe for your own use or to resell?"

Cameron is lunging for the computer now, but her grip is tight. All he can do is wrap his hands around cables that break from their ports when he pulls. "Mom! No!"

Pamela is understandably confused, her eyes wide with the instinct to run. "Oh, I'm not sure I—"

Andi doesn't give her the chance to argue. "I'd very much appreciate if you took this off our hands." She shoves the machine into Pamela's arms. "Cameron may have permission to buy it back from you once the school year is over."

At this, he howls. "How am I supposed to finish my project without a computer?" Tears threaten the corners of his eyes.

Andi's resolve falters. Her kid is hurting. The neighbor thinks she's strange as a frog wearing a hat. She hasn't thought any of this through.

Lucky for them all, Cameron's teachers have.

"You'll finish it the same way most of your classmates will finish their projects—with your school-issued iPad." Every two years, the district provides all middle and high school students with a new tablet and keyboard with which they're supposed to access classroom materials, take tests, and complete homework. She has hardly stripped her son of his only resource.

"Cameron, your dad and I have given you a thousand chances to get your work done." She feels tears burble beneath her own lids. "You ignored the warnings. So now you deal with the consequences."

That night, lying in bed, these same words replay themselves in her head. This time, however, she applies them to herself as a mother. *You ignored the warnings, Andi. So now you deal with the consequences.*

Fern

Mack has had enough of Fern's fretting about how to tell Andi, Emma, and Carolina that she optioned the book.

"Rip the Band-Aid off, Fern. You gotta do it."

They're in the kitchen making dinner. More like he's boiling pasta and Fern is a few glasses into a bottle of Zinfandel.

"But do I?" she asks. "It's only a twelve-month contract. If Dakota doesn't put the book into development by next year, she loses the rights, and my friends never need to know she had them in the first place."

Still, he's not convinced. "If our kids came to you with the same dilemma, would you advise they lie to their friends?"

"It's not lying." She searches for the words. "It's forestalling unnecessary worry."

"Their worries, maybe. But you signed the deal last month and you've been on pins and needles about telling them ever since. Neither one of us can take this much longer."

"Fine." Fern picks up her phone and shoots off a text inviting Carolina to lunch. She flashes proof of her outreach at Mack. "Happy?"

"Very."

The lunch is harder than a colonoscopy to schedule because, apparently, Carolina "doesn't really do lunch" anymore.

Too busy and nothing I eat is on the menu.

Carolina's food regimen is unnerving, even by San Francisco standards. One day she's only eating sprouted grains. The next, she's not eating grain at all. Ultimately, they settled on a restaurant in Burlingame near Carolina's condo. She has an appointment with her trainer at 2:00 p.m. and will be working from home.

When the day comes, Fern drives the half hour across the San Mateo Bridge from her house in Berkeley and meets her at the restaurant, Flora, where Carolina orders a half dozen small plates of vegetables in all forms except battered and fried. Fern wonders how she manages to get any protein if this is what she eats but chooses not to say anything. The women on her favorite podcast have been talking about how triggering it can be when people comment on your food and that it's not anybody's business other than your doctor's. She's trying to abide by what seems like a good rule.

"So, I know why we're here." Carolina is holding a forkful of spicy cucumber. "You want my blessing on selling the screen rights to the book."

Fern lets out a tiny puff of breath.

"But you don't need to talk me into it. I'm all in. Truth is, we're over fifty. We're too old to care about what other people think. And frankly, I'm too busy."

"Andi wishes I'd kept her law school drama private." Fern prods at something called a zucchini hat. "And Emma is afraid of poking the Carlton bear again."

"What is there to be afraid of? We felt threatened, and we defended ourselves. Simple as that."

"Only, it's not as simple as that."

Carolina gives her a look. "If you'd really been worried, you wouldn't have put that chapter in the book."

She has her there. Fern fundamentally agrees with Carolina—this isn't a big deal. It happened decades ago. Their choices resolved their problem. Plus, she had to put that essay in the book. They wouldn't have gone on to live the lives they did if it weren't for each other and that single defining event.

"You didn't put his name in print, so don't put it on-screen. Problem solved." There's a sprout hanging from Carolina's lip, and she struggles to brush it away. "Honestly, you've always wanted to option one of your books and you deserve success."

Fern feels a lump in her throat when she tries to swallow, and it's not because of the eggplant. "Thank you."

Carolina's fork twirls in the air like a magic wand. "Now, on to me. You're not going to believe what the CEO said to me yesterday."

"Wait—" If Fern is going to fess up, now's her chance. But Carolina's change of subject hits the air between them like a much-welcome rain. "Never mind. Go ahead."

"So, I'm sitting in the senior leadership meeting next to Mark, the CEO. He's in the middle of some diatribe when he suddenly stops and says, 'Carolina, please get your poodle under control.'" She holds up a strand of her beautifully curly, beautifully big Portuguese hair.

"No, he did not compare your hair to a poodle."

"Like Winnie herself."

Fern laughs. Carolina is referring to Fern's black standard poodle, a dog who pays as much attention to her appearance as most supermodels. "I assure you, I don't spend anywhere near as much on Winnie's products as you do on yours."

"I assure you, that's true."

This isn't at all what Fern expected to be discussing at lunch today. "Are you going to file a complaint with HR?"

Carolina looks at her like she just asked if she were going to make an appointment at the groomer. "Uh, no. That is a whole mess I don't have the energy or time for."

"But he insulted you in front of your colleagues. Belittled you. Made a borderline racist comment, even."

"Yeah." Carolina nods. "All of that."

"So, you're just gonna take it? Tell me you're not."

Carolina isn't swayed. "Every guy in that room understood what an asshole he was being. It makes him look bad, not me."

Fern wants to stand on her chair and announce to the entire restaurant what just happened to her friend. *This is not okay, people!*

"Anyway, this is not a good time to go messing with the big boss—we're in the middle of layoffs. They're not calling them layoffs, but they are."

"Oh, my God. Are you worried?"

"Not about my position; it's safe. But I am worried about my program team. If I lose any one of a handful of people, we're hosed."

"Ouch," says Fern.

Carolina scowls. "I know. The stress is killing me. Seems like I'm either running or crying."

"That's not healthy."

"It's better than having a panic attack."

Carolina changes the temperature between them again, reaching for Fern's hand. "Hey. Sign the deal. Follow your dreams. Say yes."

Fern thinks she might fall off her chair with relief.

Emma

THE PEOPLE OF THE STATE OF CALIFORNIA DO
ENACT AS FOLLOWS:

SECTION 1.
Section 691284.5 of the Education Code is heretofore
amended to read:
691284.5.
Notwithstanding Section 691284, when the literacy curriculum framework is revised after January 1, 2016, the
Instructional Quality Commission shall consider including both of the following:
Age-appropriate information…

Emma blinks to keep the words from swimming across the
page. It's nearly nine o'clock and she's been reading a single
paragraph since crawling into bed a half hour ago. She hasn't
had sex in over a year, but this is what makes her yearn for her
former husband. She would have handed this *mishmash* of legal-
ese to Devin and waited five minutes for him to explain using
real, normal human words.

Now, however, this has got her thinking about Devin, which

is terrible, because she's lying in bed. And the thoughts one thinks about in bed bring one's mind to other places. Places she doesn't want to go, especially with regard to her ex.

His perfect triangle ratio of shoulders to waist. The way his thighs stayed muscular, even during his softer, rounder spells. Pressing against her hips. Driving her legs open—

Shit!

What the hell is wrong with her.

SECTION 1.

Section 691284.5 of the Education Code is heretofore amended to read:

And again, her brain is adrift within seconds. *Heretofore.* Such a whispery word. Half of it a sigh, the rest of it rhythm.

Ripe with innuendo.

Devin's leaning in. Murmuring it.

Heeeeretofore.

Here.to.fore.

Here.To.FORE

HERE.TO.FORE.

YES! It makes her scream. But the *her* screaming isn't Emma, it's Greta, the Anglo-Amazon currently sleeping with her husband. *YES! Heretofore! Heretofore! Heretofore! OH, YES, DEVIN!*

"Shut the fuck up, both of you!" That, Emma screams for real. At which Kanga wakes and Roo yelps. "Sorry." She's instantly shamed. "I wasn't talking to you. I meant your father. He's turned me into a ridiculous woman and you're the ones living with the consequences."

In a show of penance, she pats the duvet, and after silently consulting each other about her sincerity, Kanga follows Roo up the doggy stairs to join her. They're demons, the pair of them, always getting into something or other. Except the bed. Devin "couldn't sleep with paws in his face" so prior to his departure, they had been relegated to a doggy bed in the corner.

Not that their short corgi legs were any match for the pillow-top California King with the super-deluxe bedding their father preferred, anyhow.

Emma bought the pet stairs before she had the locks changed.

"So, gals." Roo is still turning circles, ever the picky one, but Kanga is all eyes on Emma. "I need your advice on something."

Devin hasn't been the only man crossing her thoughts lately. Benjamin Guy has been texting. And, yes, he has a way with words, but who knew he has such a *way* with words?

Her phone is on the bedside table. "'Hey.'" She reads the latest aloud. "'Visited my mom today and drove down Third. Couldn't help but remember the night the group of us filled our cars with discarded Christmas trees and sped down the street with them hanging out our doors. Dumped them all in Anderson's yard, if I remember correctly.'"

Kanga cocks her head.

Emma scowls. "Don't look at me that way. We were teenagers out having fun." In her head, she's right there again, in the back seat of Benjamin's yellow Chevette, open door flapping, her hands sticky with sap from the tree she's holding, bits of stray tinsel catching the streetlights as they pass.

"Here's the good part." She peers over her reading glasses at Roo to ensure she has both dogs' full attention. "'I've thought about everyone in that group of kids very fondly over the years. But when I saw you again, I realized something: those friendships instilled a confidence in me that I carry to this day. You, in particular. In your quiet beautiful way, you made it okay for a guy to be smart and quirky and all the stuff a sixteen-year-old boy can twist himself into knots about.'"

She flushes again. For a second, she wonders if he's thinking of someone else. Certainly not Emma, who was, without fail, the last person at the party, always the most hesitant to join the fun. That night especially. She'd grabbed a tree because someone shoved it into her hands. She hadn't been given a choice but to come along.

"So, gals, you see why I don't know how to respond." The fact that she's seeking social advice from her dogs is not beyond her. "I have refused to accept his dinner invitation, but he's very persistent." Okay, so there had been no mention of meeting up in person again. But Ben's messages hadn't slowed. "And who puts that sort of a thing in a text? 'You made it okay for a guy to be smart and quirky...' Is it a compliment? Or does he mean that I was smart and quirky, too, which could be taken as an insult. Granted, it's most likely nothing but a platitude. He's just buttering me up. But still. I can't not respond to it." The double negative catches her ear, as well. "Or can I?"

Roo drops her head with a grunt.

Emma's fingers hover for just a moment before typing,

Were we really just sixteen?

Molly Ringwald is in her head now, wearing a bridesmaid's dress and sitting atop a glass dinner table across from dreamy Jake Ryan. The Thompson Twins are singing "If You Were Here." The video is wobbly, the worn VHS tape reminding her it can only be played and rewound so many hundreds of times.

She adds,

I agree with you. There was something magical about those days.

That's not too much to admit. They had been friends, after all. At least Benjamin seems to think so and who is she to argue with his memories?

She whispers her goodwill to her old friend across the digital universe. And heretofore, Devin disappears.

White linen tablecloths are lovely on nearly any occasion except a first date. Emma finds herself consumed by keeping the one in front of her now clean, lest it become a Rosetta Stone to her emotional state. Crumbs must be swept away by trembling fingers as she tears apart her dinner roll. An errant wrinkle beckons, insisting it be rubbed flat.

"What an exciting life you've lived, Benjamin." A smear of brown balsamic vinegar bleeds slowly into the tablecloth's fibers, threatening to transfer itself onto the sleeve of her blouse. "You make your fellow Spartans proud." Who is she, the head of the 1990 reunion committee?

"Every day is a different challenge. That's the part I love most."

After weeks of their text-based walk down memory lane, Ben again suggested dinner.

I know you're busy, but I leave for South Africa next week and will be gone through the end of the month. How about we squeeze all the texts we would have sent into one dinner? Might even save you time in the long run.

Emma doesn't know what drives him to want to reignite their friendship after three decades apart, but she's begun to suspect she is trying to revert to a time when the future felt ripe and full. Attempting to regain the happy "world's your oyster" sensibility she'd felt when she and Benjamin were friends. Unrealistic, perhaps. But tempting all the same.

This morning, her hips actually cracked as she got out of bed. Not creaked. Creaking was benign—the aftereffects of a strenuous workout or sleeping in a strange bed. No, this morning, they popped so loudly the dogs leaped to their feet. "Oh!" she'd exclaimed. Adding, "Gracious!" the same way her grandmother did every time her brother, Sam, filled his diaper as a toddler.

Maybe that was a good conversational topic for tonight. *Do you ever find yourself behaving like your grandparents?*

It doesn't help her nerves any, either, that she had to shoo Kent's dog out of her yard multiple times this afternoon. The last time in heels. She sank into the grass and nearly sprained her ankle. If that ever does happen, she's sending Kent the medical bill.

You're fine, she reminds herself. She didn't hurt her ankle, nor did the dog do its business on her grass. And right now, she has a salad to eat. She will not be one of those women who picks at her dinner, then goes home to swallow a pint of ice cream. No. Nope. Not ever.

They've met at a bistro in Sebastopol, far enough away from home she doesn't have to worry about bumping into anyone she knows. Explaining Benjamin would be too mortifying right now, as she's not anywhere close to ready for inquiring minds. Introducing him as "an old friend" is accurate, but no relationship other than his being immediate family would eliminate the appearance of possible romantic involvement, and that's a question she knows will tie her tongue into humiliating knots.

Then again, is this a date?

"You must feel the same way about teaching, I'd imagine."

She's wandered off, leaped forward several hours to the conundrum of whether to accept a good-night kiss. Is there a signal she's supposed to send now to help avoid humiliating him later? "Pardon me?"

"Teaching. Does it continue to stretch you after all these years?"

"Oh, yes," she manages. Though now she's having to erase the image of herself dressed in a leotard. Stretching. Probably pulling a hamstring.

Benjamin studies her quietly for a moment, and leans in. "I worry I may have come across a bit strong."

"When?" Their texts have retraced years of teenage terrain. "Back in high school?"

She recognizes instantly that she's misinterpreted.

"No. I mean with this, here." He motions between them. "I get the sense I'm making you uncomfortable. I apologize."

"Nonsense."

What is it, this need of hers to want everyone to love her,

only to grow uncomfortable when they eventually do? She's gripping her salad fork so tightly that her knuckle is throbbing, and she's looked everywhere but in his eyes. Yet, to hear him express his disappointment so early in their evening is almost enough to kill her. And she would deserve it.

Marriage to Devin was a twenty-four-year exercise in trying to convince herself she was enough. She recognizes that now, thanks to her therapist, Nikki, and the self-help section at Barnes & Noble. In fact, she's grown to accept that she had probably known she was unhappy for years but had assigned herself a penance. That if she'd been fine with the power differential at the beginning of their life together, she would have to continue to be. When she said, "I do," she'd meant it.

It wasn't as if she hadn't benefited. Devin's oversize personality came with an oversize lifestyle. Once, she'd overheard one of his partners describe him by saying, "big balls, big deals." Beautiful home, exotic travel, high-end details. He hadn't failed to dream, nor had he failed to achieve. Devin was the month of March, always coming in like a lion.

That made Emma the lamb. Which had been fine. Until it wasn't.

She finds herself drawing swirls in her vinaigrette with the tines of her fork. "I no longer know how to talk to people."

"Excuse me?" Benjamin's leaning in even farther now, palm tucked behind his ear. "I didn't catch that. My hearing is decades older than I am."

His face. It might be the first time she's allowed herself to look at it. "Why me?" That's not what she'd said before but it's closer to what she meant.

"Why you?" He doesn't understand. She's clearly flummoxed him.

"I realize I'm not making any sense. It's just, why me? Why are you here with me? You have a gigantic career and an even bigger brain. I teach second graders. Which is wonderful, and difficult. But it's a small life, and it's mine, and admittedly it's taken me too long to be able to say this, but I don't need Morocco in the fall."

At this, he sits back, refolding his napkin in his lap and smiling as if she'd just complimented him on his tie. "I met your ex-husband at the party."

So, she's a cliché. "This isn't about Devin."

"That's not what I'm implying." He raises a hand in apology. "Or maybe it is. Which probably sounds terribly presumptive and a little bit gross."

"You think?"

He accepts the admonition with a chuckle. "I guess what I mean is, if I'd asked you the same question—*why me?*—the baggage surrounding it would have been about my ex-wife."

Emma had not known he was married, though she'd assumed, and she suddenly burned with curiosity. The picture of a beautiful brunette, all legs but with a head for numbers burst into frame. She hates her instantly.

"Amelia," he offers in lieu of forcing her to ask. "She's a surgeon. She lives in Atlanta. It took me a while to get my feet back under me after the divorce."

"Do I seem wobbly?" She ought to be embarrassed at the insinuation, but she's not. Instead, it feels as if he noticed her struggling with the door and offered to hold it for her.

"Put it this way. We've been texting for close to a month. Nearly every night recently. And you just asked me why I'm here with you."

"It's a fair question." Her fingers release ever so slightly on her fork.

He nods. "Of course, it's fair. I'd just hoped it would have been obvious."

They don't say any more on the subject, too close to crossing into territory for which they're not ready. Their entrées and dessert disappear beneath the familiar gauzy haze of old memories, of people they once knew and the times they shared.

She forgets to ask the question about him acting like his grandfather.

At the valet, the lone attendant is hustling to fetch keys and return cars, and the line is several people deep. Benjamin parked in a lot around the corner but insists on waiting with her.

"I had a lovely evening, Benjamin. Thank you." This is the third or fourth time she's thanked him since the waiter dropped off the check. "I know it wasn't easy trying to wrangle a commitment from me."

She's waiting for a sign, something to indicate whether he, too, enjoyed their time together. The fact that he walked her directly to the valet without suggesting an after-dinner drink means tonight is over. This is a relief of sorts. She wouldn't have slept with him, regardless, and this releases her from having to dodge or make excuses.

There is still hope for a kiss, though. A sweet peck on the cheek, a brush on the lips—neither of those would be objectionable.

"It was lovely to see you again," he says. But with each word, he's farther away, and by the time the valet asks for her ticket, they're too far apart to even shake hands. "I look forward to keeping in touch."

She feels the rejection like a kick to the stomach.

He'd all but said her favorite word, *no*. And she didn't like the sound of it.

Andi

"MOM! You're in the wrong spot again!"

Andi is sitting in the car around the corner from the high school when Cameron throws open the passenger door.

"Dad always parks across the street under the tree. I already told you."

"Okay! Okay. I just grabbed the first spot I saw."

Cameron has lost driving privileges for two weeks after lying about having read *Fahrenheit 451* before writing an English paper about it. One would think that a kid who's currently as mad at his parents as Cam would be drawn to the novel's dark dystopia. But his teacher's comments in the margins, including, *I don't recall a character named Chip,* made it clear he hadn't even bothered to check the accuracy of the internet plot summaries he skimmed.

Now, because of Cam's choices, Andi and Dom are juggling travel schedules and client meetings to get him back and forth to school. As in, the punishment is hurting the parents as much as the kid.

"God. You never listen to me!"

Andi wants to scream. *I don't listen?*

"Fine, Cam. Tomorrow, I promise. I'll be standing under the tree waving a flag at you."

The groan comes from his deepest, darkest depths.

They don't speak for several blocks. Time enough for the nagging voice in her brain to pipe up. *You ignored the warnings. So now you deal with the consequences.*

This morning, she and Dom argued. One of those fights where whispered jabs fly from behind coffee mugs, and every facial expression says, "I hate you so much right now that I might still be angry tonight."

He'd had the nerve to tell her where to park when picking Cameron up from school. Which, in Andi's frustration, translated to an attack on her parenting.

"He'll survive," she'd hissed, already forgetting the instructions.

"What's the big deal?" Dom threw back. "He's familiar with the routine, and it's easy."

Easy. That's the word that sent her reeling. Cameron didn't need *easy.* He needed *hard.*

Or did he? In the hours since the fight with Dom, she's begun to wonder if Cameron is making bad choices from a place of emotional exhaustion. Recently, she saw a cartoon circulating on social media in which a nursery full of adolescent children sit sucking their thumbs. Only, in place of their thumb is a computer monitor, the message being that screens have become the self-soothing mechanism for an entire generation. Now she can't stop worrying whether her absence these last few years created a vacuum that young Cameron was left alone to fill.

No wonder he wants to spend all his time online. She's essentially a stranger to him.

The fog of parental guilt hanging over her head has become so unrelenting it reminds her of that scene in *The Godfather Part II*. Just when she thought she was out… Choosing to spend weeks at a time thousands of miles away from her kid was one thing. But somewhere along the line, she became so detached from his needs that now she can't even bother to show up in the place he knows to look for her.

"Sorry I barked at you, Cameron." She shoots him an apologetic look before the stoplight turns green. "Seriously. Tomorrow. Under the tree. Same place as Dad."

He glances at her. Briefly. Skeptically. "It makes a difference. I like to know where you're at."

Then, as if she'd learned nothing, the lawyer in her wants to argue. He found her today. Found her yesterday. She always comes. He doesn't need to know where she's parked to fulfill her promise.

But it's the mother who rises to answer. "I hear you, bud. I got it."

Emma

At brunch, Doris Fluke uses Lyle's trip to the restroom as an opportunity to ask Portia whether she intends to take his last name.

"Well…" Portia pauses a forkful of eggs Benedict mid-bite.

Emma has known the answer for months. They'd been on the couch sharing a pint of lemon sorbet and haunting Pinterest wedding pages. "If he had any other name," she'd said. "Portia May sounds like a question, but Portia Fluke? Absolutely not."

"The origin is Anglo-Saxon and can be traced back to the Norman conquest." Doris is wearing a look so satisfied as she says this that it strikes Emma she might be the sort of woman who has the newspaper delivery boy fired for hitting her gardenia bushes.

"Isn't that right, Sylvester?"

"So they say."

She's staring at Portia as if the girl owes them her thanks.

Emma says, "I wish I'd kept my maiden name." It's a lie, but she's in a mood, and Doris is pushing buttons. "It was Johnson. A bit generic, but it was mine. I don't understand why this is still even a question for young women."

"It will affect the monogram." Doris manages to sidestep her culpability entirely. Because Doris, Emma suddenly recognizes, is the center of the universe, the queen of the realm. How dare lesser inhabitants like Emma and Portia, who have driven all the way to Sacramento to finish the bridal registry, hold sway.

No, they have been summoned to witness this discussion, not participate in it.

Emma takes a sip of ice water to cool her rising heat.

Doris smooths a graying flyaway at her temple. "You'll have to decide by the time we arrive at the store."

Somehow, Portia manages to smile. "Or…" She's transitioned into her teacher voice, and Emma can practically mouth the words she says next. "Maybe we don't make a problem where we don't have one yet."

Doris pinches her lips, and Emma watches her shoulders rise as she fills her chest with air. "Hmm…"

Lord almighty. Has she just?

Portia continues, "You sound disappointed. Which is understandable. But Lyle doesn't have any expectations for me or my name."

Emma is momentarily so proud of her daughter that tears threaten to burst from her eyes. Had this been her, she would have sputtered and danced around her mother-in-law's inquisition until Devin returned, then lied and promised to discuss it as soon as possible.

But, of course, Emma never considered keeping her maiden name. At the time, she had considered taking her husband's name a sign of their everlasting commitment to each other. The irony.

The queen is pursing and scowling. It's no wonder she has such deep wrinkles.

When Lyle returns, he reports that the men's room is "White on white, like that display bathroom you liked." He's describing it to Portia, and Doris wriggles in her seat like the class gossip who's been caught out of the loop.

"Display bathroom? Are you looking at real estate?"

Sylvester drains his coffee. "Not a great time for interest rates."

Doris continues, "Trust me, white tile is lovely, but the grout shows everything. You'll be scrubbing it every other day."

And just like that, the two of them simultaneously engage in one-on-one conversations with their son. Sylvester says, "I thought we talked about renting. I've been looking into coverage for you."

"I suppose that explains why you originally put white linens on your registry."

"Forgot to mention that you're going to want to stairstep your way into disability insurance for the umpteenth time being. Lock in the rates when you're young and healthy."

"I know you think you want pure white Egyptian cotton, but I went back to the store and found alternatives you're going to like better."

"You can build coverage later. New bundling products all the time."

Emma is on the verge of intentionally knocking over a glass of water when she sees Portia grab Lyle's knee beneath the table.

He raises a hand. "Hey. Cool it. We were at the design center with friends. They're the ones doing the remodeling."

"Oh." His mother sounds shockingly disappointed, as if she hadn't just seconds ago been ramping herself up into a state over the horrors of a white-on-white bathroom.

"In time. All in good time," says Sylvester. He pulls a credit card out of his wallet and drops it onto the bill with a *thwak*. "Brunch is on me, Emma. Put your purse away."

No matter that she hadn't even pulled it out. And to think Emma used to accuse Devin of using money to manipulate a conversation.

It's time to right this floundering ship. She says, "Plenty of exciting things happening for you two already without having to buy a house, too. Right?"

Everyone nods. Except Doris. "You can't buy a house without a monogram. What will you put on the welcome mat?"

"What's this?" Lyle glances between the two women.

Portia raises her palms in surrender, an attempt to keep from getting pulled back into this conversational pool. "Your mom was asking if I'm going to change my name. I told her you don't expect me to."

"Right." He sounds confident, but Emma catches the slightest hitch in his tone. "'Course not. It's your name. You get to do what you want."

Doris is filling her chest. Everyone sees it.

"Mom—" Now Lyle's palms are up, and retreat is in the air. "I'm sure you can understand."

The hmm-ing has begun, and the rest of them sit uncomfortably, waiting to see if this woman can release herself from the expectations of bygone eras to step into the present.

"I never said I didn't understand."

Sylvester smacks a palm on the table, and Emma's expecting him to pledge his support to his son and soon-to-be daughter-in-law when he says, "I'm gonna hit the restroom before I go." A cordial slap to Lyle's back and he's gone.

Portia shoots a wide-eyed glare at her mother from across the table. "Of course," Emma stammers, again reminded that Devin would have known exactly what to say in this situation. Why did he have to take his good traits with him when he left? "It's difficult for all of us to adjust our expectations. I was surprised to hear that Portia is going to commute to her job from the city." Napa is at least an hour in good traffic. She'd assumed they'd find an apartment somewhere in between, but Lyle loves his neighborhood and Portia has always wanted to live in San Francisco. Things will change soon enough once they start having babies.

Doris, however, doesn't acknowledge the interjection. Emma has forgotten that her opinions are inconsequential. "I'm sorry you no longer have any use for my advice."

"Oh, Doris—" Emma is swift to redirect. "I don't think anyone was saying that."

Lyle joins the chorus and soon the table is a parade of backtracking sentimentality. Times have changed. Portia has already established a career. Her name isn't a reflection of her love.

Sylvester returns to the table but doesn't sit. "Gotta leave now if I'm going to meet Barry at the clubhouse before tee time."

Soon, the rest of them are bustling to gather purses and phones, and follow him out of the restaurant. Brunch is over, everything but the bill left unresolved.

That evening, a cold compress on her forehead to battle the headache that followed her home, Emma sees a Sacramento area code pop up on her caller ID.

"I've decided to throw a bridal shower for Portia at our house," Doris says. "As her mother, you understand her tastes. I presume you won't be offended if I ask you to join me in the planning?"

Emma's heart begs to say no. *Doris Fluke will chew you up and spit you out like bones and gristle*, it screams. But her brain remembers the commitment Emma made to Portia. *You volunteered to manage Doris. Saying yes is your only option.*

"Thank you for asking." She screws a face, pinching her eyes closed against the encroaching dread. "Nothing would please me more than to help you."

Clearly, she doesn't have a headache. She has a brain tumor.

Andi

Andi is due in court in ten minutes. She's standing in her office downtown, sliding a suit jacket over her shoulders, when her email pings. A note from Cameron's German teacher.

Bad news from school is the last thing she ought to put in her head right now. Today, a judge has finally agreed to hear arguments about whether to compel the ICE contractor accused of raping and impregnating Andi's client Abha to submit to a DNA test.

It doesn't help Abha's credibility that the baby was born last week with jet-black hair and eyes when her alleged father is fair and blond. Nor does it matter to the contractor that they hired the man despite the domestic assault conviction on his record.

When it comes to the law, past is not always prologue.

Andi stares at her computer monitor. **Following up on Cameron's progress** reads the subject line.

Don't open it.

Even if she weren't heading to court, she's desperate to cling to the quiet, lingering détente she's felt since last night. She'd been reading on the couch. Cam walked out of his room and curled right up next to her. Didn't say a word. Didn't stay for more than a minute or two. Just long enough for her to reach around and ruffle his beautiful curls, to smell his Cameron-ness, body wash and the sweet slick of sweat.

If only she knew the conditions required for her son to show up for himself, she'd manufacture them a thousand times over. And a thousand times after that.

Despite her better instincts, she hovers a finger over the mouse. And clicks.

Just a quick note to let you know that Cameron has caught up on his missing assignments and stayed on track this week. I appreciate your partnership. Whatever you're doing at home, keep it up. —Frau Mueller.

Halle.*frickin*.lujah.

The relief is almost enough to blunt the shock and frustration thirty minutes later when the judge rules to block her motion.

Not quite enough. But almost.

Fitness in the City
(and What It Did to Our Feet)

From *Smart Girls Say Yes*
by Fern McAllister

Take it from me—if you're going to adopt a Say Yes attitude, you'd better take care of your feet. You'll need them to launch yourself into new adventures. To rise tall and be heard by the powers that be. And especially to stand your ground, refusing to cede your territory to those who aim to steal it.

Plus, trust me when I say this, you'll look damn-well ridiculous trying to pair orthopedic sandals with sequins. Don't ask me how I know.

Now, if you think I'm exaggerating when I claim that your feet just might be the secret to your ongoing success, you're most likely a woman in your twenties or thirties. In which case, you definitely need to keep reading.

To commence our lesson, let's travel back to the '80s, when my suburban Milwaukee school district took the "scared straight" approach to sex ed. To walk into tenth-grade health class was to surrender oneself to an assault of shock-and-awe imagery designed to frighten our psyches and neuter our libidos.

Old man Sorenson loved to remind us that "herpes is forever, kids." But so is plantar fasciitis, and how I wish to heaven above our Dr. Scholl's insoles–wearing teacher would have thought to mention that.

Fast-forward to the '90s when, in my twenties, I could do just about anything in heels. Walk the one mile uphill from the BART station to my apartment or start the night at the Market Street end of the Embarcadero and finish it at Marina Green. I celebrated Halloween in the Castro dressed as Cher and didn't take off my four-inch platform boots to check out the party underway atop Twin Peaks.

Now, as a forty-something-year-old woman, every six months my podiatrist gives me a shot between my toes.

I'm not heroin curious. I have a condition called Morton's neuroma that, gone untreated, makes it feel as if someone cut my foot open in the middle of the night and inserted a shard of glass between my third and fourth toe knuckles. Twice a year, Dr. Feelgood fills his syringe with steroids and says, "If I had a nickel for every woman who regrets the shoe choices of her youth."

If only I had a nickel for every doctor who's ended an appointment by wishing they had a nickel for every condition with which they'd just diagnosed me. Eight years ago, I showed up at the obstetrician's office wanting to know how I could possibly have gotten pregnant a third time, never mind that I was still nursing my eight-month-old, and on the pill, and married to a man who traveled more than he was home.

The doctor smiled, shook his head, and said, "If I had a nickel for every woman who got pregnant while on birth control…"

Excuse me? Perhaps old Mr. Sorenson should have leaned on that tidbit a little more heavily in between slideshows of genital warts.

★ ★ ★

While I don't regret any of my children, I do regret not taking better care of my feet. As every philosopher from John Muir to Dr. Seuss will tell you, our feet take us places, and those places can change our lives.

Must I continue to stress this point? Yes, I must.

Let's turn to Carolina as our first example. She wasn't a runner when I first met her. She exercised furiously, aerobicizing her body into a lifelike rendition of a Reebok catalog model. Until, one day, while walking to class across the Marina Green, she eyed a running group assembling for warm-ups. The leader was just her type. "I'm a sucker for a Matt Damon look-alike."

It was a Bay to Breakers training camp, the annual 12k across the Golden Gate Bridge and through the streets of San Francisco. Carolina said, "I ran five miles in Reebok aerobics shoes that afternoon. Shin splints for days, but it was worth it."

Within a month, Carolina ran her first Bay to Breakers. Then she joined the coach's San Francisco marathon training program and ran that. Then a backcountry trail marathon. And so on and so forth.

She never slept with the Matt Damon doppelgänger. "I don't think I ever even kissed him. But I'd never have run even a mile if it weren't for that smile."

Next week, she leaves for an expedition to the top of Mount Kilimanjaro. But here's the catch: the trip was originally scheduled for last year. Only Carolina trained so hard she suffered a stress fracture in her foot and, despite Athena-esque efforts, couldn't recover in time for departure.

If you ask her about the episode, she'll downplay the coincidence. "Fractures happen," she likes to say.

To which I say, "Especially if you don't take care of your feet!"

If you take a lesson in foot care from anyone, take it from Emma. I once heard her say that "teaching is travel." I think she meant metaphorically, the transfer of knowledge leading to the transformation of minds, that sort of thing. But any parent who's ever volunteered to assist in their child's classroom has witnessed firsthand the reason that teachers are a pedometer's kryptonite.

Emma never sits down. She paces the front of the classroom, walks the hallways to and from lunch and recess and phys ed, squats desk-side for one-on-one moments with her students, but almost never places her butt on a chair.

Of all our friends, Emma demonstrated the most innate wisdom about her feet. The day she stood at the front of the conference room guiding Carolina and me through our new employee orientation, she wore a pair of brown Mary Janes I'd last seen in a sepia-toned photograph of my grandmother. Low and practical, they struck me as the white cotton panties of the shoe world. Hardly sexy, but what girl doesn't want a pair?

Late '90s shoe fashion meant chunky platforms, square toes, and three-inch heels. I swaddled my baby bunions in a pair of black Steve Madden block-heeled penny loafers with a one-inch platform sole. Carolina strutted back and forth to work in a pair of Via Spiga snakeskin peep-toe block pumps. Andi slipped on a pair of strappy red Chinese Laundry kitten-heeled sandals after work, leaving her conservative Kenneth Cole platform heels beneath her desk. Emma was all flats, all the time.

We called her Miss Frizzle and asked when her magic school bus was due to arrive.

Today, she's the only one among us who can stand upright for an hour without complaining. All four of us had plans to take the world by storm. Decades later, Emma's the only one still in the running to do it.

In college, I wore a button on my backpack with that iconic quote from Ginger Rogers. "I did everything Fred did, only backward and in high heels." Such was my twenty-something version of feminism. Now, among my forty-something friends, our version of feminism is to scream at the TV whenever a cable news head compliments the former president's former-model wife's Louboutin's. "WHY IS VIAGRA COVERED BY HEALTH INSURANCE BUT NOT BUNION SURGERY???"

Andi had bunion surgery at thirty-five.

In addition to Morton's neuroma, my feet are also prone to ingrown toenails.

Carolina wages an ongoing battle with stress fractures.

Listen to me, any of you twenty-somethings reading this. Your feet won't last as long as you think they will. Last month I bought a pair of Birkenstocks to match my favorite pair of dress pants and I wasn't trying to be ironic.

The world will soon be yours to lead, my young friends. Stand up and make your voices heard. Future generations will look to you to stop the ozone from disappearing and keep the honeybees pollinating. Nations will rise up against each other, and you will be asked to make peace. More Boomers leave us every day, and Millennials are just hitting their stride. It's my generation, I'm afraid, who won't be of much help in your life-or-death crusades. We're too busy making appointments with the podiatrist.

June

Emma

It's the first weekend in June, which means Emma has one full week of school left. Summer will hardly provide time to relax, but at least she won't be juggling students and parents and the curriculum review committee on top of the wedding planning. She'd presumed her off time would be filled with discussions about flowers and bridesmaid's gifts and honeymoon destinations. Instead, if the past couple of months are any indication, she's preparing for a summer of Doris.

Recently, she's received a series of phone calls from Doris requesting that she look at stores in "her area" for napkins in the correct shade of pink. Not Pepto-Bismol pink. Not Barbie pink. But rose-petal pink. As if the universe had created one natural shade and all others were mere bastards.

This morning, it was a phone call to inquire whether "any of her caterers" used half-and-half rather than heavy cream in their quiches. Apparently, the caterer Doris hired for the shower dared to admit she preferred half-and-half and Doris nearly fainted. Emma had no caterers to call—as if she had them on speed dial—but fibbed and said she would, *of course*, call her "people." All while pacing the bedroom in her underwear, phone glued to her ear while trying to zip up one sundress

after another and failing. She'd lost weight in the months surrounding the divorce, but it returned and brought along friends.

Now she speeds across the Richmond–San Rafael Bridge,
one eye on her rearview mirror watching for the highway pa-
trol, a half hour late for brunch at Andi's. It would be the first
time since the engagement party they'd all been together, and
Emma doesn't have the energy to be angry with them anymore.
These days, all her frustrations flow toward Doris.

It's not just Doris and Emma's shrinking wardrobe that's put
her behind schedule. She walked out the door this morning to
find not one, but *three* doggy piles in her front lawn. What on
earth is Kent feeding that animal?

She marched across the yard and rang his doorbell. It was
one of those video bells. The kind with an app that shows you
who's there and allows you speak to your guest without extending face-to-face hospitality.

"Hullo?"

It took Emma several seconds to realize that her neighbor's
voice was coming from a tiny speaker on the doorbell. "Kent?"

"Yuh."

"It's Emma. From next door."

"I know. I can see you."

She felt suddenly self-conscious. "Can you come to the door
so we can speak in person?"

"I'm not dressed."

Emma rolled her eyes behind closed lids. A simple bathrobe
would do.

"What'cha need?"

She refocused. "I need your dog to quit going to the bathroom in my yard."

"Yeah, I've seen him pee over there."

He was *aware* of this? "Frankly, Kent, it's not the pee that
concerns me. Though I'd appreciate if you put a stop to that,
too."

"I think there's a hole somewhere in my fence. That's how he's getting out."

It astonished and dismayed her how much money lazy men like Kent must be able to demand for salary. After all, he'd never have been able to buy a house in this neighborhood if he weren't bringing in at least mid-six figures. Maybe he was more diligent at the office. "If you don't want to fix it yourself, perhaps you can hire someone. I'll give you the info for my handyman."

"Sure. If you want."

Yes, she did want. Very much. "Well, please take care of it one way or another. It's happening every day now."

"Yep."

And with that, Kent clicked off. No goodbye. No thank you. Not even a promise to resolve the issue. The nerve.

Emma, however, was not finished. And she would not be dismissed by a man too indolent to put on pants. She leaned in and put her face to the camera. "Please tend to your dog," she said, no idea if he could still hear or see her. "And goodbye."

Andi

Andi wakes up already dreading the day but knowing that what she's doing will help set things right. At least, she hopes it will.

Her best friends are coming over for brunch.

This is the way it always goes with Andi, an invitation followed by dread. She's an extrovert. Loves gathering people. Can't seem to have enough conversation ever. Until the hour before her guests are due to arrive. Then, it's "What the hell was I thinking?"

By 9:00 a.m., she's racing around the house in her pajamas gathering random bits of daily mess into a laundry basket. Dom's book on the side table. Cameron's socks. A stray water glass.

"You want me to make a pitcher of Bloody Mary's when everyone arrives?" Dominick is already a full cup of coffee down and glowing in the morning sun.

She opens the fridge, hoping its contents will refresh her memory. "I can't remember what I planned to cook." The English muffins leap at her. It's eggs Benedict for three of them, and all the vegan whatevers she bought for Carolina.

Dom pats her back as he leaves. Which is fine. His happy mood is pissing her off. If she's not calm, no one should be.

Yesterday, she had a panic attack in the toilet paper aisle at

Target. Not that Dom knows that. She didn't tell him, mostly because she diagnosed herself on the internet and she's forever telling Dom and Cam not to trust Dr. Google.

She was comparing brand-name prices, when suddenly she couldn't breathe. Muscles clamped around her chest, refusing to allow the air in. Her vision became a black tunnel dotted with white sparkles. She had to reach for the shelf to steady herself, then decided to sit—right there on the white tile floor, in the same skirt she'd worn to work that day. Legs splayed wide in front of her, unladylike, blocking the aisle. One thought beating itself against her brain: *People can see my underwear.*

And then, as suddenly as it came, the feeling passed.

Just like that. It came and went. She threw a twenty-four-roll pack of Charmin into her cart and walked to the checkout.

In the car, she pulled out her phone and entered her symptoms. Dr. Google had several alarming ideas, including a heart attack, congestive heart failure, and pulmonary embolism. Surely, if she was able to stand up and pull out her credit card, she wasn't at imminent risk of death. Maybe she'd simply picked up a rare tropical disease in all her travels. But the most likely culprit was an acute onset of anxiety.

She'd panicked over toilet paper. And if her brain went haywire over ply, one bad moment in the courtroom could prove disastrous.

But she'll deal with that later. Right now, she needed to poach the eggs. Time with her friends would make her feel better. It always did. Right?

Fern

Fern pulls into Andi's driveway and blows a deep breath through tight lips. Andi has managed to wrangle all four friends together for brunch, and this is Fern's chance to break the news about optioning her book rights.

She's the first to arrive, as it's a ten-minute drive from her house in Berkeley to Andi's place in the Oakland Hills. Carolina is running a race this morning in Dublin, an East Bay suburb a half hour away. It's nearly an hour's drive for Emma down from Petaluma and across the endless span of the Richmond–San Rafael Bridge. Her house is almost in wine country.

Fern stops on the front step before letting herself in. The weather is perfect, seventy degrees under partly cloudy skies. The first Saturday in June.

"Hiya."

Andi is in the kitchen pulling a stack of plates from the cupboard. "Hey. Didn't hear you."

"I didn't bother knocking." She retrieves the dishes from Andi's outstretched arms. "Eating outside?"

"Yes, please. Thanks."

Backyards can be tricky business in the Oakland Hills, but Andi and Dom got lucky. Their yard is flat, and despite the closeness of the neighboring houses, the space feels like an urban retreat. A thicket of eucalyptus trees shades the property line, and the air smells like jasmine. The scent of California. If Fern could bottle it, she'd never have to sell another word.

Andi reappears carrying a flatware caddy. She's wearing an easy gray linen peasant dress, making her the only person Fern knows who buys linen without regret. Somehow, the inevitable wrinkles don't look messy on her. "Dom offered to mix a pitcher of Bloody Marys. You think anyone will want them?"

"I don't know why there isn't one already in my hand, frankly." It's a typical lighthearted Fern comment, and yet somehow it comes out feeling alien. As if she's just discovered after half a lifetime that she's not from the same planet as the people she loves. She shifts gears. "Okay, what's next?"

In recent days, she and Andi have spoken several times— about everything except Fern's book-to-screen deal. Life at the Abdallah house has been rocky, and Cameron continues to stir the emotional waters.

Andi leads them back to the kitchen and hands over a knife, lemon, and cutting board. "I'll tell you the whole story when everyone gets here, but Cameron got caught vaping in the women's bathroom on the school field trip to the zoo this week."

Fern stops her knife midway through the first slice. "What was he doing in the women's restroom?" She's aware it sounds as if she's missed the headline: Cameron is vaping. But there's something darker still about doing it in a place he doesn't belong. "I know this seems irrelevant, but was he the only student in there?"

Andi shakes her head. "One other. A girl."

Somehow, the presence of a female classmate lifts the veil of indecency. "And they were only vaping?"

"Yep. In fact, he says he wasn't vaping at all. He was just *hanging out*." Andi abruptly laughs like a woman gasping for sanity. "The girl's name is Persimmon. I've met her mom and she's exactly the kind of Whole Foods, Fair Trade avenger you'd expect to name her daughter after an exotic fruit."

"Have you ever eaten one?" Fern knows she's way off topic now. But she can also see that Andi is desperate to escape the burden of worry she's carrying.

"Dunno. Maybe? I can't think of what they taste like."

Fern returns to her lemon. "Armpit sweat, that's what."

The doorbell rings and Carolina doesn't wait for anyone to answer before letting herself in. "Hellooo?" She appears in the kitchen wearing two shamrock medals around her neck. "Guess who just placed first in both the women's and men's age group at the Dublin Green 10K?"

Fern and Andi stop what they're doing to welcome her with a hug.

"You smell like persimmons," Fern says.

"That's called speed, baby." Carolina winks and pulls a change of clothes from her shoulder bag. "I'll be back in a few minutes, fresh as new."

"Did you really win the men's category, too?" Andi looks wildly impressed, even though they've been witness to countless Carolina surprises.

"Meh." She waves away the awe. "It's just a community race. Not a qualifier or anything. I mainly signed up because I didn't have anything booked for this morning."

"Except for Bloody Marys with us." Fern wonders if Dom is ever going to make good on his promised pitcher.

Once Carolina is freshly dressed, Emma arrives, and the four women settle on the patio. For the meat eaters, Andi's made eggs Benedict, hollandaise on the side. For Carolina, it's tomato slices topped with micro greens and a creamy cashew sauce.

"The lady at the co-op assured me it's her favorite. Vegan. Gluten-free. Organic. Blah, blah, blah, checks all the boxes."

Carolina blows her an air kiss.

"Would we all look as good as you if we exercised like wild horses and ate less of this?" Fern holds up a bit of eggs and ham dripping with butter and lemon. "Or are we already too far gone?"

"Too late." Andi takes a big bite.

"I like being set in my ways." Emma's blond hair gleams where the sun hits through the eucalyptus leaves. "Change is mostly overrated. But don't tell my students I said that."

"Speaking of…" Fern sees her opening. "I was hoping to change your minds about optioning the book for screen." This is her new strategy—to let them assume she accepted the deal only after obtaining their blessing. "At least, I'd like to understand your concerns better."

Everyone at that table knows it's Emma who Fern needs to speak with most, but Emma is notably quiet. Finally, she says, "Before we do that, Fern, I'd like to address what happened at Portia's engagement party."

Fern's body responds as if she's a little girl about to be scolded, chest hot, stomach pinched. The urge to flee pulls at her heels.

"Perhaps I didn't express it well, but it hurt when you weren't there for my toast. It felt as if you didn't care."

"I did care, I just—" Fern's palms are sweating. "I kept getting texts from my agent and I got carried away."

Andi, too, begins to re-explain her poorly timed pop out for coffee.

Emma raises a palm. "I don't want to relitigate it. God, listen to me. I sound like Devin. What I'm trying to say is, you're my people, and I need you."

A single sob comes from Carolina's side of the table. "Ignore me. Carry on."

"Carolina!"

"No, seriously. This is pretty much my normal state these days. I just try to do it when no one is looking."

"See, this is what I'm talking about." Emma thrusts her open palm toward Carolina. "We're crying in private, falling asleep at parties—"

Andi interrupts, "For the record, I didn't actually fall asleep at Portia's event."

"Regardless," Emma continues, "we need to be there for each other. When did that stop?"

Carolina swipes at her eyes with a napkin. "It didn't stop. We're just busy, and life doesn't allow for me to call you every time I have a mini breakdown." She laughs. "That's what Queenie's for."

"But if you're crying all the time, we do want to know," says Emma.

Andi says, "I had a panic attack at Target picking out toilet paper."

"What?" they all say.

"Or, I don't know. Maybe I was just exhausted. I had to sit down for a minute."

Fern says, "Where?"

"In the aisle," Andi answers. "I was wearing a short skirt and I think people could see my underwear."

"What is happening to us?" cries Emma.

"When in doubt, blame hormones," Fern says. It's what she tells Maisy whenever she's upset but can't put her finger on why.

"Menopause," agrees Andi. "Definitely."

"This is more than hormones, you guys." Emma is not backing down. "We've overextended ourselves, taken on too many responsibilities. The world isn't going to end if we say no more than we say yes."

Fern balks. "But saying yes is our thing. More than just our thing, now. Buy Me a Drink BINGO has gone mainstream."

"That game was fun," says Carolina.

"And we played it decades ago," Emma says. "We're not the same women we were then."

"Alright." Andi raps her knife against the side of her water glass. "Let's get serious. Emma, I hear you. We're all busier than we ought to be. But it's not as easy as just saying no to a few things. Life isn't a Nancy Reagan antidrug campaign."

"But maybe it is," Emma counters. "Maybe we're just so programmed to say yes that we make saying no harder than it needs to be."

"I wish that were true," Andi says. "But I don't think it is."

Quiet falls over the table, the four of them each in their own thoughts. Fern pushes her food around on her plate like she's trying to arrange bits of broken pottery.

Overcommitment may be Emma's and Andi's and Carolina's issue, but not hers. If anything, she needs more to which she can commit her time, now with all three kids about to fly the nest and her writing mojo lying like a dry sponge in her brain. She needs Dakota Winters to bring her stories to life. She needs this yes.

"Emma?" Fern plunges back in. "What are your concerns about a screen deal?"

Emma's eyes remain glued to the drying, yolky mess on the plate in front of her.

Likely trying to break the conversational logjam, Carolina says, "Just so you both know, I've told Fern I'm okay with it. Who cares if a TV show or movie brings us a little recognition? It won't last. The public attention span is about five minutes long. And weren't we just talking about supporting each other?"

Fern studies Andi and Emma for a reaction. Andi doesn't react. Emma is studying the leaves on the trees.

Carolina goes on, "C'mon, guys. This is what Fern's whole book is about. Signing the deal is saying yes."

"And that's the problem." Emma locks her gaze directly onto Fern. "Word got out among the classroom moms that you and I are friends and now they email me to ask if we really danced in our underwear in the middle of the night at Grotta della Bolle."

Fern laughs. "That's what's bothering you? Because we did do that."

"I know we did. And it bothers me that it's not just a memory shared among the four of us anymore." She swirls a hand between them. "Now everyone who's suddenly rediscovering your book believes they have a right to it. Just imagine if it gets made into a movie. Then it's the whole world's memory."

"But why shouldn't we share it? How many people get to experience a night like that in real life?" Even at the tender age of twenty-nine, Fern knew there would be few nights in her life as magical as their night at Grotta della Bolle.

Now, twenty-some years later, she looks at Emma, who says, "If it were just about the good memories, that would be different. But it's not the good ones that scare me."

Fern knows this. Of course, she does. But she waits to hear Emma say the words aloud, hoping that speaking them will break their fearful spell.

"What if he sees it?" Emma's eyes glisten with the start of tears that never fully develop.

"What if he does?" And this is why Fern doesn't feel the same fear her friends do. "He has just as much to lose as we do."

If You Like Tiny Little Bubbles, and Getting Caught in the Rain

From *Smart Girls Say Yes*
by Fern McAllister

If you are a fan of Beauvilliers sparkling wines, you may have noted that 1999 was a particularly tasty vintage. You have my Say Yes attitude to thank for that.

But first, a bit of necessary background for those of you unaccustomed to filling your flutes with Beauvilliers bubbles. The wine is produced by the family overseeing one of Napa Valley's oldest vineyards, Grotta della Bolle. Founded by a small order of missionaries to grow sacramental wine, Grotta della Bolle changed hands several times since its 1892 inception, eventually landing in the hands of the Herman family.

Brothers Gus and Peder Herman overlapped with my time at UC Davis, and I'd gotten to know them through a mutual friend. Gus was working toward his MBA, Peder was finishing graduate work in enology, and together, they were preparing to take their family's wine business into the next century.

They graduated a year after I left campus, but I got an invite to their blowout graduation party on the vineyard, nevertheless. Beauvilliers wine labels look straight out of Versailles, gold foil on cream. Gus and Peder's invitations came via email. I still remember the subject line: *The real world beckons. Who's up for one last night of debauchery?*

I certainly wanted to be. And even as I write this, I feel the hair on my arms rise at the thought that I nearly deleted the message.

The "mutual friend" who introduced me to Peder and Gus was my ex-boyfriend, the one with the great mattress and a willingness to share it with too many women. He was sure to be at the party, and if there was one thing that tempted me more than a night at one of America's most prestigious vineyards, it was not having to see my ex there.

"What do you mean you're not going?" Hearing my news, Carolina acted as if I'd just declined to attend her birthday party. "So what if he might be there? You look fantastic. Go show him what he's missing."

Even though, back then, I carelessly bemoaned the size of my thighs and the barely perceptible curve of my belly, wisdom and time has taught me to recognize that younger me did look incredible. Carolina had me running regularly and my hairstylist was such a good storyteller I never missed an appointment.

"Can you bring a guest?" Emma asked. "One of us could go along in solidarity." Because doesn't that sound exactly like what Emma would offer, her care and support.

Andi asked to see the email. I'd conveniently printed it and stuffed it into my pocket, which was a thing people did before PalmPilots and BlackBerrys and smartphones. She read it carefully. "They don't ask for RSVPs or a head count, so there's no way they're going to be able to distinguish guests from crashers. I say we all go."

"Say yes, Ferny," Carolina urged.

And so, I did.

Which is how we found ourselves piling into Chandler's SUV and driving north out of the city toward wine country. He happened to own the only car any of us trusted in the mountains, but we would have invited him regardless. Chandler was a must-have party pro.

Grotta della Bolle was all the way up the valley toward Healdsburg, where narrow mountain roads twist their way through the coastal range. It's the land of natural hot springs and California oak, scenery ripe from the pages of John Steinbeck and Jack London. *Grotta*, Italian for cave, was an accurate description of the land the missionaries chose for their wine-making—acres of gently sloping fields came to a halt at the entrance to a yawning cavity in the mountain, perfect for storing and aging their product.

By the time we arrived that afternoon, cars were parked at least a quarter mile back along the side of the road. Through the gates, a surreal vista opened before our eyes. Lights strung between ancient oaks, illuminating the crowds of people beneath the open sky. An Eagles cover band played from a wood-plank stage and behind them, the vineyards stretched and rolled onto the horizon. The Herman family had instructed guests to bring tents and stay overnight, and a few dozen brightly colored nylon domes dotted the rows between the grapes.

Peder himself helped us find spots to pitch ours, and then led us to a table lined with more food and drink than I could ever remember seeing. The wine was homemade in unlabeled green bottles, and so great was the quantity that no one needed a glass. Guests danced with full bottles in their hands.

I sensed I'd crossed through a portal into another world.

"Is this heaven?" someone asked.

"Better," I answered. "I think it's Oz."

The moments I recall best from that night have, with time, become physical memories, sensations I can rouse by closing my eyes and falling back in time. The bead of dance sweat trickling the length of my spine. Dirt between my toes. Lifting the hair from my neck and letting the breeze cool my skin.

And the heat. That hot, hot dancing heat of which I couldn't get enough.

There's a mystical allure to the fever generated by a group of friendly strangers come together to dance. A galvanizing magnetism. A rushing current of crashing ions, giving birth to a moment that will never come again. Not in this combination. Not with these people, under this full moon, breathing this fertile air.

Because except for Gus and Peder, this wasn't anyone's real life. Grotta della Bolle was a magical dream that we guests were allowed to inhabit for this one and only night.

At some point, it began to rain. Only briefly. Just enough to cool our heated bodies and wet our clothes. Someone took off a shirt, and soon everyone was stripping down to essentials. I hung my denim dress from the bowing branch of an ancient oak to dry, drinking in the feel of the evening breeze on my bare belly. Curves and all.

Isn't it ironic, as Alanis might say, that this is when I spotted my ex? He was in the boxers I'd bought him for our first Valentine's Day, dotted with tiny red hearts. His fingers traced the delicate pink bra straps of a brunette I'd never seen before.

"She's not as pretty as you," Emma whispered.

Carolina grabbed my hand. "Don't look at that. I've got something way better to show you." She led me to the small line of porta-potties and opened one of the doors.

"Gross." I recoiled.

"Trust me. Look on the wall." She nudged me forward.

I laughed out loud when I saw it. "Who wrote that?" I didn't recognize the handwriting. It hadn't come from my ex. But someone had found a black Sharpie somewhere, and they'd used it to leave me a message.

I ♥ Fern

"Where's Chandler?" I knew this was his kind of prank. "Go check his pockets for a marker."

Carolina's smile glowed beneath the string of soft white lights. "He swears it wasn't him."

Don't let that fool you, whispered my ego. My heart fought back. *Oh, come on. Let this former ugly duckling of ours believe she's a swan, even if just for tonight.*

We never solved the mystery. I didn't want to. Because as long as I didn't know, I could believe that Grotta della Bolle had chosen to sprinkle a dusting of magic onto my head and turn me into one of its treasures.

There is a point in every wonderful night—a great party, an incredible date—when the clock breaks your heart. When time reminds us that it's not ours to control. On that evening with the Herman brothers, the moment came when people began to scatter, trading the intimacy of the dance floor for the privacy of their tents. *How can you leave?* I wanted to call. *Night isn't over until the sun tells us so.*

But eventually, we, too, found ourselves making the same trade. Maybe the band packed up and went home. Maybe we were so exhausted we could no longer stand. Either way, I paused before crawling into my tent and looked at the grapes all around me, glowing greenish white beneath the moon. "I'll never forget you," I whispered. "Never, never, no way."

Finally, I zipped the tent flap behind me. The air inside smelled of nylon and fresh rain. My pillow called. I lay down.

And without warning, the night's revelry lurched in my stomach. I made it just in time, barfing all over the vines outside my door.

As I said at the beginning, 1999 was a wonderful, magical vintage year.

Carolina

Carolina turns off the car radio so she can think. It's been a good day with friends, but ripe with big questions and few answers.

Was she overstretched, as Emma implied? Queenie was all over her these days about cutting back. "You're online before I get up in the morning and you're still online when I go to bed. Somewhere in between you disappear, and I can only assume you're at the office."

She was working a lot. But it was justified. "Do you really think I can cut back at work when there's a layoff happening? How does that look to my team? How does it look to Sandra?"

Queenie's answer had been cutting. "Live your priorities, Carolina." As if it were that easy.

"That'll work great. Because when I lose my job, you'll see me even more."

Queenie didn't deserve such a careless dismissal, and she regretted her words as soon as she'd said them. Then she cried, as was her pattern. Not because she wanted or even deserved her partner's forgiveness, but because the bottomless well of tears inside her overflowed, flooding her face and drenching her soul.

Every southbound lane on the 101 suddenly came to a crawl,

nothing but red taillights stretching into the horizon. Carolina was five miles from her exit. At this rate, it would take her an hour to get home.

A single tear trickled down the side of her nose. Why did everything, *everything* have to be so difficult?

Or, as Andi had said, "Some days, I just want to stand up and scream 'somebody fix it!' And by *it* I mean *everything*. There's only so much a person can take on, you know?"

Last week, Dom had brought Andi's car in for an oil change and the next day, driving to work, the brakes started smoking. After filling Carolina in, she said, "It's like, what the hell—I just need *one thing* to go right for a change."

Fern said the financial aid forms they'd submitted for Maisy's freshman tuition went missing "somewhere in the internet ether" and she missed crucial loan deadlines.

Emma said Devin has quit picking up her phone calls, so every time she needs him to cut a check for his portion on the wedding costs, she has to leave a voicemail. "I feel like a little girl asking Daddy for money. And I'm sorry, but I refuse to request a two-thousand-dollar down payment for the reception venue via text."

Andi said, "Nearly every day now, I get to the point where I throw my hands up and wonder, *Why do I bother?*" She went on to tell the story of having to pick Cameron up from school after he lost driving privileges for some reason or another (Carolina missed that part because she was having to process the idea of little kid Cam being old enough to drive).

"Heaven forbid," Andi said, "if I don't pick him up in exactly the same spot as Dom does. 'I like to know where you are!' he says. So, fine, if it makes him feel better, I can park in the same spot every day. But another part of me wants to say, 'Do you really expect the world to cater to all your whims?' What's going to happen when he leaves home and realizes everything doesn't revolve around him?"

Not having kids herself, Carolina tries not to comment on

her friends' parenting dilemmas. They mostly want her to listen, and she's good at that. This time, she couldn't help herself.
"Is that really fair, though? I mean, I know I'm not a mom, but
don't we all need a basic sense of security?"

Andi said of course, but also that it's also complicated. "The
line between security and dependency can be hard to spot."

Security, though, is certainly top of mind for everyone at
work right now, worrying about whether to take the severance package or roll the dice; about the tightening job market;
about the threat of a recession, inflation, social unrest, global
warming, their family's future.

As suddenly as it jammed, traffic clears, and Carolina is on
the move again. It's almost four o'clock. If she makes it home
soon, she'll have a full couple of hours to spend with Queenie
before she has to log on and check email. If nothing's blowing
up at work, the two of them might even have time to open a
bottle of wine and watch something.

Turning off at her exit, she considers stopping by the store to
pick up dinner, but that will only eat into their time together.
They can order in.

She pulls up to their building and drives around back to the
lot. Queenie's car is in its space, and just seeing it makes her
smile. She does love her nerdy, adorable boy.

Carolina kills the engine and throws open her car door. As
she steps out, her knee gives out with a painful snap, and she
falls, face kissing the blacktop.

Andi

At last, the school year is over, and the fat lady is singing. Literally. Cameron comes home from his final day of sophomore year and hits repeat on a YouTube video of Ethel Merman singing "Everything's Coming Up Roses."

He pops his head into Andi's room where's she's packing for another trip. "'You'll be swell!'" he croons. "'You'll be great!'"

"Are you still planning to drive me to the airport?"

He's doing the Tom Cruise *Risky Business* slide across the wooden floor. "'Gonna have the whole world on a plate.'"

"We need to leave in ten minutes."

Now he's heading down the hall to his bedroom doing the Molly Ringwald, Ally Sheedy dance from *The Breakfast Club*—heel-toe, heel-toe, heel-toe. "Startin' here. Startin' now."

Like a hurricane, Cameron had thrown himself into schoolwork at the end of the year. He got himself semi-organized, put his head down, and dropped overdue and coming-due projects on his teachers' desks like falling houses.

Grades are already coming in. There's even a B in Civics. Maybe miracles are possible. Fingers crossed.

The trip she's packing for, however, is less heartening. A Guatemalan client recently admitted that the men she'd paid to help her across the US border forced her to marry a migrant from Honduras on the journey. The coyotes claimed it would make the US more likely to grant them both amnesty, and that the government considered dual-income families more desirable. They also charged the bride and groom a hangman's sum for the privilege. Now the groom is being deported, and Andi's client is fearful of being sent back to an unfamiliar country with a man who's not her rightful husband.

Andi has to appear before a San Diego judge first thing in the morning to argue for the annulment of a marriage she's not even certain took place. It's also forcing her to break her "no overnight trips if I can help it" rule.

But even twenty-four hours away is better than what she'd been doing. Judging from Cam's sudden burst of responsible behavior, being home is good for everyone. Her and Dom's sex life is back on track, too, which makes Dom especially pleasant.

Yet, just as one pool of guilt begins to dry up, another begins to flood. A lawyer on her team resigned, citing burnout, and they've had to cut back significantly on the ICSW cases they take on as a result. Last week, her legal assistant, Issah, blocked fifteen minutes on Andi's calendar and used the time to request a transfer back to the division she'd been working in before joining the team.

"I can't stop worrying," Issah had said. "And I can't sleep. My life feels like a hamster wheel that I can't get off."

Andi knew how she felt. And yet it had been her need to cut back that hastened her team's unraveling. Where was the justice in that?

On the way to the airport, she reminds herself that she can't do anything about staffing concerns right now. She ought to take advantage of this still-scarce one-on-one time with her son. "We're really impressed by the way you wrapped up the year, Cameron."

"I know. I'm the best." He laughs at himself, practically giddy with relief. "I told you not to worry, didn't I?"

He wants her to give him credit, to praise his ability to grab a rabbit out of a hat. She won't. The lesson Andi and Dom want him to learn is the importance of working hard and fulfilling one's responsibilities. Not shutting the blinds and pretending like your lawn isn't on fire.

"Like I said, I'm impressed by the way you pulled yourself together. But I don't want you to think you'll always be that lucky. Your teachers could have docked you a lot more points, considering how late some of those assignments were."

In law school, she'd lost a full letter grade on a paper for missing the deadline by one minute. Upon returning it, the professor wrote in red pen: *Deadlines matter. Had you been one minute late to file in court, the judge would have been justified to not read at all.*

She's already told that story to Cameron a dozen times so doesn't repeat it now. She does say, "Being bright is no excuse for being sloppy."

"I know. I know." He pulls up to the Departures curb, his tone of voice matching the one Andi uses with her own mother.

"I'll be home tomorrow. In time for dinner. Promise. We'll celebrate the end of school, order pizza or something."

"Maybe." He unlocks the doors, shooing her out. "If I don't have plans with friends."

Andi stands on the curb and watches him drive away.

He needs me. He needs me not.

Carolina

Carolina hasn't moved from the couch in four hours. Somebody kill her.

Per doctor's orders, she's flat on her back, her right leg propped on pillows above her heart to reduce the swelling. As a leg, it's unrecognizable, entombed from thigh to ankle in a black steel immobilizer straight out of *The Terminator*. Queenie even has to help her to the bathroom and moved her useless crutches across the room to ensure she doesn't get frisky and go for a wander.

It's unnatural for the body to be still like this. Every nerve cell screams at her to *move*! The muscles in her left leg twitch every few seconds in the same way Mrs. Roper noses at Carolina's shins when she wants to go outside. *Hey. Pay attention. You're cramping my style.*

Right this minute, however, Mrs. Roper snoozes, curled against her hip. Her orthopedist is recommending surgery. Both her ACL and MCL, two of the major ligaments in the knee, have torn beyond the point of self-repair. She's injured them too many times before.

"I can get you up and walking again," Dr. Chung had said. "But the days of strenuous runs are over." To top off the bad-news sundae, she strongly encouraged Carolina to start thinking about finding a new outdoor passion. "Your body is begging you."

Maybe that's true. But every time Carolina tries to picture a life without running, her throat begins to close, and the tears threaten.

She is too tired to cry anymore.

Instead, she's on her insurance provider's website looking for a new orthopedist. Someone who can fix her knee and make it strong enough to run again. Carolina will surrender herself to surgery, but not if, as Dr. Chung warned, it requires nine to twelve months of recovery and leaves behind a disappointing, dysfunctional limb. Her good leg twitches as she googles.

In the procedure Dr. Chung recommended, the surgeon creates a whole new ligament by grafting a piece of one of her other healthy tendons into the torn ligament's place. The article she's reading comes with photos that make her so queasy her blood pressure drops, and her stomach prepares to empty itself.

"Queenie? Where's the barf bowl?"

"Under the coffee table." He's working from home but left everything from power cords to painkillers within her reach. She grabs the empty Tupperware container. Her stomach stills. *This. Sucks.*

She's also had to take several days of personal leave from work after discovering that email and painkillers don't mix. Unfortunately, she cc'd the CEO on a lunch order she sent to her administrative assistant at 2:47 a.m. Hours later, she woke to an email from the head of HR, copying Sandra. Per the employee handbook, it is strongly recommended that you not return to work while taking prescribed narcotics.

Carolina has no memory of that email. Which leads to the question: Who else did she write to that night?

Following the mishap, Queenie took away her work laptop and replaced it with her personal iPad. It effectively feels as if he's left her with nothing. Without her work tether, there are no meetings to attend. No Slack chats. Stuck here in the condo, there are no flybys at her desk. No break room run-ins.

Nor can she relieve her stress with a midday run. Not even a walk in the fresh air. Couch Potato is not a woman Carolina understands, and she wants this stranger gone.

The intercom buzzer startles her from her malaise. It's the most excitement her heart has had in days.

"Queenie? Did you order food? Someone's in the lobby."

He's already heard the buzzer and bustles toward the door while pulling a sweatshirt over his head. "It's freezing in here. Did you jack up the air-conditioning again?"

When he presses the intercom button, the voice that emerges is Andi's. "I was in the neighborhood and thought I'd check in on Carolina."

"In the neighborhood?" Carolina says from the couch. "Baloney."

She told her friends she didn't need fawning over. Fern sent flowers, anyway. Emma a card. All of them chipped in on an Uber Eats gift card, since Carolina won't be cooking anytime soon and Queenie, the carnivore, isn't likely to become vegan literate overnight.

And now Andi is at her door. Queenie buzzes her up.

As soon as Carolina sees her face, she knows this wasn't simply a get-well call.

"What's it like to lose a piece of you?" Andi asks.

Queenie puts the kettle on and retreats to the office, closing the door behind him. Andi sits in a lounge chair, holding a mug of tea. Carolina's mug is on the coffee table, growing cold, since it's impossible to drink hot liquids while lying flat without getting second-degree burns on your chest.

"What do you mean? Like with my knee surgery?"

Following the appointment with Dr. Chung, she'd texted her friends with the news. "She says my running days are behind me, but she may as well have told me to just lay down and die."

They'd predictably responded with blind encouragement.

We can do hard things! You got this! You'll find something new to love! Carolina threw her phone out of reach to keep herself from replying, Yeah? Would you find something new to love if you lost one of your kids?

Andi shook her head. "I mean, what's it like to lose a part of your identity? A piece of you that's so fundamental you don't recognize yourself without it. The way you've lost your ability to keep running."

Carolina flinches at what is anything but a foregone conclusion. "Are you having an identity crisis, too? No offense, but I don't know if our friends can handle more than one at a time."

She's kidding, of course. Sort of.

Andi doesn't laugh. "I've never been so fulfilled as a lawyer than I am right now. I love the ICSW work. It's what I envisioned for myself in law school—at the crossroads of institutional injustice and real people's lives. The problem is, all the work I'm doing for other families is hurting my own."

Carolina frowns. "Cameron in trouble again?"

At this, Andi does laugh. "No. Can you believe it? Just the opposite. He's turned a corner for the better. Less moody, got a job at the grocery store and is making some money. He even comes out of his room from time to time. Yesterday, he smiled at me without prompting."

"And that's—" Carolina doesn't know the ins and outs of raising teenage boys.

"Huge. Gigantic. A unicorn riding a phoenix."

"Okay. So that's great progress."

"I know." Andi slumps.

"I don't see the problem."

"All of this improvement happened after I quit traveling. It's better at home when I stay home. But I can't do this kind of work if I don't travel."

"Ah." Carolina doesn't bother to argue otherwise. If there was a way to stay in town and be effective, Andi would have found it.

Andi says, "Why don't men seem to experience this impossible pull? When I'm doing my best work, my family falls apart. And when I give my family the time it needs, my clients pay the price."

It's the same dilemma they'd tried to solve at brunch.

"What if you cut back on the cases you take on?" Carolina asks. "You said the partners aren't going to let your team exist forever."

"That's the other problem," she answers. "We've brought great international exposure to the firm, but even that perk has its limits. At some point, if I want to keep my job, I've got to start bringing cash to the table."

"The almighty dollar."

"All hail the king."

"Shit."

"With a cherry on top."

Neither speaks for a moment.

Carolina understands what brought her friend all the way across town for this face-to-face pop-in. It's a question as old as womanhood itself.

Lacking answers, she picks up her painkillers and shakes the bottle. "I'm happy to share. One of these will buy you a few hours of peace, but you may wake up with more trouble than you went in with."

"I've got plenty of troubles already, thanks." Andi's eyes glisten with tears as she laughs.

Carolina's well up in loyal response to her friend. "I wish I had wisdom to share." If she did, maybe she wouldn't be desperately googling for a new orthopedist. "As I'm sure you can already see from my glamourous appearance, losing a piece of yourself feels pretty terrible." She holds up a matted strand of hair. "There's only so much that dry shampoo can do for a gal."

Andi pulls a tissue from the box on the coffee table and dabs her cheeks. "I'm worried that no matter what I decide to do, it'll feel wrong."

It probably will, Carolina thinks.

"If it's any help, my doctor said something that I haven't been able to let go of. She told me that my knee injury wasn't an accident. It was avoidable. She's been telling me to cut back for years, warning me that the next injury could be catastrophic. But I didn't believe her. I thought I was strong enough to do it all."

Andi says, "Running is your stress relief. It keeps you physically and emotionally healthy."

"Or so I thought." Carolina motions to the cage on her leg. "Queenie says he thinks I'm compulsive. That I don't need to work as hard as I do, and that if I'd just cut back on my stress, I wouldn't have to push my body so hard to compensate."

Andi gives her a sympathetic smile. "But what do you think?"

Carolina dodges the question. Queenie may be right, but she's not ready to admit it. Instead, she says, "Here's what I think: I think I'd rather lose my knee than lose my son."

Fern

Fern is in the laundry room shoving wet sheets into the dryer when she hears cable news announce that Carlton Willis is running for Senate. In response, she slams her finger in the latch.

"Shit!"

She hustles into the next room, nursing the wound in her mouth and cursing herself for putting off her appointment at the hearing-aid place. Carlton Willis? That can't be right. She'd be less shocked to see her neighbor's pug, Priscilla, on the ballot.

But sure enough, there he is, larger than life on the bedroom TV. The man she knew in her twenties has gone gray—and, dammit, if he doesn't look better for it. He's shaking hands with the employees that everyone in the state of California knows he underpays and overworks. In the edited footage, they act as if they're meeting the Pope.

Carlton cofounded a company that makes tax preparation software. There's a TaxAware accounting suite and a TaxAware app. Come January, temporary TaxAware offices pop up in every strip mall across the country where minimally certified tax preparers will file your returns using Carlton's software in exchange for a generous slice of your refund. Their motto: Tax Know-How for Every American.

Irony of ironies, he's also made a name for himself on social media by bloviating in favor of eliminating the IRS, calling it unconstitutional in a republic governed by and for its citizens.

Fern shouts at him, "Your suit is too well tailored to be seen as a man of the people, dumbass!"

He turns to face her. Obviously, she knows he's facing the camera, but she and Carlton have a history. She'd say the same thing to him in person.

"I'll bring the productivity and profitability mindset we've developed at TaxAware to Washington, where it's needed now more than ever. Let's be honest. We need less dysfunction at the federal level. And Californians have seen me turn a messy regulation-burdened chore into a streamlined, job-producing global enterprise. If I can do it here, I can certainly bring the same know-how to the Senate."

Fern responds by blowing *thhbbbbfffftt!* until her tongue goes dry.

It's not until that night when she's lying in bed that she realizes she hasn't discussed the development with Andi, Carolina, or Emma. She spent the last several hours lecturing Mack as to why Carlton's announcement is a "master class in egotism," and watched as countless local and national talking heads debated the likelihood of his electoral success.

Now, in the quiet, she's even more unsettled. The friends' text chain has gone eerily quiet.

Cue the four horses of the apocalypse.

Carolina

Carolina is still on the couch when she hears Carlton's news, though she's finally working again, free of the mind-altering painkillers and in rightful possession of her laptop. Sandra's on her screen via video conference and she's just notified Carolina that so far, no one on team MAVERIK has volunteered for a separation package. "Here's hoping your concerns were overblown."

Carolina winces. It's not as if she'd been hysterical. "There's still two weeks left. Let's not jinx it."

Sandra changes the subject. "I assume you've heard the news."

The words send a jolt of panic to Carolina's brain. "The *news*—" She draws the word out as if there's too much news to track. It's better than admitting ignorance.

"Carlton's news."

"Carlton Willis?"

"Oh, so you haven't heard." Sandra's tone shifts to that of the mean girl on the playground, the one who knows all the gossip and revels in its power.

Carolina doesn't bite. "Well, he and I aren't close."

"You might want to change that soon. He's running for Senate."

"You're shitting me. Is that why he was meeting with Mark? To gin up campaign contributions?"

Sandra merely smiles.

Carolina wants to ask if they gave him their favorite advice: *do more with less.*

When she finally disconnects, Queenie brings her a fresh bottle of water and says, "Alright. It's zero hour. What have you decided?"

She promised to make a decision about knee surgery by five o'clock. The orthopedist who gave her a second opinion said she could try rehab and physical therapy, but it would take months and favorable results weren't guaranteed.

"I don't know yet," she says.

"That's not an option. We agreed—there'll be a decision today." Queenie, who is pro-surgery, looms over the couch. All six feet of him. He knows better than to tell Carolina what to do, but he also knows her ability for skirting difficult conversations.

"I'm too distracted. The layoffs—"

"Nope, you've already used that excuse."

"Fine. But I did just learn that Carlton Willis is running for Senate. That ought to buy me a day."

Queenie knows Carolina and friends' sordid history with him. He also knows better than to talk about Carlton and to never ever buy a TaxAware product. "Even more reason to get the surgery. You'll need strong legs to go door knocking for his opponent."

"I don't want surgery." The tears come, and Carolina doesn't try to stop them. "I don't want to lose my knees. I don't want to have to change my lifestyle. I don't want to be getting older."

Queenie sits gently and rubs her good leg. "It happens. Even this masterpiece of a physique—" he gestures at his doughy torso "—isn't as magnificent as it was ten years ago."

She laughs until her nose starts to drip. He wipes it away with a tissue.

"I'm going to be a nightmare to live with if I can't run."

He raises an eyebrow. "And right now, you are…"

"The word you're looking for is *delightful*."

She cries for ten more minutes, then calls Dr. Chung's office and schedules the surgery.

Andi

Andi doesn't hear anything about Carlton Willis's senatorial ambitions until Dom tells her at dinner over take-out chicken vindaloo. When the news drops, she's at lunch with Connie Trujillo, a social worker who consults on their ICSW cases.

Connie has also led workshops to help Andi's team understand the social, familial, and cultural challenges facing the populations they represent. During one, Connie warned team members to be on the lookout for something called "compassion fatigue," saying it wasn't uncommon for people whose work requires them to witness others' trauma to also suffer mental and physical setbacks.

This is why Andi has invited her to lunch.

"My team is burning out. I've already lost one attorney and a legal assistant. If I lose any more, I'm concerned we may have to cease our ICSW cooperation altogether."

There's a crash in the kitchen, shattering glass and porcelain. She knows it's just a server dropping a tray, but the noise sends her blood pressure sailing, her heartbeat into her ears.

Connie notices. "You okay?" She's one of those people who seems to have been physically designed for her profession. Brown eyes that widen when you say something good, or droop when you need sympathy. A face that's uniquely hers in conversation, but completely forgettable afterward. What you see is what you get. And right now, Andi sees a woman who smells trouble.

Andi says she's fine, even though her hands are trembling. "Anyway, my fellow partners aren't going to let me poach any more resources from the firm, and I can't hire from outside with the money we earn."

Frankly, she's amazed the firm has allowed her team to continue this long. If it weren't for Andi's glad-handing of prominent intergovernmental and human rights agencies, she wouldn't have been given six months of runway, let alone twenty and counting.

"I asked you here because you once talked about compassion fatigue. I need to know how to stop that from happening with my team. Or, if it's already started, from getting worse."

Connie asks, "How long have you been representing ICSW clients? A couple of years now?"

"Almost. Two years this September."

"With the same legal team?"

"Until a few weeks ago, yes."

Connie's brown eyes grow big. "Congratulations. That's a long stretch of time to retain your resources, especially with the types of cases you've seen." She knew what she was talking about, as she'd consulted on some of their most egregious.

"Well, our streak appears to be over. Though the work isn't anywhere near finished."

"You want to know the average tenure of a caseworker in our office?" Connie asks. "Eight months."

Andi isn't surprised. "You're asked to work for practically nothing, though. No offense."

"None taken." Connie has somehow managed to keep a smile on her face since sitting down. She hardly flinched at the crash in the kitchen. "It's not all about the money, though. People drawn to my profession tend to be highly empathetic.

We know going in that our salary won't be anywhere near commensurate with the work, and yet we choose to do it, anyway. We're wired to help people. Problem is, the more we give to helping those in pain, the less mental emotional energy we have to care for ourselves."

"So, you burn out?"

Connie hmms. "More than that. The body begins to show internal stress in external ways—inability to sleep, headaches and stomachaches, mood swings. That sort of thing."

"I've yet to meet a lawyer who sleeps well," Andi says. "It starts in law school and never ends."

"That's too bad." Connie's brown eyes shift to sympathetic.

"I'm kidding, of course."

"I know." She shrugs. "But how are you coping with all this? You're handling some pretty hefty cases, and you're the public face of the work."

Andi brushes away the question. "I'm fine."

"What does *fine* look like for you?"

Maybe it's because Connie is still smiling that Andi chooses to answer, even though they've strayed from the topic she'd hoped to discuss—the well-being of her team members. "About six weeks ago, I made deep cuts to my travel schedule. My son was acting out as a result of me traveling so much. The change seems to have made a difference."

"For you?"

She finds the question surprising. "I meant for my son. And my husband. It's made a difference for the family, and that's good for me, too."

"But how are you doing? You said 'fine.' And yet you're asking about compassion fatigue. I'm curious if maybe you ask because you're beginning to experience some yourself."

The words *I'm fine* nearly escape Andi's lips a third time before she catches herself. "I'm coping, let's put it that way. Trying to control what I can and roll with the rest."

"Like quitting the travel?" says Connie.

"Exactly. That's something that made a difference."

"Good for you." Connie sits back in her seat, beaming.

She doesn't say anything more for a such a long time that Andi finds herself filling the silence.

"I mean, of course, my team has had to pick up the slack. And that's been rough. I'm sure it led to a good part of their burnout."

"Meaning, people on your team quit because of your choices?"

Connie's question cuts like a razor blade in the shower— so quick, you don't notice the injury until the water runs red. Andi agrees with the insinuation; her inability to keep up with the work put an undue burden on others. She also hates hearing the words aloud; Connie has made her sound presumptuous and self-centered.

Andi says, "You sound as if you don't believe me."

"Did they complain about the extra workload?"

"Not directly. But I know firsthand they had to travel more because I had to be at home."

Connie leans in and says gently, "What I'm saying is that you seem to be taking a lot of personal responsibility for other people's choices."

Without warning, Andi's chest tightens. There's a siren screaming in her head. She grabs the table.

"Andi?" Connie's voice sounds a mile away. "What's happening?"

It's not until she feels Connie's hand on hers that she snaps back. "I was at Target." She means just now, in her head, though she also means when she'd slid to the floor of the toilet paper aisle. "I think I had a panic attack. Suddenly, I couldn't breathe, all the symptoms. But I didn't know what started it until you just said that."

Connie waits without speaking.

Andi explains, "Personal responsibility. You just said it. But the other week, there was a mother berating her kids. I couldn't see them, they were on the other side of the aisle. But she was

TIRED LADIES TAKE A STAND

hollering, 'You're not getting this back until you learn to take personal responsibility.' And then I don't know what happened, but the kid just started to scream."

Her mind drifts back to the scene and her palms begin to sweat, her face clammy. She refocuses her gaze on Connie. "Am I losing my mind?"

Connie's brown eyes turn to deep pools. "No. You heard a child crying and your brain connected it with something terrible—a kid in real trauma, maybe. Think of all the frightened and vulnerable children you've seen over the last few years. It rewires one's circuits."

Andi nods. Perhaps that was true. She liked to believe that she was strong and resilient enough to separate her personal and professional lives. What she doesn't tell Connie is that the face that flashed before her eyes was Cam. Screaming for her.

Emma

Shortly after Carlton's news drops, Emma is packing a mass of shopping bags into the trunk of her car. Not only does Doris have her running all over the North Bay looking for exact shades of pink, but she's also having a crisis of confidence about using paper products at the bridal shower. *Would Emma mind looking for linens, as well? Tablecloths of various lengths. A few dozen napkins.* "The 'no iron' variety, of course," she'd added. *Unless Emma thought she might have time to press them?*

It reminds Emma of an old joke. A mother buys her son two shirts. The next morning, he comes down to breakfast wearing one of them. She says, "What? You don't like the other one?"

It's eighty-six degrees in Napa today and the heat radiates off her dashboard in waves as she climbs inside. She starts the engine, blasting the air-conditioning. The KQED meteorologist comes on to announce this will be the coolest day of the week. Emma's armpits weep in response.

"In state political news, California entrepreneur and founder of TaxAware, Carlton Willis announced his bid for the US Senate today…"

"WHAT?" Emma screams at the reporter as if expecting a response. "No! No! No!"

With her windows rolled up tight, it appears to the man pulling in alongside her that she may need to be medicated.

900 Brides

From *Smart Girls Say Yes*
by Fern McAllister

Hear me out, friends: I think we ought to start an annual race called the Running of the Brides.

Just imagine… Runners as far as the eye can see, dressed in taffeta and satin and silk. Bustiers and bustles. Veils turned loose on the wind. People in attendance from near and far. Hundreds strap on running shoes. Hundreds more, their cameras.

One bride is running to raise money for breast cancer research. Another, in honor of the sister who died at the hands of her abuser. Every bride has a purpose, though none of them run toward the altar. It's not the vows they're sprinting for.

Some may even be there to run away. A few brides run after walking in on sights they can't unsee, and after reading texts that secret lovers assumed would always remain hidden.

A handful of jilted fiancées chase their runaways like the bulls in Pamplona.

But a wedding isn't the destination for any of them.

We run to wear the dress. Because we can't return it. Because it may not fit tomorrow. Because we're sick of waiting for the ring. We can all worry about marriage later, but the dress we love today has an expiration date. I think it would save the country a lot of heartbreak, though it might drive a hefty proportion of divorce lawyers out of business.

If I had the gumption, I'd make it my mission to bring the Annual Running of the Brides to life. My friends ran something similar once. Everyone ought to get the chance.

In late 1998, Emma broke off an ill-fated engagement. Only the groom and his mother had trouble understanding her decision. The rest of us breathed a sigh of relief and assured her she'd done the right thing. We bought her drinks and held her hair as she worked the grief out of her system.

Gradually, with time, the shock of losing the life she'd envisioned faded away. But one regret remained: her wedding dress was nonrefundable.

"Take it from me, girls," she said. We were drinking cherry bombs at the Moana Loa Club. "Buy your gown off the rack and keep the receipt. Alterations ruin everything."

We ordered another round and rubbed her back. Then I had an idea.

The following weekend, we hosted a cocktail party. We called it the "Aisle of Broken Dreams" and took decor inspiration from *Rudolph the Red-Nosed Reindeer*'s Island of Misfit Toys. We invited everyone we knew—except for ex-fiancés and former boyfriends. Attendance required a costume.

I dressed as a doctor in scrubs and a stethoscope.

Andi wore a bathing suit and life preserver in honor of her long-abandoned hopes of becoming a Cypress Gardens water-ski star.

Carolina turned circles in a leotard and tutu, the ballerina her mother always believed she could be.

Chandler put on a suit coat and stuck a name tag to his lapel. "Dad's favorite."

Emma, of course, looked stunning in a Vera Wang knock-off, the one with the peekaboo back that only a tiny thing like her could pull off.

That night, she fell asleep on our couch—too danced out to make it the three blocks home—and woke in the morning hungover but happy in her "runaway bride" skin. Over coffee and eggs at the Balboa Café, she said, "I'm not ready to take this off."

So, the next week, the three of us without dresses haunted vintage shops and thrift stores for bridal gowns of our own. Andi's had lace like wisteria blossoms dripping from her bosom. Mine had a detachable train and a butt bow the size of a Honda Civic. Andi's came with a matching floppy hat.

The four of us donned our gowns and sat together in the Saturday afternoon sun, pouring tea and eating cucumber finger sandwiches in the tiny back garden behind Emma and Carolina's apartment. We repeated silly Britishisms like *cuppa* and *biccies* until our sides split from laughing. Andi brought a tin of Marmite, which we spread on water crackers and wondered aloud how anyone could enjoy such a strange salty treat.

Later, too in love with ourselves to shed the taffeta and ribbons, we walked arm in arm to the Palace of Fine Arts and, like thousands of brides before us, took pictures beneath the soaring stone rotunda. Had Emma gone through with the wedding, she'd planned to have her bridal party surrounding her in the very same spot.

Let's call Emma's jilted ex-fiancé Ted. I named him in honor of Ted Bundy. I don't care if he reads this. I don't need him to like me. I do need you to understand that Emma did the right thing by running.

Ted and Emma met at a party in Andi's Haight-Ashbury apartment near University of San Francisco Law School. The place was barely the size of a closet on the second floor of a four-bedroom Victorian split into six rental units. Somehow, a few dozen of their friends squeezed in and brought a keg of Anchor Steam with them.

Of the four of us, Carolina met Ted first. She made the mistake of putting her red plastic cup down and turning her back. When she turned around again, a guy she didn't know was drinking from it.

"Dude, that's my beer."

"Nah," he said.

To this day, when Carolina tells the story, she leans heavily on the *nah*. No one with a degree should have permission to give single syllable responses.

"See that bite mark on the rim?" she continued. "That's my sign."

"Well, I'm a Scorpio. That's my sign." Then he took a long pull and capped off his disdain by finishing the cup. "Ahh. Cold and tasty."

"You have mommy issues," she said and walked away, intending to never speak to him again. It would have been an ordinary Saturday night for Carolina if, a few hours later, she and Andi hadn't spotted Ted and their dear friend Emma mashing faces under the streetlight below.

"Oh," Andi remembers saying. "That is not going to end well."

It took almost two years, but the end eventually did come. And, no, it did not go well.

Ted wasn't a man used to hearing the word *no*. Indeed, he did have mommy issues. But like I've said before, that's a story for another chapter. What I'll tell you now is that Emma was lucky enough to wake up before saying "I do."

"You know, I bought another dress before this one." The four of us were in the back garden drinking our tea. "His mom insisted on seeing it, so I invited her to my first fitting. She said she loved it. But that night at dinner, he commented that I needed to make sure the dress I chose would be 'timeless.'"

"What does that mean?" I asked.

"It means his mom didn't love the dress," Andi answered.

Emma sighed. "Apparently, I looked *busty*."

"Jealous," said Carolina. Emma filled out a bikini the way none of us could.

"Tell me you got your money back on that one, at least." I remember cash registers ringing in my head. The money. The *money*. The MONEY!

"The shop gave me in-store credit to find something else." Emma floofed her skirt. "This was my second choice. And now I'm stuck with it."

"I like it," said Carolina. "The only thing it's missing is a giant floppy hat."

"And a butt bow," I said.

Carolina ripped a sprig of polyester wisteria from Andi's bodice and stuck it between Emma's boobs.

"I really do love you guys," Emma said. Even though we already knew.

Sometime later, Carolina came home bursting with enthusiasm and waving a copy of *SFGate*. "A production company is filming in San Francisco and there's a casting call for nine hundred brides."

Word was out. The movie was titled *The Bachelor* and reportedly starred two of the late '90s hottest hotties, Chris O'Donnell and Renée Zellweger. We dialed the 1-800-number and were told to report for costuming at a warehouse in China Basin at five thirty Saturday morning.

It was still black as night when Andi poured me a cup of coffee and said, "We must really love Emma."

If you're wondering what nine hundred film extras packing a warehouse parking lot before dawn looks like, think: your first day at summer camp. Makeup was fresh and attitudes peppy. Conversation buzzed with star sightings. Was that Renée? Oh, my God, did I just see Brooke Shields?

To that image, add a run-down warehouse. Through the front window, one can see nothing but white, as if the infamous San Francisco fog had rolled in off the bay and got trapped inside. Finally, create a line of people marching for the door.

Before entering, they look like your friend, your sister, your neighbor, even the guy in the apartment upstairs who dances in a drag show on Columbus. When they exit, however, they're transformed. Sheathed beneath billows of cream and white and pearl polyester. Lace upon beads upon ruffles. Brides marching as far as the eye can see.

Given that Emma, Andi, Carolina, and I came dressed in our very own gowns, we didn't have to undergo bridal transformation, so we had time to mess around with the small and insanely expensive digital video camera Carolina borrowed from Chandler. "I told him I wanted it in case we saw one of the stars. He agreed to loan it to me if I promised to capture a video of a beautiful woman reciting her phone number."

Carolina recorded the line of brides going in and coming out of the magic warehouse. She caught us trading the rest of our coffee thermoses for a packet of gum. Mostly, though, she can be heard on the microphone saying, "Can you believe all this? It's beyond words!"

Eventually, one of the production assistants saw her with it and hollered, "Hey! No cameras allowed. Get rid of it."

"As if," Carolina muttered under her breath, then hitched up her crinoline and slid the camera into the waistband of her bike shorts beneath. "I knew I wore these for a reason."

Around midmorning, the costuming crew loaded us on buses and drove us to the set on Grant Street, where we were met by production assistants sporting matching production company T-shirts and name badges. "Matilda" herded us all the way to the curb and gave us our direction. "When the brides in front of you run, you run."

As you can imagine, nine hundred brides lining the San Francisco streets eventually stretches into several city blocks. Whatever movie magic was underway for the stars, we didn't have line of sight into it. For the next several hours, we ran, retreated, and ran again.

Here's how it worked. Somewhere in a galaxy far away, a

director would call, "Action." Presumably, Chris O'Donnell, dressed in his tuxedo best, would then run, and the brides behind him would give chase. Two, five, seven minutes later, that wave would ripple back to us, and we would follow, lending our feet to cinematic history.

"I wonder if you'll be able to see us," we each asked in turn.

When the movie came out that November, Emma thought she saw Carolina's floppy hat. Andi thought she caught a glimpse of my face. I knew all of it was simply wishful thinking.

Late in the afternoon, it began to rain, and soon herds of brides trudged back to wherever they'd come from, veils soaked and feet aching. Emma's hem turned black with mud. I lost my butt bow somewhere on Grant Street. We skipped the buses and walked home.

"That was quite possibly the best day of my life," I said.

"Definitely the best wedding I've ever been in," said Andi.

Carolina dialed Chandler and told him to make dinner reservations.

Emma said, "You guys must really love me." And we did. We really, really did.

July

Emma

Flying north toward Sacramento on I-80, Emma realizes she's taking her exasperation out on the speedometer. Nearly twenty miles over the limit. A ticket would put enough points on her driving record that she'd have to hitch a ride to her own daughter's wedding. She slows, reminding herself she's helping Doris to help Portia. And Lyle is not his mother. Her daughter's new life with her fiancé is all that really matters.

"You're simply frustrated and exhausted." She says this aloud to the empty car. And it's true. Her to-do list has no bottom. She isn't sleeping well, hot flashes soaking her sheets every night. Daily texts from her credit card company warn her she's approaching her spending limit. And she constantly endures the squish of dog shit under her shoes while taking out the garbage.

Damn that Kent for being so careless with his dog.

Speaking of shit, her ex-fiancé is running for US Senate, which means she can no longer watch television. His ads are all over broadcast TV, and last night, while trying to bliss out with a mini–*Schitt's Creek* marathon, Hulu had the nerve to use her private streaming sanctum to promote that insipid, beige, nebbish face of his. "Let me do in Washington as I've done for California."

She threw a fistful of popcorn and rage howled. *What, like steal its mail and haunt its dreams, asshole?*

Crap. She's speeding again.

Also, she can't forget that Benjamin's month in South Africa has come and gone and so far, there's been no word from him. Not a text, not a call, not a peep. Nothing but a black conversational hole since their dinner in Sebastopol.

"Why are you here with me?" she'd asked. She may as well have sprayed herself in man repellent before leaving the house. It would have been better if she'd said, "I occasionally get lockjaw during blow jobs." At least with those odds, he might have chosen to stick around and try his luck.

Not on the first date, though, she reminds herself. If it even was a date. And who was she kidding. She wasn't anywhere near ready for a relationship yet. Or ever. The only career she intended to support was her own, thank you very much.

"You are plenty. You are already enough," she says. She'd said the same words in the mirror this morning. And when struggling to zip up her skirt. And while trying not to panic that she was already twenty minutes behind schedule.

She says it again, "You are plenty. You are already enough. You are a perfectly capable woman." Then she repeats the words until they meld with the thrum of asphalt skimming beneath her tires as she pulls into the Flukes' driveway.

"You can unload through the garage," Doris calls from the front doorsteps, dressed in a pantsuit nearly identical to the one she'd worn to the engagement party, but in buttercream yellow. Unlike the lavender, the color makes her skin look sallow and strips any chestnut undertones from her hair.

"You must be excited about today! The weather is beautiful." It's actually unseasonably hot but Emma is doing her best. She is enough.

Doris flicks a fingernail toward the driveway. "I'll open the side entrance for you. Once you're finished unloading, you can park on the street." Then she closes the door, leaving Emma to whisper under her breath, *Well, screw you very much, too.*

So much for the self-talk.

Thankfully, Andi and Fern are due to arrive any minute. Carolina would have come, too, if she weren't on the couch paying the price for ignoring her body. Emma hadn't asked permission to add her own friends to the guest list, she just did it, a rogue act she found unexpectedly thrilling. Now she's wondering if it wasn't some sort of premonition, that she knew she was going to need her friends as a safety net.

By the time she hears the doorbell ring and Fern's voice in the entryway, Emma's trudged so many bags in from the car that she can feel a line of sweat forming along the underwire in her bra.

Moments later, Fern appears in the kitchen. "I get the feeling Portia's future mother-in-law is the kind of person who meets someone for the first time every time she sees them. She just acted like we'd never met." She's holding a ridiculously large gift bag with every color of pink tissue paper billowing out the top and Emma loves her friend so much in this instant her heart physically swells. "I met her twice at the engagement party and now just again at the door. Three times makes you besties, right? That's the rule?"

"For sure." Emma tries to relieve her of the gift, but Fern slaps her hand away.

She disappears into the house while calling, "I'll be back to relieve you of your indentured servitude in a jiffy."

Old Emma would have gasped at the thought of Doris overhearing such a comment. New Emma wishes Fern had spoken louder.

Andi is still in the front hall, patiently listening to Doris give a verbal history of every photo hanging on the walls of the entryway. Lyle at Disneyland. Lyle with his grandparents. Lyle receiving a certificate of good citizenship for helping trim the shrubs outside the local library.

Emma, meanwhile, has been instructed to "try to make some sense of the disaster left by the caterers," which, so far as she can surmise, is a disaster that consists of three quiches, mini croissants, a bowl of fruit salad, and a tray of macaroons. Though how that qualifies as calamitous, she has also surmised, is a series of calculations that exist only in Doris's head.

In other words, Emma knows a narcissist when she sees one.

Back in the late '90s, when their friendships and careers were new, Emma worked at the consulting firm McKay & Goodwin along with Carolina and Fern. M&G was the sort of company with its fingers in nearly every international corporation across the globe, but had near-zero name recognition among anyone over the age of fifty. "Management consulting" wasn't a career aunts and uncles and grandparents understood, and whenever Emma tried to explain what she did, eyes glazed. "I just don't understand all this computer business."

Never mind that Emma didn't "do" computers; she worked in the human resources department.

Her title, "Employee Onboarding Assistant," sounded more impressive than the tasks she was expected to perform, which were mostly making copies, filling out paperwork, and sitting in on the training courses her boss conducted. Mostly boring, but a job that, on the whole, changed her life. It led her to teaching. It was also where she'd met Fern and Carolina, helping them complete their employee tax forms.

And then there was her boss, Flora, a woman who doubted everyone's skills but her own. Years later, in a graduate seminar on childhood behavioral psychology, Emma would learn the clinical definition of the term *narcissist*, and reread the text until her eyes burned. If words were dots, this cluster connected one to the next until all she saw was a picture of Flora staring back at her from the page.

During her tenure at M&G, Emma was too young and naive to understand her boss's behavior. Instead of recognizing the emotional abuse for the rotting black rose that it was, Emma wholly internalized Flora's criticisms as her own inability to do anything right. She believed it was her fault she hadn't stapled packets exactly one inch below the corner or triple checked—rather than double-checked—that the A/V guy was coming a half hour early or had a backup A/V guy on reserve in case the first guy was late.

Her most prominent memory of those years is of riding home on BART, willing the tears away, chastising herself for not having been careful enough in her wording of a particular email, rereading the notes in her planner of the "professional guidance" Flora had provided her that day—to never say "sorry" but rather "my apologies," and that she tended to break eye contact when she was thinking through her response to a question and it made her look as if she lacked seriousness. Also, perhaps a compression camisole beneath that blouse?

In retrospect, Emma can see Flora for the insecure woman that she was. Her standards for others (and likely herself) were not only unclear, they were unattainable. But Flora was also a mean girl. After all, how many times had Emma heard her say, "I need to take these extra five pounds off because on my tiny frame, five pounds is a lot"? That's some A+ passive-aggressiveness right there.

Point was, thanks to that experience, Emma had learned that there is no pleasing people like Doris. The same behavior that brings a smile one day can bring a dressing-down the next. Because these people either don't know how to be satisfied or they don't want to be. And, yes, Emma may have invested an inordinately obscene amount of time buying, and returning, and then buying again the lidded cake stand at Williams Sonoma that Doris had seen online but couldn't find the time to personally look at in the store. But Emma was doing it for Portia, hoping that, with any luck, a happy mother-in-law might just equal a happy bride.

That *was* the reason, wasn't it?

Emma ever so carefully slides an entire spinach quiche out

of its tin pie plate and guides it into a pink glass pie plate she bought on a hunch for this very situation. She's been so involved in perfecting the quiche's presentation that when Portia comes to find her in the kitchen, the party is well underway, the house abuzz with voices.

"Mom, please stop. Andi and Fern just told me they keep trying to help but you're shooing them away."

Emma is on the verge of letting loose with a particularly choice description of Doris's latest complaint about the new linen napkins leaving "dust" on the guests' clothing, but she catches herself. This isn't Portia's problem.

"You're right." Her hands surrender their tools and the quiche lands in the glass pie plate with a *splooch*. The fall leaves a crateral crack down the middle, but Emma can't bring herself to care. "We're here to celebrate you."

She wrings the water out of the clean dishcloth she'd been asked to retrieve—a small compromise she knows won't placate Doris but at least Emma can say she tried—and loops her arm around her daughter's waist. "Let's go meet some of these new friends and family you're about to inherit."

"Doris keeps introducing me to women by describing what their husbands do." Portia raises the pitch of her voice and mocks, "'This is Anne Binghamton. Her husband, Charles, is the head of sales for a multinational hedgehog conglomerate. They live in a lovely house on the river and have their cars upholstered with the leather of an endangered frog found only in the deepest rainforest.'"

Emma winks. "Are you worried Lyle will want endangered-frog leather seats?"

"I'm worried she thinks we're moving to Sacramento. Why else would she keep whispering, 'You should ask for the name of their *Ree-la-tor.*'" Portia emphasizes the misalignment of vowels, knowing how much it drives her mother wild when people say jew-la-ry instead of jewel-ry, or Ree-la-tor instead of Real-tor.

Emma fills her lungs and begins to hmm.

"Don't. You. Even."

"Buckle up, sweetheart. Your future mother-in-law is in a league of her own."

After the divorce, Emma had basically quit dealing with Devin's mother altogether, leaving communication entirely up to him. Most days Mother May sits alone in her assisted-living apartment watching *Jeopardy*. Devin often goes several weeks between visits. It isn't ideal. But then, it isn't Emma's problem anymore, either.

Crossing into the dining room, Emma's stomach growls at the sight of the buffet.

"My God, Mom, have you even taken a minute to eat anything?"

When did she last eat? Does coffee with cream count?

Portia doesn't wait for her to reply before loading a paper plate—in the color Rosé Blush, from the bridal supply store in Santa Rosa at $16 for a pack of eight—with a mound of fresh fruit and a slice of unbroken quiche. It's mortifying to realize that your twenty-three-year-old daughter is better at sticking up for you than you are.

"Thank you, sweetheart."

"I'm the one who should be terrified of Doris. Not you."

Technically, the woman shouldn't be able to terrorize anyone. But her daughter knows that.

Emma is just gliding her fork into her mouth when Queen Doris appears. A frown flickers briefly across her face at the sight of Emma's food. She straightens and smooths her suit jacket.

"Shall we start the games?"

Whether or not to have games at the shower had elicited several days' worth of emails. Once they'd agreed that, yes, games would be fun, several more rounds followed in which Doris debated which games and how many. And did Emma suppose she could print up a word-search puzzle that included

the names of Portia's bridesmaids, as well as her wedding colors and honeymoon destination?

Emma had done it, of course.

"Did you bring the word search?"

"No." The word tumbles from Emma's mouth, accompanied
by an electrifying *zing!*

Portia disguises a snicker with her hand. She knows her
mother is lying.

Emma suddenly can't stomach the thought of handing over
that stupid, vapid, grade-school girl's fantasy of a word search—
"Find the bridesmaids! Find the parts of a wedding dress!"—
that she'd stayed up until 2:00 a.m. one night to finish and then
paid to have them printed on the only pink paper available at
Kinkos. Nope, she couldn't do it, especially knowing that her
product would be met with a sigh and, "Hmm. You didn't print
them on card stock?"

No, I didn't print them on card stock, fork you very much.

"Oh, Doris." She pinches her thigh until her face cracks in
pain, the nearest expression to a smile she can muster. "My
to-do list is simply too long to accomplish everything on it.
Didn't the decorations come together beautifully, though?"

That last bit may have verged on wicked—a solicited compliment is a narcissist's kryptonite. She watches Doris struggle
to free herself from the trap.

"Well. No matter," Doris says. "I am prepared with a more
engaging game, anyway."

And…point goes to the mother-in-law.

Having narrowly avoided the conversational quicksand thrown
in her path, Doris turns her attention once again to Emma's plate,
staring holes into her yet untouched slice of quiche.

"Perhaps you should throw that away so we can get started.
The quiche is delightful, and I'll be sure to give you my caterer's card."

It's as if the woman is trying to torture her.

They follow as she ushers them into the living room. Emma

is promptly dismissed with a flick of the hand and she squeezes onto the couch between Andi and Fern. Portia is planted beside her mother-in-law in front of the fireplace.

One of the guest hands them cups of punch, and Doris clinks a teaspoon gently against the glass. "I'm pleased as my drink here—" pause for titters of polite laughter "—that you're all here to join me in celebrating this lovely new addition to our home."

She doesn't say her name and the guests are left to presume Doris is referring to Portia, though from the phrasing she could just have easily been talking about a new couch or grandfather clock.

"As many of you know, Sylvester and I struggled to start a family. I had two miscarriages, and soon after, we lost our son, James, who was born prematurely at twenty-four weeks. It was simply devastating and obviously I wondered whether I was meant to be a mother at all. Maybe God didn't have it in his plans for me."

She pauses and a few sympathetic noises briefly fill the quiet. Emma feels a rush of compassion. Loss is loss, and the devastation of losing a child? Presumably ineffable.

"This is a story, perhaps, for another day but I believe it was the pesticides the neighborhood lawn care company used that were making me sick."

And here we go... Emma thinks to herself.

"The woman down the street got ovarian cancer. A nine-year-old one block over died of leukemia. And I kept losing babies. I told Sylvester we had to move. Plain and simple. If we wanted a family, we needed to escape that toxic cloud."

The theorizing continues long enough that a woman in the corner clears her throat uncomfortably, and either Doris takes the cue or is getting to the point anyway, because she concludes with, "This house brought us Lyle, and I've always considered it lucky. So, let's play!"

Fern leans in. "What kind of sick shit was that?"

"I have no idea…" Emma pauses, equally perplexed. "Maybe

the opening salvo of a woman who doesn't have any idea what she's supposed to do with the rest of her life?"

"She makes me sweat," says Fern. "I've got swamp pits."

Doris's tinny voice fills the room. "This game is called, How Well Does the Bride Know Her Fiancé? There are ten questions. Each of you write down how many of them you think Portia will answer correctly and whoever comes closest will win a small prize."

Andi turns to Emma. "What happened to your crossword puzzle or whatever?"

She shakes her head. "Don't ask."

One of the neighborhood lackeys hands a pen and a slip of paper to each of the guests. Meanwhile, Portia is escorted to a velour wingback chair that looks strikingly throne-like.

The queen takes her own throne and begins. "Question one: How many hours of television per day was Lyle allowed to watch in elementary school?"

Portia smiles amiably and laughs. "I don't think we've ever discussed this exactly. But I suspect you encouraged him to focus on his schoolwork and playing outside." At this, she beams at Doris as if giving her the greatest compliment. "So, I will guess...no more than an hour per day?"

"An hour!" Doris hoots with such verve that her jacket shifts and she has to pull it straight again. "No. Zero television on school days, one hour on Saturdays and Sundays."

The guests murmur, some with appreciation, some with surprise. One woman who'd apparently predicted Portia would score a ten out of ten calls, "Well, I'm out!"

Doris continues, "What grade did he receive in ninth-grade biology?"

It's a ridiculously specific question, again, but Portia plays along diplomatically. "An A, of course!"

"An A+, but I'll give you credit. Next question: With whom did he dissect a frog in ninth-grade biology lab?"

Emma hears herself scoff before she's able to stifle it. Is Doris kidding?

Portia tries to pass. Doris says passing isn't an option.

"How about if she gets to ask a guest for help?" Emma suggests. One woman even raises her hand. A few others clap genially like congregants in the church of Doris.

She cruises right past Emma and her interlopers.

"What was the first book Lyle ever read all by himself?"

Portia's answer is a brilliant deconstruction of her future mother-in-law's character. *"The Children's Bible?"*

"No. *Oliver Twist*. Next question: What was he wearing in his fourth-grade picture?"

"Hang on!" Emma springs forward on the couch, bouncing Andi enough that she splashes punch into her lap. *"Oliver Twist?* That can't be true."

Doris blinks once. "And why is that?"

"It's just—" Eyeballs turn to her from throughout the room. But she's in this now, no turning back. "I've taught elementary school for twenty years. I know kids don't jump from *Clifford the Big Red Dog* directly to Dickens."

"Perhaps not with your teaching methods, but I was Lyle's first and lifelong teacher. Question five—"

"My *teaching* methods?" The nerve of this woman.

Emma tries to stand but Fern grabs her waistband, tugging her back down. She whispers, "She's not worth it."

Emma turns just quickly enough to glare at Fern for stopping her. "I'm fine. It's not like I was about to hit her."

But Doris has moved on. "What is Lyle's favorite Bible verse?"

Portia's attention is now split between Emma's rising temper and this dreadful game. She hits her mother with a dead-eye stare, the one Emma knows from experience translates to "Mom, seriously! Do NOT!"

Doris presses, "Any guesses?"

"Uh..." Portia's focus is still locked on Emma. "The 'For God so loved the world' one?"

"No, wrong again. It's 'Jesus wept.' The shortest verse in the Bible." Then she titters as if the selection proves her son is the wittiest creature in the universe, and if Emma didn't already know and love Lyle, she'd hate him from this anecdote alone.

"Doris," Emma says, trying her utmost to keep the exasperation out of her voice, "how about a few questions Portia and Lyle are more likely to have discussed? I know I certainly didn't know Devin's favorite Bible verse or high school grades before we got married."

"Oh. I see." Doris lowers her gaze to the floor and places the index card full of questions on the table next to her. She takes a deep breath, beginning to hum quietly. "How do I put this?"

Doris smiles, but Emma girds herself. An insult is coming. The air buzzes with it, standing the tiny hairs at the back of her neck on end.

Fern preemptively hooks her fingers into Emma's waist. Andi leans in, driving her shoulder into Emma's chest, attempting to pin her against the couch.

Someone coughs. Another clears her throat.

Portia whispers, "Mom, it's fine."

But Doris puts a hand on Portia's knee, silencing her. "May I say, Emma, that given your recent divorce, perhaps you yourself should have gotten to know Devin better before walking down the aisle to him."

Did she just? Did she seriously JUST?

"And may I add that perhaps if you'd prepared the bridal word search for Portia's party as you promised, I wouldn't have had to come to the rescue with a game you seem to dislike so much."

"Come to the rescue? Come to the—" Emma thinks her throat might be closing up. She can't even strangle the words out.

"While this game is certainly not what we planned on, it is

what we have available." Doris's face is smug, her tone pedantic. Emma immediately thinks of Nurse Ratched from *One Flew Over the Cuckoo's Nest.*

If Emma doesn't leave the room right this second, she's going to lose her shit. She drives her elbows into Fern and Andi and stands.

"Mom." Portia's tone turns from anger to pleading.

"No. It's okay, honey. I'm just going to take care of something in the kitchen." *Move*, she tells her feet. *Get out, get out, get out.*

Doris tsks, which Emma is prepared to ignore. Until she adds, "Refill the punch bowl while you're there, wouldn't you?"

And that's when something snaps in Emma. Her resolve, her positive affirmations, the devotion to her daughter, her manners, and her cool. Emma is flat out of fucks to give. "Certainly, I can, Doris. Is there anything else you'd like me to do? Hand-wash your bras, perhaps? Iron Sylvester's boxer shorts? Because it's not as if I've done much to help with this little party."

She's aware she's standing in the center of the room, and hyperaware of the shuffling feet and fidgety hands all around her. She hears Andi's hushed, "Don't do this, Emma," and catches a glimpse of Portia's face in her hands.

It's too late. The rage train has left the station.

"I just haven't helped at all, have I, Doris?" Emma grabs a guest's empty plate from the nearest side table. "It's not like I drove to three stores in Napa, four in Marin, and one in Santa Rosa to find these plates. These perfectly pink-blush plates that you couldn't quite explain but insisted they had to be just the exact color you had in your head. This precise fucking shade."

She flings the plate across the room. It hits Doris's sister-in-law in the chest.

Emma cackles. "Good thing they're paper, huh? And not cheap paper, either. No, sixteen dollars for a pack of eight, in fact. Doris, you can go ahead and pay me back the sixty-four dollars I spent on them anytime now. I won't charge you for my time or my gas."

"Are you quite finished?" Doris does not rise from her chair. This is her kingdom. Her citizens.

"No! I don't think I am, in fact." Despite her every instinct, Emma marches into the dining room and returns holding the Williams Sonoma lidded cake stand by its glass stem. "There's this, too. A hundred and twelve dollars without tax. You found it online. But could you spare the time to go to the store in Sacramento to look at it? Heck, did you even try to order it online? Of course not! You had me go buy it. Then, before even looking at it, you changed your mind and made me return it. But wait! *Sorry about all that trouble, Emma, I think I would like that lidded cake platter, after all.* This stupid, generic, 'could have bought the same thing at Target,' 'made in China cake' stand. AND THEN YOU DIDN'T EVEN SERVE CAKE!"

She thrusts the platter, emphasizing her point. The lid flies from its perch and crashes, hitting a chair on the way down, shattering into a thousand pieces.

"MOM!" Portia springs to her feet, along with Fern and Andi. They're on her in seconds, dragging her from the room by her elbows.

But not before Emma hears Doris announce, "Well, I'm certainly not reimbursing her for that."

Fern

The sight of Emma trying to beat back tears in the face of a suburban tyrant is all it takes to convince Fern she's not going to tell Emma about the screen rights. At least not until Portia is married. Once the stress of the wedding eases, maybe. But not today.

When she returns home from the bridal shower, Fern throws her car keys on the counter and makes straight for the couch. She needs her shoes off and her feet up.

"Mack? Maisy? I'm home."

Winnie the Poodle curls at her feet as Mack emerges from his office. "How'd it go?"

She'd sent cryptic texts like shit show = this party all afternoon, and Mack sat down in his chair, ready for the tea.

"What makes people so terrible?"

"Well, let's see." He begins to tick off on his fingers. "Mercury poisoning. Lead. Falling on one's head as a child. A hit to the head as an adult. Rabies. And cable news."

It's moments like this that remind Fern why she loves her Mack with the loyalty of a penguin and the ferocity of a hyena. "The only reason Emma didn't walk out that door was because of Portia. Maternal love is a superhuman force."

She describes the afternoon in broad strokes. Doris's ability to shame, even while giving praise. Emma's tireless sacrifice in the face of it. And, of course, the episode with the pickles.

"Emma wasn't letting us help with anything, so Andi and I finally took matters into our own hands and started assembling the charcuterie board—meats and cheeses and crackers, et cetera, including some bread and butter gherkins. These tiny little sweet pickles from this farm-to-table boutique near Emma's place. They probably cost twenty bucks a jar, and they're delicious. So, we shove cocktail sticks into them and scatter a few across the board."

She looks at Mack to ensure he's getting how miniscule this issue ought to have been. "We're talking baby relishes. You get that, right?"

He nods.

"Good. Because you would've thought we'd sprayed a syringe full of cyanide on the food. Doris literally gasped when she saw them. Pickles. I mean, how dare they!"

"I take it she's not a fan."

Fern can no longer keep telling this story lying down. She's upright and talking with her hands.

"Apparently not. Only, that's news to us. But she's pointing and squirming and doing this thing with her face." Fern tries her best to imitate the look, a cross between angry duck lips and the expression a "lady of the manor" might give upon discovering that one of her staff took a shit on the floor of her boudoir.

"Wow." Mack's enjoying every second of this. "Imagine what she'd have looked like if you put out dill spears."

Fern stifles a laugh before continuing, "As it was, she'd walk up to anyone with meats or cheeses on her plate and say, 'Apologies if that has a pickled aftertaste. The caterer went rogue.'"

"You're a caterer now, huh? Lemme guess—Doris is a great tipper?"

Her adrenaline purged, Fern falls horizontal again. "My guess is that she's the kind of neighbor who gives out raisins on Halloween."

Mack stands and grabs her toe gently as he walks by. "Can I make you a cup of tea? Glass of wine?"

She requests rose hip tea and reaches for the television remote. Moments like this call for numbing out in front of one of two things: a good cult documentary, or one of those real-estate shows where a couple comes to the verge of divorce before finally agreeing on a property.

As she flips channels, Carlton Willis's face is plastered across every news station.

"Oh, yeah. You probably haven't heard." Mack hands her a steaming mug. "A female member of his campaign staff quit and is accusing him of harassment."

Fern's brain suddenly feels as if it's swelling beyond the confines of her skull. The chyron at the bottom of the CNN screen reads: *California Senate candidate and TaxAware CEO accused of sexual misconduct.*

She hopes with every ounce of her best juju that Emma doesn't hear about this today. Not after what she just went through.

"Are we seeing the natural progression of the #MeToo movement in this woman's willingness to come forward so soon after making her accusations?" The anchorwoman probably wouldn't have chosen the orange vegan leather blazer she's wearing if she'd known what would break during her programming time slot. Saturdays usually aren't big news days.

It's also not a great look for a white man to be her expert guest on #MeToo. But there he is. And he has an answer. "She'll have to prove her accusations, of course. But yes, I think this is another indication that women feel more emboldened to tell their stories publicly. To make it clear that they don't intend to tolerate the same behavior they have in the past."

Fern groans. "Gosh, thanks for explaining that to me, Mr. White Dude. My vagina didn't make sense to me before you came along."

This is, of course, the moment Maisy chooses to emerge from her bedroom. "Gross, Mom!"

"Not nearly as gross as this." She points to the screen, where the chyron is now explaining that the allegation includes accusations of digital stalking. The revelation catapults Fern off the couch, and she throws her arms around her daughter. "You know that nobody, no woman or man or anyone, gets to be in your space without your permission, right? That means physical space. Bodily space. Social media space."

Maisy's voice comes muffled from the depths of Fern's shirt. "For example, your choice to hug me right now?"

Fern squeezes tighter. "Yes. That's the perfect example of what I mean."

Damn. That fuckin' Carlton.

Carolina

"I'll entertain you," Chandler says, "but in exchange, you have to show me your scar."

"Deal." Carolina can't stand one more minute at home. Only problem is she can't drive with her knee in an immobilizer, and she can't ask Queenie. She hasn't been exactly easy to live with lately. All she wants is to do something or go somewhere, but he acts as if just walking from the couch to bed is going to tear her knee open. The surgery happened a week ago. Nurses had her up and walking, albeit with support, only a few hours later. Plus, she has crutches. All the world should be her stage.

Chandler doesn't have anywhere he needs to be, anyhow. His kids are at school for the day, his wife is at the office, and his only job is overseeing the remodel of their house, which has been ongoing for more than two years. The extended timeline isn't because he's overly picky, though that could be part of the problem. It's that he's working with a trust fund money budget. He can afford the kind of remodel in which you debate whether to install an elevator. The permits alone probably cost more than Carolina makes in a year, and she's Bay Area–comfortable.

She texts Queenie, who's at the dentist for a cleaning. "Chandler's taking me to lunch. Back in a bit."

Chandler is illegally parked at the curb when Carolina gingerly exits the building. Just getting from the elevator to the front door feels as if it takes an hour, and the hobble to Chandler's car an hour-plus. She hands him her crutches and slides the front seat all the way back to make room for her unbendable knee.

"So," Chandler says by way of greeting. "The assistant. You think he paid her off?" He doesn't need to say Carlton's name. Chandler lived through the women's turn of the century drama firsthand.

Carolina adjusts the air-conditioning vents to blow directly on her armpits. "She didn't change her mind without significant coaxing. I just hope it hurt when he wrote out the check." Carlton's assistant has publicly withdrawn her accusations and is refusing to say why.

"Nothing hurts that guy. He's too rich to feel anything but the feigning praise of his cronies."

Chandler witnessed a lot back in the day, and he knows there's one weighty caveat to his statement. A caveat that involves Carolina, Emma, Andi, and Fern. *They* can hurt Carlton, and he knows it.

"Where are we going, anyway? What do you feel like eating?"

"Nothing," says Carolina. "You're driving me to the office."

Chandler is none too pleased, which he demonstrates by roaring the engine and taking a corner fast enough that Carolina has to grab ahold of the "oh, shit" handle.

"You dragged me halfway down the peninsula when you could have just taken an Uber?"

The idea of ordering a car hadn't even occurred to Carolina. Her waistline *and* brain must be getting soft. "Fair enough. Lunch is on me. Then, you're taking me to work."

"Why do I have the feeling Queenie's gonna kick my ass when he finds out?"

They eat vegetarian at an Indian place near the corporate campus. Between forkfuls of eggplant vindaloo, Chandler says, "You know he's called me for campaign donations. It's always him, and he always starts by saying, 'Chandler, buddy!'"

Carolina thinks she might gag.

"The only reason I'd consider giving him money would be to speed up our building permits."

"US senators don't have any pull in city politics." She doesn't know if this is an overgeneralization, but it feels good to say. "Plus, he's not going to win. Keep your money."

"Probably not. But I doubt the allegations hurt him at all. If he loses, it'll be because voters see that he's a straight up dick of a human being."

"Maybe you should say that to him the next time he asks you for a donation."

After lunch, Chandler drops Carolina and her crutches at the front entrance of the building on campus where the MAVERIK team works. She hobbles inside shortly before two.

At 6:15 p.m., Queenie calls her cell phone.

"I hope you're not where I think you are."

"I swear. I'm out of here in fifteen, twenty minutes, tops." The team had been in the throes of another data glitch when she arrived, and she'd lost track of time. It resolved within an hour or so, but since she was at the office…

To work effectively, she'd made a standing desk out of cardboard boxes from the mail room and set her computer on top. If she propped one of her crutches under her right armpit, she could lean on it enough to take nearly all the weight off her left leg. In fact, Queenie shouldn't be scolding her; he should be praising her ingenuity.

"You're on authorized medical leave, Carolina. Legally, I don't even think you're supposed to be there."

Technically, he might be correct, but she'd scored significant points for showing up. Sandra actually did a double take walking by her office. "I'm impressed to see you."

"Some things are better handled in person," Carolina answered. "Data hiccup. We resolved it. Program's back online. I'm waiting on one set of reports and then I'm calling a Lyft."

She doesn't share this anecdote with Queenie. He's trying so hard to tamp down his frustration that he's huffing. "Carolina, why take the leave if you're just going to work, anyway? You're a wreck about your running life being over, and yet you won't even stop long enough to give your knee a chance to heal."

An email from Sandra pops up on her screen. **Subject: Excellent show of leadership today.**

"Leaving in thirty minutes," she says. "Promise."

Fern

"Holy SHIT!"

Maisy's screams send Fern flying from her bedroom and down the stairs where she trips, bashing her baby toe against the baseboard at the bottom.

"Bugger! Bugger! *Bugger-all!*"

"Mom! I did it! I got in!"

Fern gathers herself, recognizing the weight of this moment, and soon they're both jumping up and down, Fern on the foot she hasn't just broken, and Maisy holding an acceptance letter in her hands from Amherst College.

"Congratulations, Maisy!"

She'd been wait-listed by Amherst in the fall and elected with a fractured heart to attend her second-choice school, UC San Francisco. Too many people in her life had gone to UC schools. Her brothers currently attended Fern's alma mater, Davis. Half her graduating class was scheduled to attend either UCSF or San Francisco State. Maisy wanted to blaze her own path.

Fern could certainly understand that.

But why did she have to go all the way across the country? And to a school with a price tag Fern refused to think about. Now there's no choice but to figure it out.

"I'm proud of you, girlie." She pulls Maisy in and wraps her up. Her hair smells like coconut and mango and teen anxiety. "Sometime between now and your first day of classes, I'll even let go of you."

Maisy squirms. "Mom."

"Nope. Another few seconds, please."

"I need to text my friends."

After dinner, Fern tells Mack the good news. "Doubly glad I optioned the book now. We're going to need the money for Amherst."

He hmms absentmindedly, a dad still glowing about his daughter's success. "Speaking of, I forgot to ask. How'd it go when you told everyone you signed the deal?"

She doesn't answer.

Mack, correctly interpreting the dead air, looks at her sternly. "Fern."

"I know. I know."

They finish loading the dishwasher in silence.

Emma

Emma rarely answers calls from unknown numbers, but she's waiting to hear back from the florist with a final estimate and is anxious to strike one more item off her to-do list.

"Emma?"

The voice sends her sliding to the kitchen floor. "Carlton."

He chuckles. "I didn't expect you to recognize my voice."

"Yes, well…" It's all she can spit out, given the sudden pain shooting through her body. Something inside her is twisting, rearranging itself into an unnatural shape. Tanking her blood pressure. She lies down on the tile before she passes out.

"So, I trust you've heard I'm running for the Senate."

He cannot hurt you. You owe him nothing. Carlton is your past, not your present. Her therapist's voice strains to be heard against the thrum between her ears.

"And I suspect you've also seen the accusations made by my former assistant."

Her twisting gut lurches. She wants to scream. But her breath is gone.

You're okay. Nikki's voice rises again from somewhere deep inside. *He cannot hurt you.*

"Emma? Are you with me?"

Find something real, Nikki reminds her. *Break the momentum of your fear.*

Emma lays a hot palm on the cool stone tiles. The temperature contrast ricochets across her nervous system, bringing her back to the present moment. Her eyes refocus on the blue color of her shirt, to the fingerprint smudge on the dishwasher. And to her paralyzed grip on the phone.

She loosens her fingers and slowly sits up, leaning her back against the cupboard door.

"Emma?"

Her breath remains uneasy, but it comes. "Yes."

"I asked if you're with me."

"Yes. I said I'm here." Her fingers tremble. She moves the phone to the opposite ear.

"But are you with me?"

"I don't—" As in, physically? Is he asking for her vote? "I don't know what you mean."

"You will." She hears him smile. "In time. You'll decide."

She's still spinning when he says. "Really lovely to hear your voice again, Ems. I'll stay in touch." Then he hangs up before giving her the chance to answer.

The phone call lasted all of two minutes and Emma is spent, her bones barely able to support her weight. She stays on the floor, knees to her chest.

When her Fitbit buzzes on her wrist, commanding her to move, she stands carefully and opens the fridge, pouring the entirety of what remains of the bottle of Pinot Gris. She pauses, and then pulls a second bottle from the wine rack. If she needs it, she'll drink it on ice. It's a trick she learned after Devin moved out. And this is no time to be precious.

As she heads outside to the patio, wineglass (and bottle) in hand, she leaves a message on Nikki's voicemail. "I began to spin out this afternoon. Lightheaded. Shooting pain. Couldn't catch my breath. But I did what you told me to do. I found something real and focused on it. Brought myself back to the moment. Cut off the momentum of my panic. And, well, I guess I'm just calling to say that it worked. Thank you. I snapped out of it."

It's not until she hangs up that she realizes she made no mention of Carlton's call, of what sent her spiraling in the first place. Maybe it's a fear hangover, as Nikki calls them. The ability to only process so much at a time. She'll try to fill in the details at their next appointment.

The sun is hot on the front of the house at this time of afternoon, but the backyard is shaded and cool, bringing her more deeply into the present moment. The air smells of bougainvillea the way it always does after a full day of soaking in the heat, and she briefly considers lying in the hammock beside the flowering bush. Except she can't drink and swing at the same time. Once, on a particularly low day during the dissolution of her marriage, she'd tried sipping her wine through a straw, but it made her feel ridiculous.

Devin had nearly destroyed her. And before Devin, there was Carlton. He'd come close, too. He may have even succeeded in his emotional demolition if it weren't for her friends. The day she and her friends took matters into their own hands, Carolina wore a look Emma has never seen since. Which, considering the circumstances, is a good thing. It was the sort of expression that means something deep and lasting is underway. As it was.

These two men. They'd crowded every therapy session for the last year. Why had she been attracted to them? Why had she put up with that sort of behavior? Why did she believe she was in those relationships as much for the men's sake as for her own?

Why, and why, and why? Too many days it felt as if she'd learned nothing, but that couldn't be true, because if it were, she wouldn't be sitting here, calming herself, and sitting (mostly) upright. Yes, she was leaning on the wine tonight. Yes, she might be on the verge of ordering an entire carrot cake and eating it with her fingers. But she wasn't hysterical. She wasn't blaming herself for answering the phone, or for not hanging up as soon as she heard his voice. These men had once been her world. Now, she just wanted them out of it.

She's still on the deck a few hours later, her belly happily full of buttercream frosting, when a text from Portia pops up on her phone.

Did u know about this?

She can tell Portia sent a photo, but it's struggling to load. Emma waits, imagining what the picture may be. A surprise gift from Lyle. Something from their registry.

Her screen lights. The photo is there. She zooms in.

It's a picture of Devin's girlfriend, Greta. She's cradling her belly. Emma estimates she's five or six months along.

Fern

When the bat signal comes via text, Fern picks up Andi and drives the hour to Emma's house in under forty-five minutes. They stop at the store for reinforcements and arrive at Emma's with every variety of chips and dip that Trader Joe's carries. Carolina is already on the couch, having been dropped off by Queenie with a box full of vegan-bakery cupcakes. "I haven't eaten sugar in nearly a month, but this is worth the sacrifice."

Andi heads to the dining room to grab wine from the rack. Emma is down the hall putting clean sheets on the extra beds. "Nobody's driving home tonight," she calls.

They've all brought their overnight bags. Devin at least had the decency to announce his girlfriend's pregnancy on a Saturday night, meaning no one has to be at work in the morning. The runway is clear for staying up too late, drinking too much, and bitching their problems into oblivion.

As Fern assembles snacks, Andi returns holding two bottles. "What goes better with heartbreak and blinding rage? Cab Franc or Sangiovese?"

"I've got Verdicchio chilling." Emma appears, dressed for an evening of commiseration in sweats and a sweatshirt that reads You Say Potato. I Say You're Wrong.

Glasses clink. Middle-aged bones sink into sofa cushions. Oofs and aahs punctuate the air as they settle in.

"Thank you so much for coming, ladies." Emma's stress pulls at the bags beneath her eyes and plumps the wrinkles along her forehead. "I know it's a lot to ask."

"Couldn't get rid of us if you wanted to," Andi says. Fern and Carolina echo the sentiment.

"Me, especially," says Carolina. "I'm here until someone piles me into a car and drives my limp ass home."

The joke goes over about as well as a white man wearing a beret.

"Has the universe conspired against me?" Emma asks. "Because I don't think it's expecting too much to enjoy my only daughter's wedding."

The friends assure her it's not.

"I mean, maybe the universe needs to temper my happiness by tossing in a needy, passive-aggressive mother-in-law, but Portia has made it very clear that I'm officially off Doris duty."

"Wait." Fern pauses the conversation. "We'll return to Devin in a minute but what do you mean you're 'off Doris duty'?"

Emma bats the question away as if it's of little consequence. "Oh, you remember. Doris was being so passive-aggressive about the wedding plans that I offered to step in as a buffer."

"You *volunteered* to help with that shower?" Fern scoffs. "I thought you were the queen of saying no these days."

"Oh, come on, Fern. As if you wouldn't do the same for Maisy?"

Fern can't believe Emma doesn't recognize her own hypocrisy. "Sure. But Doris treated you like the caterer and maid." She realizes this probably isn't the best moment to pick an argument with a vulnerable woman, but the duplicity is just too obvious.

"I was trying to help."

"Okay," Andi interrupts while shooting Fern a look to *cool it*. "We all understand why you'd want to do that."

Emma straightens, her hackles apparently up. "For what it's worth, after the squabble at the bridal shower, Portia told Lyle that he is exclusively in charge of dealing with his mother. I don't know where she learned them, but my daughter has boundaries."

Carolina raises her glass. "To Portia. The prettiest, most bad-ass bride-to-be there ever was."

"Here! Here!" they say in unison.

Fern grabs a handful of sour cream and onion chips and passes the bowl. "Okay, back to the subject at hand, the man who brought us all together tonight. Let's talk about that ass-hole Devin." She and Mack never clicked with Devin. In their opinion, he talked too much about money and winning, but almost never about humanity and humility.

Emma had already forwarded the photo of Greta's taut, rounded belly. Beneath the picture, Portia wrote, Did u know about this? Apparently, Devin hadn't said a thing to any of them, not even to his daughter. He thought it better to spring it on her in person at dinner.

Emma scoffs. "She's going to be eight months along at the wedding. No way of hiding that in the photos. Not that Devin would consider it."

Fern can't help but chuckle. "Well, that's one way to steal the spotlight. Usually the mother of the bride pulls the prima donna antics, not the father."

"He's met his match in Doris," Carolina adds.

Emma's face lands in her palm. "Lord help us all."

Andi snorts into her glass, and the room erupts in the kind of laughter that only comes on the heels of exhaustion, exasperation, and the knowledge that whatever is coming next only has a fifty-fifty chance of killing you.

"I'm sorry," Emma catches her breath. "But can I just say... who looks *that* good pregnant? Seriously. Her cheekbones are so tight they look like she just had a facelift. I know she's only five months along, but by then, my face was so puffy people thought I was having an allergic reaction to something."

"You were," Fern says. "To pregnancy."

Carolina shrugs. "She probably got filler. Nothing is natural these days."

"Can you even do that when you're pregnant?" Fern wouldn't know. She's too cheap to buy anything more expensive than drugstore cosmetics.

Andi chimes in, "My doctor took me off everything, including caffeine and my antidepressant."

"That's just asking to get punched," Fern replies.

"I know, right?"

"A male doctor?"

"No, surprisingly."

Carolina returns the conversation back to Emma. "It must feel pretty crappy, though. Finding out the way you did. The timing. Having a baby with the woman he cheated with. All of it."

She nods. "Thanks. And, yes, it does. Pretty crappy, indeed."

A few hands reach for hers, a chorus of sympathetic tsks and clucks.

Then, "But what a dummy, am I right?" Emma is laughing again. "Devin is fifty-four and he's about to start all over again. With the lack of sleep, and the hormonal wife, and the bills."

"And all of that lasts a hell of a lot longer than the first few months," Andi says. "He's not going to get a full night's sleep for years. Not when there's ear infections coming and stomach bugs."

"Teething. Nightmares. Tummy aches," adds Fern.

Carolina says, "Think of how much more expensive a college education is going to be by the time this kid leaves for school."

"Exactly."

"Let's hope it doubles."

"He'll probably be dead by then." Emma's as shocked by her

casual cruelty as the rest of them. "Oh, my God, I can't believe I just said that. But it's true, no? He'll be seventy-two."

"Statistically, he'll be close," agrees Carolina. "At a minimum, his nut sack will be down to his knees."

"Gross!"

"Does that happen?"

"God, I don't even want to think about it."

Emma takes a long sip. "Oh, but there's more! Guess who called me today?"

Fern says, "The IRS."

"Or Doris," says Carolina. "She wants you to come clean up the mess you made."

Andi adds, "Was it Greta?" Which makes Emma nearly shoot wine out of her nose.

She wipes her face with a napkin. "You're all wrong. It was Carlton."

"Willis?"

"*The* Carlton?"

"*The* asshole?"

The news has everyone pitched forward in their seats.

"What the hell did he want?" asks Carolina.

Emma holds her hand out to the group and tells them to appreciate the fact that, after over two decades, she's finally able to say his name without shaking. "I'm not even sure what he wanted, to be honest. My head got muddled when I heard his voice."

Andi looks directly at her. "What did he say, exactly?"

She thinks about it. "He was like, 'Hey, Emma. I'm sure you've heard I'm running for Senate. And I'm sure you've heard about the accusations from my former assistant.'"

Her friends wait quietly while Emma retraces the conversation in her head.

"Then what?" Andi presses.

"Then… I wasn't listening for probably half of it. But I know he said, 'Are you with me?'"

Carolina scoffs. "He called to solicit your vote?"

"That's what I wondered!"

"No," says Andi. "He was asking if you're *with* him. As in, are you going to keep your mouth shut." She makes a circle with her finger. "Are we *all* going to keep our mouths shut."

"Oh." Emma's face goes red. "Really?"

Andi nods. "And he left the question vague so that if you do ever speak up, you can't say that he told you to stay quiet."

"That asshole hasn't changed a bit, has he?" Carolina says.

Fern says, "It sounds like he's gotten worse."

"Do you think I should say something?" Emma asks. "I mean, I can't, right?"

The rest of them shake their heads. "It's mutually assured destruction," adds Fern.

"Then again…" Carolina equivocates. "Do you still care about *that*?"

None of them are saying the words aloud. Because they don't need to. And because they took a vow of silence that day.

Emma, however, makes it clear that she very much does still care about that. "My daughter gets married in six weeks!"

Carolina raises her hands in surrender. "Fair enough. Just asking."

"But you still have what you have, right?" asks Emma.

"I do."

Tracking this evasive back-and-forth is giving Fern a headache. "You gotta block his number. Gimme your phone. I'll do it for you."

"Can't." Emma frowns. "The call came through as an Unknown Caller."

"Identity blocking," Andi says. "Not surprised."

Emma reaches for the gummy bears. "Let's just drop it, okay? I answered a call I shouldn't have, but I know better now."

"What if he shows up at your door?" asks Fern.

"Don't scare her!" says Carolina.

"But what if?"

Andi catches Emma's eye and shakes her head. "Then she won't answer the door. Easy as that."

"Changing the subject, as I requested..." Emma loudly clears her throat. "How do I get the neighbor's dog to quit pooping in my yard?"

Fern makes a face. "Seriously? Gross."

Carolina says, "Sorry, but Mrs. Roper is a lady. She minds her potty manners."

"Honestly, I wish I could electrify the grass, or something," says Emma. "Not enough to hurt the dog, but enough to teach him a lesson."

"Have you talked to the neighbor?" asks Andi.

"Yep. And he hasn't done anything about it."

Carolina says, "Start leaving the poop bags at his front door. Then at least he has to throw it away."

"And he'll see actual proof of the crime," says Fern. "It is a crime, isn't it, Andi?"

She laughs. "I specialize in immigration law."

"And this is a dog who's migrating into Emma's yard to poop!"

Andi rolls her eyes. "Okay. I'll be sure to look for case law precedent as soon as I get home."

The evening goes on like this, unfolding just as it should for friends who've shared as much as the four of them. The small group of women who'd share just about any secret, any fear, any dream.

Including thoughts about the past they'd naively believed would play no part in their middle-age lives.

It's Carolina who returns the conversation to Carlton. "I'm not sure if this is bad news or not, but our CEO, Mark, had a meeting with Carlton. Next morning, Sandra told me Carlton dropped my name. Said we went 'way back.'"

"You do." In fact, Fern considers "way back" an under-statement.

"But was it a signal? Another way for Carlton to warn us?"

Emma visibly sinks.

Andi sits up. "He knew the message would get to you."

"Oh, come on, you guys." Fern's the writer. Of all of them, her brain is supposed to be the most naturally conspiratorial. "Don't get paranoid. He knows Carolina's boss has deep pockets. He could simply be trying to turn a personal connection into a campaign contribution. Politics 101."

Carolina smirks and shakes her head. "It's like you never even watched *House of Cards*."

"We don't talk about Kevin Spacey here. This is a safe space."

"Chandler says he's called him, too."

"Because Chandler has money!" Fern is about to reiterate her confidence in Carlton's past remaining in the past when Emma slams her wineglass on the table.

"I just want Portia to have a beautiful, peaceful, memorable day. Why is the universe trying to fuck that up for me?"

Emma

Emma looks at the women sprawled out in her living room and knows a gal couldn't ask for better friends. Even if they do fall short occasionally and drive each other to the brink from time to time.

"I know we covered this, but I still can't imagine what Devin is thinking." Andi tears into a bag of salt-and-vinegar potato chips, then pauses and sprints to the kitchen to retrieve a serving bowl, hollering as she goes. "Does he think Greta is going to do all the work?"

"He's having his midlife crisis. His brain is addled." Fern opens the barbecue chips, sending Andi back to the kitchen for a second bowl.

Carolina grabs a handful directly from the bag and calls to Andi, "Just let us eat like heathens!"

Fern says, "I know it's a cliché to say men think with their dicks, but for some of them, it's true. There's a reason women can't have babies at our age."

Emma isn't listening. Or, she is, but mostly she's letting the warmth of the evening wash over her. This is what friendship is, why the four of them have never truly drifted. When hard luck falls, girlfriends show up. She ought to make that into a sweatshirt.

"Mack was great with the babies," Fern says. "We had a whole system worked out because I'm a morning person and he's a night owl. But that still didn't make it easy."

Carolina crunches on a chip. "Queenie would've been great with babies. I would've been a mess. Eight hours of sleep a night, minimum, or I can't function."

"Still. It's amazing what hormones can do." Andi is finally back, arms loaded with extra bowls, napkins, and a pitcher of water. "Some days I functioned on zero sleep like a superhero. I believe those stories about mothers being able to lift cars off trapped children or whatever."

"Isn't that thanks to adrenaline?" asks Fern.

Nobody knows exactly.

"Girls, why do I feel like such a cliché?" Emma groans, feeling the self-pity set in. "I keep thinking of that scene in *WHMS*." The friends have watched *When Harry Met Sally* so many dozens of times it's earned its own shorthand. "At Marie's wedding. Sally and Harry are fighting, and Sally says, 'Is one of us supposed to be a dog in this scenario?' And he says, 'You are,' all self-righteous like, even though he can see how much he's hurting Sally."

"And?" Fern asks.

"And that's me—I'm reliving that scene. Devin's gone and gotten his much younger über-Anglo goddess-looking girlfriend pregnant, and yet I'm the cliché. I am the dog."

"How?" Andi wants to know.

"Because I'm the jilted older ex-wife. Of course, he's going to procreate with Greta Magnussen. Who wouldn't?"

Carolina scoffs. "Lots of guys, obviously. Isn't she in her thirties already?"

"Oh, my God—ageist, much?!" Andi squeals, pointing an accusatory finger.

"I was being sarcastic." Carolina scowls, then returns her attention to Emma. "My point is, Ems, you are neither the dog nor the cliché in this scenario. And anyway, I always disagreed with Harry. If anyone, he's the dog."

"Agree." Fern raises a hand. "Harry is totally the dog."

Andi snuggles up to Emma and wraps her into a squeeze. "I'm happy to let you be a cliché if it means hanging here with you. All of us together."

Emma leans in, soaking up the love.

Andi continues, "Watching the girls at Cameron's school reminds me of what a good thing we've got with each other." She reaches for a blanket and pulls it across her lap and Emma's. "There's this group of girls that always stands together while waiting for their rides. They're obviously friends, but the whole time, they hardly speak to each other. Then their phones light up at the same time and they all laugh."

"Snapchat?" asks Fern. "Insta? TikTok?"

"Who knows." Andi rolls her eyes. "But it's just so weird. Is that what qualifies as conversation now?"

"That is what passes for conversation now—interaction via screen," Fern explains. "My boys do it, but to the extreme. They play video games online with their friends and threaten to kill each other several times an hour. We'd never know if someone was actually being murdered in our house because Mack and I tune it out."

Andi sighs. "I know. Cam does that, too. But this seems different. Does Maisy have friends the way we're friends?" She gestures at the four of them.

"She does," says Fern. "But it is different. Social media facilitates friendship, but it also catalogs it. Since nothing can be deleted, it's never truly forgotten—every insult, slight, and misunderstanding can be dredged up with a few clicks. It can be devastating."

"How are kids supposed to learn to trust anyone growing up fearing the worst?" Carolina asks.

"Right?"

"Portia went through that." Emma's mind drifts to entire evenings spent trying to console her brokenhearted daughter. "She'd fall apart if an Instagram post only got a hundred likes. There was this girl in her high school who doled out exclamation points like she was a Michelin food critic. I remember she commented, 'Cute!' with one exclamation point on a picture of Portia in front of the DMV with her new driver's license and Portia came home so upset you'd have thought she'd run over a pedestrian during the exam. This gigantic milestone and a single comment ruined the whole day for her. It's ridiculous."

Andi groans. "And people wonder why there's a teenage mental health crisis."

Fern passes the tray of cupcakes. "Why are we so terrible to each other? I mean, yes, something needs to change with this whole climate of toxic masculinity that's taken hold, but it feels like women should have figured out how to end the pattern of keeping each other down."

"The cards are stacked against us." Carolina takes two cupcakes and grins. "I'm going big on the sugar tonight."

"What do you mean the cards are stacked?" Fern asks.

"I mean, okay. Here's the reality. I try to mentor the strongest people on my team, regardless of gender or race. But I especially try to reach out to the women because there are so few of them. You get past a certain level and the numbers just dwindle."

"Don't you have a female CIO?" asks Fern.

"We do. But I've worked for nearly a dozen CIOs in my career and she's the first woman. That's a bad ratio, even for tech."

Andi nods. "Same with lawyers. It varies by field of course, but you wouldn't believe how lopsided the profession can be."

"Anyway," Carolina continues. "We're going through this pseudo layoff. Long story short, my biggest fear from the beginning has been that I'll lose one of my team leads. Yesterday I found out that not only am I losing one, but I'm losing my only female team lead."

"Crap," says Fern.

"She's leaving for a better job, so I can't blame her. But now there are no women in the leadership pipeline."

"Shouldn't that make it easier for a talented woman to rise in the ranks?" asks Emma.

"Not necessarily. When we were hiring for her position, HR sent over a huge bundle of candidate résumés they wanted me and the former CIO to go review. My boss flips through them like, 'Okay…interview this one, this one, and this one.'"

She flicks her wrist as if tossing cards from a deck one by one into the air.

"The whole effort takes five minutes, tops. And I say, 'You haven't selected a single woman or person of color to interview.' But he's suddenly all defensive. 'These are the best candidates for the position. None of the others have the necessary relevant experience.' Which is exactly the problem!" She throws her arms in the air. "How are women going to get the relevant experience if we don't give it to them? It's a self-perpetuating cycle. You give the men the opportunities, they get the skills."

Fern asks, "What does that have to do with girls outside Cam's school?"

"Because females are forced to compete on every level, at every stage, when we really ought to be looking out for each other. It's even biological. Think about it. The world's population is 51 percent female, right? So simply to complete one of our most fundamental biological functions—to have babies— we're fighting for resources."

"As in, one Devin for two women," says Fern. "See, Emma? You're not the cliché. It's just biology."

"Well, in that case—" she holds out her glass "—someone please refill my wine. It appears I'm off baby duty for the rest of my life."

Fern obliges. "Don't forget about grandkids."

"Oh, my God." Emma drops her head against the back of the

couch. She can't believe she didn't think of this before. "Portia's kids are barely going to be younger than Devin's."

Carolina peels the paper from her cupcake. "At least she and Lyle will be young enough to enjoy them."

"How did we get on this subject?" asks Fern.

"Because men think with their ding-dongs, and women are expected to either celebrate that or get out of the way," Andi answers.

Fern laughs. "Did you really just say 'ding-dong'?"

"It's a legal term."

"What about meat stick? Would you use that in a court briefing?"

"Absolutely."

"Mr. Silly Business and his pals, Billy and Baldwin?"

"I've got a case pending against them right now."

"Brilliant. Can I come to the trial?"

"Of course. Though I'll warn you, Judge Palmer can take a long time to finish."

Andi

Before tucking herself in for the night, Andi tiptoes into Emma's bedroom.

"Hey, you awake?" She doesn't turn on the light in case Emma has already drifted off to sleep.

"Yeah," Emma whispers. "I'm exhausted but my mind is spinning."

She pats the mattress beside her, and Andi sits down, glad her friend doesn't reach for the lamp. It feels easier to talk about this in the dark.

"I just want to make sure you're not worried about Carlton." The wine and junk food sit at the base of her throat as she speaks, an acidic reminder of things not quite vanished. "I'm sure he's just trying to keep you from showing your hand. I doubt he'll call again."

"What do I say if he does?"

Andi doesn't have a quick answer. She's not used to lingering in the gray areas of the law. "I suppose you can just tell him nothing's changed."

Emma grunts. "Do you think that's true? What sort of a man clings to a grudge for twenty-five years?"

"It's more than a grudge, though, isn't it?" The sad truth is that none of this had to escalate the way it did. "Carlton Willis is not a good man. I'm so thankful you left him."

Emma is quiet for a minute. "He really makes Devin look like a saint, doesn't he?"

"Not a saint." Andi won't give Devin that much credit. "Just a lesser devil. The second level of hell variety."

"Lust," says Emma.

"What?"

"The second layer of hell in Dante's Inferno. It's full of sinners driven by lust."

Andi can't help but laugh. "Wow. I guessed that one right, didn't I?"

"I wish I had." Emma's chuckling, but it's wistful.

Andi grabs her hand. "Meh. You got Portia out of the deal, and she's pretty fantastic."

"Thank you." Emma squeezes back.

"Hey, whatever happened to that guy you were texting with? Lyle's uncle, or whatever." Andi didn't remember the details. She was too consumed with screwing up her own life to pay close attention.

"Benjamin Guy," says Emma. "We went to dinner, and I embarrassed myself so he ran away to South Africa."

"You're lying."

"I'm not. I am exaggerating, but only slightly. We did go out, I did embarrass myself, and he did go to South Africa. But it was for work. I haven't heard from him since."

"What could you have possibly said that would have driven him off?" Andi hasn't gone on a date in more than twenty years, but she can't imagine Emma being so out of practice that a guy loses her phone number on purpose.

"I said, 'Why are you here with me?'"

Andi shrugs. "That's not so bad."

"It is when his question was 'do you still love teaching?'" Emma pushes herself up against the pillows and bunches the sheet between anxious fingers. "I was a conversational wreck."

"Well…" Again, Andi doesn't have a quick answer. "Maybe you were just nervous. You'd been texting for a while, right? It takes time to shift to meeting someone face-to-face."

Emma kicks her gently. "You're such an optimist."

"No one has ever called me an optimist."

"Okay, then. Naive. Trust me. It was awkward. He practically ran to his car at the end of the night."

"Uh-huh." Andi doesn't buy it. "You're rusty. Devin stomped on your heart and your confidence. Next time will be easier."

"Not with Ben." Emma slides back under the covers. "He's supposedly been back for a couple of weeks, and I haven't heard a peep."

"Photoshop your face onto the picture of Greta and send it to him. That'll get his attention."

Emma kicks her harder. "Get out before I shove you off this bed."

Fern

Throughout the rest of July, Fern feels hot—in all the best possible ways.

She and Maisy end the month with a post-graduation mother-daughter trip to Calistoga Springs. It's two days of mud baths, mineral soaks, and heated stone massages. A masseuse even gets the knots out of her back, which he calls "ropey and stubborn." Fern likes the description so much she considers adding it to her social media bios.

Shortly after returning home, Fern signs a contract for a new book. Her writing mojo has risen like a phoenix since optioning *Smart Girls*, and she wants to ride the tailwind as long as possible. Plus, she likes getting checks.

She's already started the collection of essays—an examination of the daily micro-humiliations experienced by middle-aged women. Yesterday, she went bra-shopping, intending to write about the experience. Her conclusion? That any woman who isn't clinically depressed after eight hours of tucking, strapping, boosting, and cupping her sagging boobs ought to be elected the first female American president.

"I know income doesn't equate to worth, but I'll admit... I like myself even better today than last week." She and Mack are on an after-dinner walk with Winnie the Poodle, who, Fern also knows, will consider herself the lady of the estate no matter how much money her owner makes. Poodles don't do hoi polloi.

Mack says, "I always believed you'd get the recognition you deserved. Maybe it didn't come as quickly as you'd hoped, but a victory is sweeter the longer you anticipate it."

"Speak for yourself." She's kidding, of course. "Though it does feel better than expected to prove you right for once."

"Wait. Say that again." Mack cups a hand behind his ear. "Repeat that part about me being right."

"You're right." It comes out barely audible.

"Excuse me?"

"You're right, Mr. McAllister."

He's frowning and shaking his head so vigorously Winnie takes notice and begins to yip. "I'm going to need you to speak up, little lady."

An elderly couple is approaching from the opposite direction, and since Fern doesn't want to send them to the hospital under cardiac arrest, she waits until they're several yards past before opening her lungs. "JOHN JACOB MCALLISTER. YOU ARE CORRECT AND NEVER TO BE DOUBTED AGAIN!"

"Good." He laughs and nods approvingly. "Now, hold this." It's Winnie's doggy bag.

Come September, she and Mack will be empty nesters. Owen, their oldest, graduated from college a week after Maisy got her high school diploma, but he's already accepted a fellowship for graduate work and started the research program. He didn't even want a graduation party. They drove up to Davis and took him to lunch.

The new book will consume much of her time, although she's never written anything of significance while juggling so few responsibilities. She wonders if she'll have the willpower to drive herself to the keyboard every day. When the kids needed a ride every twenty minutes and a snack every ten, writing felt like a five-minute vacation. She got to escape, one sentence at a time. Now, her life will be nothing but escape.

Maybe she'll sign up for one of the writing retreats in Italy or France she's drooled over for years. Or, on second thought, not yet. They do still have two kids in college.

There's always a writer's fellowship. If she gets organized, she can apply for a spot at an expenses-paid writer's residency. Live on nothing but inspiration, walks in the woods, and as many bags of almonds as she can fit in her suitcase.

The only decision Fern ultimately makes is to take the remainder of the summer off. The new book will have to wait a bit. Maisy will be gone in less than three weeks and there's shopping to do and hugs to be stolen and, yes, a few tears to be wiped. The reality that Massachusetts is very far away has hit, and the last few evenings have brought frightened tears.

"What if I don't like it there?" Last night, Maisy came home from a friend's house ready to email Amherst and cancel her enrollment.

Mack goes directly into "Dad the Problem Solver" mode. "Believe that you'll love it, and you will."

Maisy's tears turn from streaming to pouring, so Fern sends Mack up to bed and grabs her daughter's hand.

"I guarantee you're going to hate it from time to time." Maisy's skin is sweaty from trembling. "Think about it—some days, you even hate it here at home. Because no place is perfect. Utopia doesn't exist. But I don't think you're going to hate Amherst all the time. In fact, I suspect you're going to grow to love it. You'll make friends. You'll settle in. Then one day, you'll call me as if you never doubted your choice for a second."

"And if I don't?"

God, she looked so much like her dad when her eyes turned to frightened saucers.

"Well, if you do hate it, then call me and we'll talk about what needs to happen next. Don't forget, I came to California from Wisconsin, and besides being America's leaders in cheese production, those two states don't have anything in common."

Fern and Mack both believe much of the reason Maisy chose to venture across the country for college was because Fern spoke so fondly about her decision to do the same. That she'd been so open about how it changed the direction of her life.

"Maisy, look. Even if I'd stayed in Wisconsin, I'd have a great life because I'd have kept looking until I found the people and activities I wanted to fill it with. And that means I won't fall apart if you change your mind and decide to stay in San Francisco. But we both know that if you don't try your college life elsewhere, you'll always wonder what you might have missed."

She reached out and stroked the length of her daughter's hair. "I wouldn't have blessed you with such a beautiful long neck if I didn't want you to stick it out from time to time."

Maisy went to bed with her Amherst enrollment intact.

Now Fern is in the kitchen debating whether tonight's dinner will be pasta or pasta.

"Mack? Curly or tubular?"

He answers, but she can't hear him over the TV. It's blasting because she still hasn't gone in for a hearing evaluation. She sweeps the counter with her eyes, looking for the remote.

Orchestrated sirens announce a *Breaking News* alert as the anchor segues from a discussion on interest rates. "The *Daily Beast* has just published reporting with a second bombshell accusation against California US Senate candidate Carlton Willis in which a former TaxAware colleague claims 'I'm not the only woman he assaulted.'"

Emma

Emma's dragging a loaded grocery cart across the parking lot, trying unsuccessfully to steer with one hand while holding her phone in the other, as she's made the dual mistake of dressing in a skirt without pockets and leaving her purse at home. Her back and shoulders tweak from the strain.

She bought biodegradable doggy bags. As soon as she gets home, she'll leave them on Kent's front porch with a keenly phrased note about his dog's ongoing bathroom habits. She'd tried to speak in person with him again, but he didn't answer the door. Even though his car was outside, and it was Sunday afternoon.

"Helloooo! Kent?" She rang the doorbell and stuck her face directly into the camera. "I need to talk to yoooou." Then she tapped on the lens like a child terrorizing aquarium fish.

He was probably ignoring her.

When he ultimately failed to appear, she slid a polite note under his door. *Still having trouble with your dog in my yard. Let's discuss. Emma (the house on your left).* This time she'll be all business. Perhaps she'll even say, *You leave me no choice but to...* What? Call the police? That would escalate the issue well out of proportion. Do they even have an animal-control division anymore?

Oh, to return to those heady days when dropping Devin's name and firm got her out of nearly any pinch.

Out of the blue, a Tesla traveling too fast for any parking lot zooms past, nearly clipping her cart. "Watch it!" she hollers. The absolute last thing she plans to do today is die. Particularly while pushing a shopping cart bearing a jumbo box of panty liners for her perimenopausal bladder which, judging from the state of her underwear right now, she absolutely, positively needs.

What a humiliation this aging thing can be. She'd had her roots touched up last week and already her grays are peeking through. "It's not the dye," her stylist said when Emma called to complain. "It's the hormones. Your body's fighting back."

Against what, she'd like to know. Because her body definitely isn't fighting back against her perpetually dry skin or middle-aged acne. And by the way, how is it possible to have both?

"You are not defined by your appearance," she says aloud to herself. Nearby, a couple still young enough to think they know everything steps out of their car. She doesn't care if they hear.

Like Frogger successfully crossing the stream, she makes it to her car and is loading the trunk when her phone rings. It's her darling Portia. "Hello, love!" She could not have chosen a better time to call.

"Hey, Mom. How're you doing?"

"Other than nearly getting plowed by a Tesla just now, I'm fine!"

"What? Are you okay?"

"Yes, like I said, I'm fine." Her therapist Nikki's voice echoes in her head. *Feel your feelings. Don't stuff them away for other people's comfort.* "Actually." Emma drops the last shopping bag into the trunk and closes it. "To be honest, I'm angry. That driver was exceptionally careless. But physically, I am unhurt."

There. Score one for her evolving mental health habits.

"Well, I'm sorry that happened to you, but I am glad you're okay. Anyway, Mom, I'm calling with sort of a sensitive question."

Emma starts the ignition and sets the air-conditioning to *blast*. "I'm ready. Go ahead."

"So, Daddy called me last night."

Lord. She was not prepared for a Devin discussion.

"He asked if I would be okay with them using my cradle for the new baby."

"HE WHAT?"

"I know, Mom, just hang on. That's why I'm calling. To give you a say in the matter."

Emma punches the horn, *waaah-wa-waaaaah!* It echoes across the parking lot.

"Are you driving?"

"No. I'm pissed." Devin knows with 100 percent clarity that the cradle is not Portia's to give. She may have slept in it, but the piece is a family heirloom passed down from Emma's grandmother. Her mom slept in it, Emma slept in it, Portia slept in it. But Greta Magnussen's *bébé* gigantesque will not so much as lay a hair between its delicate spindles. "You know that the cradle was handed down to me by my grandmother, right?"

"I do. And Dad says he'll give it back. But he also claims he wants to create traditions for both his daughters to share. Like, sleeping in the same cradle."

"His *daughters*? He's having a girl?" *Waaah-waaaaaaaaaaaaaaaah!* The news kicks Emma almost as hard as learning that Greta was pregnant. Would he be asking for the cradle if he was expecting a son? No. Of course not. He'd be hiring a decorator to make the nursery look like the basketball court at a Lakers game.

"IT'S A GIRL?"

"Ugh, Mom. I'm so sorry." Portia sounds more exhausted than apologetic. "I should have said no as soon as he asked. I wasn't thinking."

Emma groans, rubbing her eyes, even though you're not supposed to do that for fear of wrinkles. But what does she care? She's ready to buy a dozen cats and never leave the house again.

When she's steady, she says, "Portia, it's not your fault. Your father should not have asked you about my property. He put you in the middle."

"But now I feel terrible for upsetting you."

"Which is why he did it. To play on your tender heart. I'll bet he was probably surprised you decided to ask me at all. If I know your father, he likely assumed you'd say yes simply to avoid having to broach the subject with me."

"He's not that manipulative, Mom."

Emma's jaw drops. This, from the same young woman who refused to let Queen Doris Fluke get the best of her. But, just as Emma once did, Portia has a giant blind spot when it comes to Devin. Thanks to his charm. His ease. His bountiful affection for "his girls."

"Look," she says, "I'm not going to nitpick your relationship with your dad. Heck, now I even feel bad for making you feel bad. But I am going to encourage you to take a minute, when you're calm, and think about what he asked of you. How did you feel when he asked you, and how do you feel now?"

"I'm going to call him back right this second and tell him no." Portia's ire is up; Emma can hear her breath tightening.

"No. I'm going to call him. My cradle, my issue."

After they hang up, Emma sits in the cooling car debating whether to call Devin now or wait until she gets home. She's so riled up that if she tries to drive, she might go right off the road. Then again, talking to Devin may make her angrier, and then what will she do?

"I'll walk around the block to cool down," she says aloud. "And if that doesn't work, I'll march back into the store, buy a dozen eggs, and smash them in the parking lot."

She dials.

Devin picks up just as it's about to go to voicemail. "Hey, Ems."

The nickname rankles; he lost the right to it eighteen months ago on a Xerox machine.

"Why did you ask Portia for my family's cradle? You know damn well it's not hers to give."

"I do not, in fact, know that." He's put on his smooth "nothing ruffles me" voice. "In fact, you said many times that you were giving it to her, for her babies."

"*Exactly!*" Spit flies from her lips onto the steering wheel. "For Portia's babies. Not your pollywog's!"

"My what?"

"Your—" She catches herself. "Never mind. What I'm saying is that the bed is Portia's. Not yours."

Now he sighs, all good-naturedly and genial, the same way he did when Portia broke into such blubbering tears as a child and neither of them could make sense of her words.

"Don't you sigh at me, Devin!"

"Well, which is it, Emma? First you say the cradle isn't Portia's, and now you say it is."

"I didn't say that. I said it will be."

"Actually, you said, 'The bed is Portia's. Not yours.'"

"Quit doing that lawyer thing."

"Quoting you?"

"Twisting words. Placing blame where it doesn't belong." What's that term everyone uses these days? She can't think of it. Devin has once again twisted her into knots. "GASLIGHTING! You're gaslighting me."

"Emma." He's Stern Dad now. The one with his hands on his hips, declaring, *Quit it with this nonsense.* "I called Portia to ask for *temporary* use of what you've long said is her cradle. I'm trying to do something meaningful, keep a family tradition going. I did not ask her to call you."

Something's burning deep inside her. A fire licking at the edge of Emma's being, of who she is at her very core. Nice Emma Johnson. The maternal, patient one. The teacher of all children. Not just the easy ones, but also the ones who need all the extra care and attention they can get. Emma Johnson, the girl who never ever turned her back on a person in need, and who grew into a woman compelled to carry the burdens, worries, misfortunes, and toils of the less fortunate. Because she can. Because she ought to. Because it's right.

Little Emma Johnson is aflame. Her image of herself, a conflagration. Emma May reborn as ash and smoke.

"The cradle is up in the attic." The fire inside her is out, its fuel spent. And it's changed this body that she inhabits. As if her bones are lighter. The oxygen entering her lungs purer. She smiles. "Come over to get it, Devin...and when you do, I'll have you arrested for trespassing."

"Emma!—"

She hangs up, delighting in the sound of his indignation.

She taps gingerly at the skin beneath her eyes, recycling the beads of sweat as moisturizer. "Well. That was fun."

Four Weddings
and a Wake-Up Call

From *Smart Girls Say Yes*
by Fern McAllister

Ella and Carmine married beneath a chuppah overlooking the San Francisco Yacht Club's million-dollar view of the bay. She was the taller of the two; he had the brighter smile. As research partners, they were poised to take the academic world by storm. As husband and wife, they were two blissful nerds confounding their upwardly mobile parents, together.

It was May, and the burgeoning summer sun on the water foretold a promise that every day forward for the happy couple would be luminous.

"They're disgustingly happy, but I can't hate them." Emma, Andi, Carolina, and I were seated at a table with Ella's teenage cousins from Los Angeles. They were the closest thing to male companionship that she could rummage up for us, and the boys were intent on getting us to fetch them drinks from the bar. We were intent on getting them to quit showing us the loathsome messages they sent each other on their beepers.

I'd met Ella in my graduate program at UC Davis. Carmine was already deep into his PhD dissertation, and they were deep into each other. Even so, the three of us managed to strike up a friendship, and I introduced them to Andi. Fast-forward, and Ella joined our book club, closing the circle of friends.

And now here we all were, witnessing their great step into the future together.

"I'll know I've met the right guy when he looks at me the way Carmine looks at Ella," I said. I'd never had that. Smilers, yes. But adorers, definitely not.

"I don't need to be adored," Andi said.

"Are you kidding?" said Carolina. "Out of all of us, you need it the most."

"I do not."

"Yes, you do. I need someone who's not going to get in my way. Fern needs a cheerleader. And Emma is the one who does the adoring in her relationships. You, however, need a man who loves you for the hard-ass that you are, but who also admires you for so much more."

"Like my boobs?"

I laughed. "If you got 'em, you may as well work 'em."

It was also at Ella and Carmine's ceremony that Emma said she'd briefly considered having a chuppah at her own wedding.

"You're a Methodist," said Andi.

"I know. But it's just such beautiful symbolism, you know? A representation of the couple's new home, of communal hospitality. I'm very warm and welcoming. It suits me."

Andi reiterated. "Again, you're Methodist. Haven't the Jews suffered enough without you hijacking their traditions?"

"Well, I think it's a lovely sentiment, Emma," I said. "And if it still matters so much when you do get married, I will personally hold a roof over your head for the entire ceremony."

"Your Methodist ceremony," added Andi.

Carolina grabbed the beeper from the kid sitting next to her. "That's it. I'm showing this to your mother."

Melanie and Patrick got married at home in Ohio but threw a party in San Francisco to celebrate with their west coast friends. They were college sweethearts, a match made at the Ohio State University. She'd been recruited by a burgeoning start-up called eBay. He followed Melanie and the sun hoping to find his purpose. As a couple, they were opposite poles bound by fire.

"I give them a year." Carolina had met Melanie in a Bay to Breakers training group and fell under the spell of a woman more outgoing than herself. Soon, Melanie and Patrick were joining the group for memorable nights out.

It was during these nights that we witnessed what a truly fiery relationship looked like. Emma said, "Oh, come on. They fight like cats but imagine what it's like in the bedroom."

"I bet he's the one wearing the lingerie," said Andi. "And not because he has a fetish."

I recoiled. "Sexist, much? So what if Melanie is the assertive one in the relationship?"

"Assertive is good. But Patrick is just…man goo. Nothing he does is his own idea. It's like the last thing he heard becomes a long-held belief. Do you know I spent a night at the Moana Loa listening to him argue that the Y2K bug was planted in the government's computer systems back in the sixties by a disgruntled contractor? He read a pamphlet about it."

"A pamphlet?" I said. "Maybe we have time-warped back to the sixties."

"Opposites might attract, but those relationships never work in the long run," said Carolina. "It's the whole reason I broke up with Julius. I need a guy who's as active as I am. Someone who likes to taste the wind in his face. Not a couch potato like Julius."

Emma frowned. "You said you broke up with Julius because he couldn't keep a job."

I chimed in, "No, it was because he spent all his money on pot."

"I thought you caught him selling pot from your apartment," said Andi.

"You've all just proved my point. There are certain things in a relationship that are nonnegotiable, and for me, being energetic and goal-oriented is one of them."

"So," I said, "Carolina wants a sporto. Andi wants a man who's done evolving out of the primordial goo. What about you, Emma?"

She sighed. "I want to be the kind of woman who doesn't have to answer that question?"

I asked what that meant, and she told us we talked about men too much. "Aren't we worthwhile on our own? You don't even need a man to have a baby anymore." This, from the woman who'd come closer than any of us to binding herself to another human being for life.

"We're at a wedding," said Andi. "Relationships are an obvious topic of discussion."

"All I'm saying is that we shouldn't focus so much on the future that we miss the fun that we should be having today. Have we forgotten that we're supposed to be saying yes, ladies?"

We remembered. And we collectively decided that the first yes of the evening should be between Carolina and the guy in the Dolce & Gabbana tie who'd been checking her out all night.

The next morning, Carolina reported he had been a good kisser. "Until he forgot it's bad form to mention your girlfriend while making out with another woman."

Teresa and Ezio stood face-to-face beneath the great dome of the Greek Orthodox church, holding hands while a priest wrapped a silken rope around their wrists, declaring them bound as man and wife for all eternity. She was barely five feet tall and eye level with his naval. He was the fifth Ezio in an unbroken lineage of large Greek men who only answered to E-Z. Together, they looked like that famous gorilla and his pet kitten.

They'd dated ever since high school, classmates of Carolina. She was one of Teresa's eight bridesmaids. Emma, Andi, and I were there as her dates, because according to Teresa, "The more the merrier at a Greek wedding!"

Sitting in the church made me dream of escaping to Santorini, with its white plaster walls supporting a domed ceiling painted the same color as the sea. Everywhere you looked, flashes of gold dotted my view. And I had plenty of time to gaze upon our surroundings because the ceremony itself seemed to go on forever. In Greek.

I suggested we plan a trip to the Greek Isles, but Emma shushed me.

I commented on E-Z's resemblance to the kitten-hugging gorilla we'd learned about in my college psychology course, but Andi corrected me. "The gorilla's name was Koko and she was female."

When my watch told me we'd been in the church for over an hour, the bored little girl in me took over. Problematic given our environment, because as soon as my brain goes quiet, my mouth likes to pipe up. These were a few of the musings I shared with my pew mates:

How does he keep from splitting her in half when they have sex?

He's cute when he smiles, but when he frowns, he looks ready to put Teresa on a spit, roast her over a fire, and strip the meat from her bones.

I wonder if the priest has ever been tempted to pocket one of those gold candlesticks when he was short on cash.

Carolina says E-Z is the sweetest man she's ever met, but also one of the dumbest.

It wasn't until I heard a woman whisper, "Do you have a tissue?" that I began to see the error of my bored ways. Neither Emma nor Andi needed a Kleenex. Nor had the lady in front of me turned to request one, and the pew behind me was filled with a line of Teresa's younger cousins. The voice wasn't nearby; it was coming from somewhere in the church.

Now, if you ever paid attention in school, you learned that some buildings are far superior to others acoustically. Among the very best, the dome. Think of the world's most famous concert venues—the Hollywood Bowl, Radio City Music Hall, the Sydney Opera House. All renowned for the way their design carries sound, and all domed.

Across the sanctuary, in the front row of E-Z's side of the aisle, I saw a woman blow her nose and blot her eyes.

"Thank you," she whispered when she was done.

I could hear the groom's family with the clarity of a Bette Midler at the Hollywood Bowl in *Beaches*. Which meant they could also hear...

"Of course, they heard you!" Carolina was draped head to toe in seafoam taffeta. We hadn't had to venture far for the reception. It was in the church basement. There was baked chicken, a full bar, and a gaggle of Greek grandfathers mixing the strongest Long Island iced teas any of us had ever tasted. "Mrs. Bratakos will probably skin your hide if she figures out it was you who said all that stuff about her beautiful Ezio."

"Maybe you shouldn't sit with us," said Andi. "We don't want you to taint our reputation."

"You guys! How was I supposed to know the sound would carry like that?" I was a full iced tea in and letting the alcohol soothe my bruised soul.

"Math," said Andi. "Arcs and angles. The Pythagorean theorem."

I, however, had always hated math and this did nothing to assuage my distaste.

"Sorry to tell you this, Fern." Emma grabbed my hand. "But you have a habit of saying things you're not supposed to say out loud."

Andi piled on as the iced tea floweth. "And of not asking permission. You're an 'act now, beg forgiveness later' kind of gal."

Isn't that what we were supposed to do, though? The '90s rules of business were full of such colloquialisms. Think outside the box. Grab the low-hanging fruit. Push the envelope.

"Someday I'm going to accomplish something great and you're going to regret ever having given me a hard time tonight."

That prediction, like the future, has yet to unfold. The only thing we regretted the next morning was just how charming those Greek grandpas were when pushing their teas.

Molly and Wes said their vows with their toes in the sand of Ocean Beach on a chilly day in September. She looked sad. He looked like he hadn't slept since Tuesday. As husband and wife, they didn't stand a chance.

"If I look as forlorn as Molly does on my wedding day," Carolina said, "I want you to throw me into a car and get me the hell out of there."

"Ditto," said Andi.

"Deal," I said. "And ditto."

"Her face says everything I was feeling while I was engaged," said Emma. "Carolina's right. Let's not ever stay in a relationship that makes us sad."

It rained as soon as the vows were complete.

Molly and Wes made it less than a year.

Two lives happened to come out of our year of weddings, and the first was a baby named Beau. His mother, Julie, was a friend of Carolina's from high school and she met a guy named Chris at Teresa and E–Z's wedding. A couple of Long Island iced teas later, they went back to Chris's apartment. A couple of months after that, Julie told Carolina she was moving to Florida to be near her mom.

"She's pregnant," Carolina reported. "She doesn't want to

have an abortion, but she doesn't want to get stuck in a relationship with a guy she doesn't love. Her mom moved to Florida after she retired. Julie wants to be near family while she raises the kid."

Emma was full of empathy. "That couldn't have been an easy choice."

Andi and I were full of piss. "Why the hell does she have to give up her life?" Julie had an MBA from Cal and a great job in Silicon Valley.

Carolina said, "It's the choice she's made."

"Yeah, while this Chris guy gets to go on living his life, carefree as ever."

There were no answers, of course. Just another glass of wine and the reminder that one can never be too careful. That motherhood was a goal for each of us, but not yet. And when the birth announcement arrived several months later with a picture of baby Beau, Carolina hung it on the refrigerator door where we could all stand and look at it, taking whatever lesson we needed in the moment from that beautiful boy's face.

And as for that second life I mentioned… Andi met her husband, Dominick, at that sad wedding on the beach, running for shelter from the rain. She made him wait almost a year before accepting a date. First came love, then came marriage, then came baby Abdallah in a baby carriage.

"Deep down, I knew I wasn't ready to get serious, and yet we never panicked about losing each other. Somewhere during our friendship, I think we spoke this silent agreement to each other—I knew he was the one, and he knew he would wait until I was ready. It gave me a sort of confidence I'd never felt with anyone else. He gave me back myself."

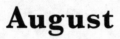

August

Emma

Every year, August fills Emma with melancholy. Though fall brings the thrill of fresh school supplies, fresh students, and a fresh start, it's August's job to toll the bells on summer. Soon, Emma will return to the classroom, and gone will be the deliciously lazy mornings over coffee and a crossword, sleeping in and staying up too late, reading whatever book she feels like reading for as long as she can keep her eyes open.

When Portia was young, they went to the country club to swim in the pool and buy treats at the concession stand—ICEE Pops and fudge bars and too-salty popcorn streaked yellow with artificial butter. As she grew, Portia attended tennis camp and golf camp and a one-week theater intensive called "Midsomer Mayhem" for which the club hired actors and directors straight off the stages of the San Francisco Theater District. Those hours Emma spent taking walks and reorganizing drawers and completing all the tiny household projects she could only dream about during the school year.

Summers beheld a secret garden–like charm.

Then August would arrive, and each morning she'd wake with a thin new layer of accountability that, by the end of the month, would have hardened around her, a shell just thick enough to survive the upcoming nine-month teaching journey.

Today, August 1st, Emma wakes feeling the early ticklish signs of her annual metamorphosis. The sun filters through her bedroom curtains, and yet she has no sense of the time, of whether she's overslept or ought to close her eyes and drift away.

"Hey, Siri." Her phone lights on her bedside table. "Do I need to get out of bed?"

Until Devin left, Emma didn't realize that he was the clock around which she graduated time. Every morning, he rose at 5:30 a.m., went for a run, showered, and left for work. During the school year, she'd shower while he was running, then wake Portia. Come June, his stepping out of bed started the day's passage. Though he was so quiet she hardly stirred, her mind took note. She hadn't used an alarm for twenty years.

Of course, it's the natural way of things for a child to grow up and leave the nest. When Portia left for college, Emma eventually adapted to being alone in the house while Devin was at work. After the divorce, she even began to enjoy quiet evenings all to herself.

But waking up alone continues to leave her disoriented and unmoored. Thirty-two days from now, Portia and Lyle will become their own family, Devin will be preparing for second-chance fatherhood, and she will return to a house in which the only voice she hears is the stunted robotic tenor of her AI assistant.

Siri says, "I'll let you decide if you wish to wake up. But if you'd like me to play your Morning Mix playlist, just ask."

"No, thank you." Even Earth, Wind & Fire's "September" won't break this spell. Emma needs a jolt to the system, the benefits of electroshock therapy without the subsequent memory loss or the sensation she imagines feels like being plugged into an electrical socket. Boredom isn't the problem; there's no end to her to-do list. Her life simply lacks…something she can't put her finger on.

"Hey, Siri. Am I depressed?"

"Depression is a clinical condition that should only be diag-nosed by a medical professional. However, I can tell you that some of the main symptoms of depression include feelings of sadness or hopelessness, loss of interest in pleasurable activities, a shortened temper, fatigue—"

"Siri, stop."

Emma speaks to her therapist every week. If she were de-pressed, Nikki would have said so.

She turns, angling her face to the windows. It's late, prob-ably already 9:00 a.m. Now that the brain fog has begun to lift, she can see that morning is fleeing. And still she lies, un-prepared to move.

This encroaching listlessness isn't entirely mysterious. Try as she might to deny it, Emma misses Ben, and it's his fault. He charmed his way into her life, reanimated the quiet moments of her days and nights, made her laugh, got her to talk. And then, he walked away.

She knew she wasn't ready to date, and she said no. Repeat-edly. But he persisted. Broke her down. And now here she is, missing him and hating herself for it.

"Dammit." Emma throws back the covers and swings her feet to the floor. Kanga and Roo startle; she never moves this quickly.

"Hush," she says. "I have a bone to pick with someone and I don't want to lose my nerve."

Emma did lose her nerve, of course. As soon as she had heard Ben's voice, her anger went running for cover.

"Emma!" he'd trilled. "This is a welcome surprise."

She steeled herself against his charm, knowing that she only wanted him because he'd rejected her. And she'd picked up the phone to tell him he'd broken his promise to reach out as soon as he returned to the States.

"I missed you, Ben." *Where the hell had that come from?* She smacked her forehead hard enough to see stars. "What I mean is, would you like to meet me for dinner?"

Clearly, she was having an aneurysm.

"I would love nothing more. I'm so pleased you called."

And so, here they sit, facing each other over a round bistro table at Emma's favorite, Plum River. The restaurant is only a mile from her house, meaning that any of her friends or neighbors might see them. Oh, well, let the gossip begin. She is saying *Yes* to dinner with an old friend.

Or is she saying *No* to caring what other people think?

"Ben, would you like to choose the wine?"

He picks up the list. "I'll be happy to. But didn't you say this was one of your favorite restaurants? I'd love to hear what you recommend."

"Oh—" Emma knows wine. But she doesn't know what it's like to dine with a man who doesn't flaunt his enological expertise like a silverback gorilla beating his chest. "I suppose I could."

Suppose she could? Good grief.

Ben hedges. "Unless you'd prefer not to?"

"Actually," she reaches for the wine list and snaps it open with a flourish. "I know just the thing."

Half a bottle in, Emma and Ben share an heirloom tomato salad and relive the night they attended a "Weird Al" Yankovic concert at the state fair.

"I can't believe he's still around," she says. "We only went because the tickets were practically free!"

Ben's face is lovely when he laughs. "He's more successful now than ever. A millionaire several times over."

"Maybe I should quit teaching and learn to play the accordion."

"I'd pay to see that."

He winks, and Emma goes hot and sweaty in all her unmentionable places. She leans in, knowing her blouse is likely falling into the salad, but what the hell does she care? She wore black for a reason. "Ben, I have to ask—"

He anticipates her question. She can see all the knowing signs in his Bradley Cooper grin.

"Emma?"

This is not Ben's voice. This is Carlton Willis. And he's standing too close, having appeared out of nowhere. All her good sweats go cold.

"What a wonderful surprise bumping into you. We haven't seen each other in, what is it now, ten or fifteen years?"

It hasn't been anywhere close to ten years. He called her last month.

From the look of him, he's in politician mode—dark suit, white shirt, classic tie. His haircut can't be more than an hour old. "Carlton." It comes out as a statement rather than a greeting, though he's lucky she says anything at all.

"I'm here with a few members of my campaign staff. Let's connect soon, what do you say?" Nothing moves on his face as he speaks, nor are there wrinkles where a fifty-something-year-old man ought to have them. He extends a hand.

Emma does not take it. "Carlton, meet Benjamin Guy. Ben and I went to high school together."

"Benjamin Guy…" Carlton pauses. "Have we met?"

Ben stands, displaying his professional side, extending his own hand toward Carlton's. "Not officially. But our worlds do overlap from time to time."

"Ah. Perhaps we've shared the stage at a conference or two."

"Something like that." Ben takes his seat again, and Carlton takes the hint.

"Well, I'll leave the two of you to your dinner and go join my team." He doesn't turn before meeting Emma's glance one last time. "It's been too long."

When he finally departs, Emma's hands are shaking. Two coincidences in as many weeks confirm to her that this wasn't a coincidence at all.

"So, Carlton Willis, huh?" Ben keeps his voice low. "You keep some heady company."

"No." The word comes so quickly she feels as if she's vomited it. "Not anymore."

The evening is ruined. There's no recapturing the light-hearted spirit of repartee she'd been enjoying.

"Something about the expression on your face tells me Carlton won't be getting your vote next year." Ben's expression is gentle, but he's skirting the edges of a topic Emma is not ready to discuss.

She smooths the already smooth napkin across her lap. "We have a history. In that we dated." Ah, but they'd done so much more than that. "Before Devin. It didn't end well."

"I see." Ben doesn't push, though he looks as if he has more to say.

Anyone would have a thousand questions, and the fact that he doesn't ask them opens a tiny door in Emma's heart. "Let's just say that I wasn't surprised to hear the recent allegations from his colleagues."

"Oh."

Neither of them speaks for the next minute.

"Is it rude to say I kind of hate him?"

"Rude? No." Ben exudes a forgiveness she hasn't felt outside of her therapist's office in a long time. "In fact, I'd go so far as to say you're not alone in that sentiment."

She assumes he's referring to the assistant.

But she's wrong.

Ben doesn't just lean across the table this time. He stands and moves his chair until they're sitting side by side. It feels a little too "teenagers sharing a drink at the malt shop" for her, but she also wishes he'd come closer.

"There's some well-informed scuttlebutt going around the PR world right now. Suffice it to say, Carlton has reason to worry about people coming forward with complaints."

"I see." The news is meant to help, but Emma wishes she

hadn't heard it. For the past two and a half decades, she's consoled herself with the belief that their dynamic together allowed for Carlton's behavior. That surely no other woman provoked him the way she had, and therefore no other woman had experienced the same pain and fear.

How dare Ben bash her delusion against the rocks.

He senses her agitation. "I'm sorry. I shouldn't have said anything."

"No, it's—" A familiar anger fires deep inside her. "You just apologized for telling me about another man's behavior!" She won't say his name. Won't risk giving Carlton the sick thrill of hearing it on her lips. "I hate people who slither away from disasters of their own making. At some point, they need to face the music."

Ben loops his tie between two fingers, smoothing it. "You're right. I ought to know better. Especially given what I do for a living."

The waiter arrives with their entrées, stopping when he sees their modified seating arrangement.

"I'll move," Ben says, and returns to his place across the table.

Emma feels a lonely draft where he'd just been.

Fern

Mack is reading in bed beside her when Fern says, "Let's drive to the airport and buy a ticket to anywhere."

He lowers his book and looks at her through his reading glasses. "I would think you'd know not to joke about that with me."

December 30, 1999, a younger Mack had stood in line with her at the Milwaukee airport while she waited to check in for her flight back to San Francisco. They'd known each other four days, and only because Fern finally decided to trust the high school friend who insisted she "just had to meet this guy she worked with."

She was only convinced to accept when their other friend, Sarah, added, "Hey, free dinner."

Fern was home for the holidays, staying at her mom's house and making the social rounds. "I won't be out late," she'd told her mom. "I'm just meeting this guy for food, then I'll probably have him drop me off straight after."

The last words her mother said before she got into the car of the man she would soon marry were, "Okay, hon. Have fun, Ferny!"

She returned home at 3:00 a.m. with her bra stuffed into her pocket.

Whirlwind days and nights followed. Not in the "never managing to get out from between the sheets" sort of way, though there was plenty of that. What Fern couldn't get enough of was the feeling that this guy would never leave her, no matter how much of a pain in the ass she became. She knew because she tested him. On day three, they met for lunch, and she dedicated the entire meal to explaining why they couldn't date.

"One: we live in different states."

"Likely not a permanent hardship."

"Two: you don't make me laugh enough."

"The past two days notwithstanding?"

"Three: your sideburns are too long."

"I'll make a note of it."

"Four: you don't wear enough black. You have dark hair and fair skin. You need contrast."

He pulled out his wallet and handed it to her. "Then let's go shopping."

She could not shake this guy. There was something magnetically sexy about it.

The evening of day four, he drove Fern to the airport and insisted on walking her inside. In those pre-9/11 days, airports were full of couples and families saying extended goodbyes. Fern liked that she would get hers.

"I wish you could come to Lake Tahoe with us." Carolina, Emma, Andi, and Fern were heading to Tahoe for three days of skiing over New Year's Eve. Chandler had a time-share near Heavenly and was generous with his offers of extra beds and floor space. They were leaving from San Francisco the next day at noon.

"How do you know I can't come? You haven't invited me."

Back in those days, Mack wore a lusciously thick double-breasted leather coat that smelled like high-end cologne. It was black. And possibly the physical aspect she most liked about him besides the perfect triangle formed by his broad shoulders and narrow waist. She curled her fingers into the grain and squeezed. "John Jacob McAllister, will you come skiing in Tahoe with me?"

"Excuse me for a moment, please." He abruptly turned and left.

"Where are you going?"

By the time he returned, she was fuming and nearly to the front of the check-in line. "What the hell was that?"

"My car was in short-term parking."

"And? My flight leaves in less than an hour."

"Exactly. But I'll be gone for a few days."

She didn't have time to ask what he was talking about because the check-in agent ushered her to the counter. Fern surrendered her itinerary, suitcase, and asked for a window seat.

"Put me next to her, please," Mack said.

"Yeah, right." As if they were living in a Norah Ephron movie.

"I called the airline while I was moving my car. It's not a full flight, correct?"

The agent shot eyes at Fern as if asking whether she wanted this bear of a guy in his big black coat following her across the country.

Fern wasn't sure. "Tickets have got to be ridiculous expensive, Mack."

He bobbled his head. "Expensive, but not ridiculous."

She pointed to her bag. "You don't have any of your stuff."

"I'm assuming they have stores in California?"

"But skis!"

"Are available to rent at every resort."

Fern suddenly woke up to what he was doing. This was Mack's version of a test. Would she stop him? Or would she take the leap?

"Do it. Buy the ticket." She turned to smile encouragingly

at the agent, then returned her attention to Mack. "I'll say yes if you say yes."

He handed over his credit card. Which, given how much she'd made him charge on clothing yesterday, had to be approaching its limit. "I already did."

As they boarded the plane, giddy with the realization of having finally met each other's match, Fern had only one ominous thought: *Andi, Emma, and Carolina are going to think I've lost my goddamn mind.*

Two and a half decades, three children, and four homes later, one of the few decisions in life Fern has not ever doubted was her decision to marry Mack. Perfectly imperfect in his own right, he is the calm to her frenzy. Which means that if he gets out of bed right now and pulls out a suitcase, she will follow him without hesitating.

Instead, he continues to lie there, looking at her with his gigantic alien eyeballs. The magnifying lenses on his reading glasses make his already prominent eyes look straight out of a 1950s sci-fi movie.

"Can you at least take your glasses off while I talk to you?"

He obliges. "What's got you tossing?"

She hesitates for a moment, and then hands over her phone. "I just received this."

Mack reads the three-sentence email in as many seconds. "Dakota hired a screenwriter? Fantastic! That means the book is going into development, right?"

She nods.

"Then why the—" He stops. He gets it now. "Fern!"

"I couldn't help it! Andi's been dealing with a family-versus-work crisis, and Emma's a complete mess between the wedding and Devin's bombshell." She pulls the covers over her head wishing she could hide until this all went away.

When she can no longer breathe in the hot stuffy hole, she throws them back and sits up. "It wasn't supposed to happen!

Do you know how few book options actually go into development?"

Mack looks at her as if she just said she didn't know morning came *every* day. "Holly told you how enthusiastic Dakota was. She said if anyone brought this book to screen, it would be her."

"Not yet!" Fern sounds the same way Maisy did when they turned her light out at night.

All Fern wanted was the thrill of seeing her book brought to life. She'd waited more than a decade for the honor. What was a few more months?

"Do you think I should email Dakota back and ask her to hold off until after the wedding?"

"You know you sound like you've lost your mind, right?" Mack inches away from her with every breath.

"It's only a month."

"Fern! You signed a contract. These aren't your calls!" He throws back the covers and stands. "I gotta pee. I'll be back."

While he's gone, Fern bounces her legs on the mattress, trying to get her heart pumping. Maybe a boost of endorphins will give her the brilliant idea she needs to get out of this jam.

"Mack?" she calls into the en suite. "So, about that airport idea…"

Carolina

Carolina is back at work, though doing her best to limit her hours. Queenie had been genuinely angry when she'd used Chandler to help her sneak out of the condo and into the office.

"It's like you don't even care," he'd said.

"Of course, I care!" She'd barely closed the door behind her when he started in. "In fact, I'm following doctor's orders. She told me that I'm supposed to be moving around every day. She said as long as it's not painful, it's okay."

Queenie was so angry he couldn't speak, his face flush, his eyes narrow. Which was when Carolina finally caught on that this wasn't just a little spat. Something was brewing.

"What? Just say it."

"You don't see it, do you?" His voice came just above a whisper, though loud enough she could hear it tremble.

"See what, Queenie?"

He laughed—the kind born of astonishment rather than amusement.

"This isn't funny!" It wasn't. She actually felt fear. Queenie looked as if he were on the verge of a nervous breakdown. "Just tell me, please."

At last, he said, "You act as if the injury only happened to you. But it didn't. Never mind the time I took off work for the surgery and recovery, the sleep I lost getting your meds and helping you to the bathroom. I care about you, Carolina. It hurts me to see you in pain, but it hurts more to realize that you don't see me."

"I—" The defense came so easily, she felt it in her body. A need to tell him that he was wrong. That not only did she see him, she loved him. "I do."

"You do what?"

This was a game they played, Queenie getting her to repeat his words back to him to ensure she'd been listening. At the same time, this wasn't the game. He didn't want her words; he wanted her heart.

"Can you help me to the couch?" She pointed her crutch at the pillows that required intricate configuration beneath her leg, her back, her head. Perhaps it was poor timing to ask him for even more help, but she had overdone it today, and pain was screaming up her leg, scrambling her nerves.

Queenie obliged without fuss or argument. Because he loved her. Because he demonstrated his devotion every day, without fail.

By the time she was settled, tears hung like storm clouds behind her eyes. "I do see you, Queenie. And I'm sorry." She wanted to reach for his hand, but the coffee table between them may as well have been an ocean. He was too far away, and she had run herself ashore.

There was no escaping her choices.

Carolina behaved herself for the remainder of her medical leave, and once she had been cleared by the doctor to return to the office, she intended to show Queenie that she'd heard him. Caring for herself was caring for them.

It hasn't been easy. In the aftermath of losing her team lead, Mila, work has felt like trying to outrun a tornado. The last day of the severance window, three additional team members submitted paperwork to leave. That left four vacancies on a team that could barely withstand one.

Mila's absence is the most crucial, and with no one to fill it, Carolina has taken on most of the responsibilities. She's effectively trying to perform two full-time jobs, and as predicted, is highly ineffective at doing so.

This evening, she's doing her best to wrap up and go home when Sandra calls her into her office.

"The deployment of the security patch," Sandra says. "Where do we stand?"

A recent change one of their third-party vendors made to its software had inadvertently left a small segment of MAVERIK customer data vulnerable to corruption. Prior to the first round of layoffs, Carolina's team would have resolved the issue within twenty-four to forty-eight hours. Even afterward, the team likely could have deployed the fix within three days. Now, thanks to the "voluntary" packages that Sandra told her likely wouldn't affect the MAVERIK program at all, they were going on a week with little visible progress.

"I don't have an ETA for you." Carolina was too preoccupied to finesse her language. "Deploying the patch is a priority, but we are juggling several priority issues right now. It's a resource issue."

Sandra says, "I get it. But you also need to know that this one is on Mark's radar."

Learning that a problem on her team has garnered the attention of the CEO should send Carolina's blood pressure spiking. In a previous life, it would've had her reaching for her running shoes and telling the team she'd "be back soon with a solution," pounding out the miles until she had one.

Tonight, her blood pressure does spike. But this time, it's from anger, not fear.

"I raised this as a risk months ago. And you said leadership was confident that if anyone left, you could find the resources in-house to backfill."

Sandra either doesn't remember that conversation or she doesn't want to engage. "Mila left for a better position elsewhere. It has nothing to do with the severance packages."

"No." Carolina isn't prepared to let Sandra whitewash this. "Mila happened to get a better job because as soon as she learned of the severance packages, she started looking. She left MAVERIK because she'd lost faith in leadership's commitment to the program." Mila had told Carolina as much before leaving. Carolina had taken her to lunch to say goodbye and thank her for her excellent work. Mila thanked her, too, for her leadership, advice, and mentorship.

"Any chance I can get you to reconsider?" Carolina had asked.

Mila answered, "No. It's done."

Now Carolina asks Sandra if Mila's suspicions were true. "Has leadership lost faith in the program?"

Sandra shakes her head.

"Are you certain? Because you also don't seem to be protecting it. I asked you to exempt my team from the voluntary packages."

"Every division is making the same cuts. No one was exempt. This tide will eventually turn." Sandra, Carolina notes, is wearing a pair of plain black flats today. They don't look expensive. "But as the program lead, Carolina, it's your job to work with the resources you have. I know it's not ideal. Believe me, I don't love having to make cuts, either. I'd much rather be offering people jobs than taking them away."

Carolina's phone vibrates in her hand. It's Queenie confirming she's still good for him to pick her up at 6:30 p.m.

When they negotiated the time, he'd wanted her to leave at 6:00 p.m. "Ten hours on your feet is too much."

Still, she'd argued for seven o'clock. "I could work until midnight and not finish everything." But that only proved Queenie's point. She couldn't control the amount of work she had, but she could control the time she dedicated to it. They settled on 6:30 p.m.

Now, it's 6:15 p.m and she has important emails to send before leaving. "I have to go," she says. "My ride's coming in a few minutes."

"Send me a status from home later tonight," Sandra says. Her tone is tighter than before, meaning she doesn't love that Carolina is hobbling out the door, but there also isn't a whole lot she can do about it right now.

As Carolina returns to her desk, she thinks of Andi, and of how many nights she must have grappled with either pleasing the law partners or going home to her family. Carolina and Queenie never planned to have kids. She'd always considered that an advantage. She wonders now if she was just deluding herself. No company she's ever worked for has taken everything she can offer without asking for more. There is no "enough."

Sandra won't fire her for walking out the door tonight. MAVERIK is already struggling for resources and losing Carolina would set off a crisis. The decision to leave may go on her performance review, which in turn might take a bite out of her next raise or bonus. So be it.

What she doesn't expect is the feeling that overtakes her as she moves. Her knee aches—Queenie was right that ten hours is too long. And yet, she's stronger than she was five minutes ago. Her backbone can be a steel rod when she needs it.

Andi

Andi is standing outside an airplane hangar in a far corner of the San Francisco International Airport. She hugs her trench coat to her body against the morning chill. It's 7:00 a.m. In a few minutes, the generic white 737 on the tarmac will take off, bound for Honduras with two hundred deportees inside. Among them, the Guatemalan woman who followed the coyotes' advice and married a Honduran stranger believing it would reduce the chances of this very moment.

There had been one more attempt to annul the marriage since Andi's appearance in court on her client's behalf back in June. That, too, was denied.

She's here this morning out of a sense of duty. To show this terrified woman now bound for a country that is not hers with a man who owes her no fealty a small sign of humanity. She does so knowing that it may be the last show of kindness the woman may witness for a long time, if not the rest of her life. Poverty and violence await her in Honduras, just as they had in Guatemala, where eighteen months ago she'd run for her life.

The cabin steward raises the plane's stairwell and latches the door. As the engines roar, Andi raises her hand and waves. She doesn't know if the woman sees her farewell.

At least she tried.

When the plane is in the air and out of sight, she returns slowly to the main airport and the lot in which she'd parked before dawn. She closes the door, blocking out the noise of the world beyond, and dials.

"Are we sure?" she asks.

Dom says, "I'm sure. Though this isn't my decision."

There's just enough time to drive downtown before her 9:00 a.m. meeting with Harold Ennis, the firm's managing partner. It was Harold who recruited her almost twenty-five years ago. At the time, he'd only just made partner himself and was looking to make a name for himself. "You're part of my strategy," he'd told her. "If the firm is to grow, it will have to go international. I believe you can help us do that."

Andi kept her end of the bargain.

"I expect this will come as no surprise," she begins. "But I notified ICSW just before our meeting that we will no longer be taking on new cases. I withdrew from the newest cases and from those in which there has been no substantial progress. We'll see the remaining half dozen or so through or, if necessary, refer them to new counsel."

Harold grins. He looks delighted by her news. "I commend your decision. Of course, it was no secret that our ability to fund the work was coming to an end. But even if I've said this before, I haven't said it enough. The international exposure you brought to this firm measurably heightened our legal profile. I'll need you to lead a number of the cases we've taken in as a result."

She expected this. Andi not only expanded the firm's reputation, she helped land a number of their new clients. "I wish I could promise to give you my all, Harold. But there's a second reason I scheduled this meeting. As soon as the ICSW work is wrapped, I'll be dissociating my partnership and leaving the firm. Though I hope it goes without saying that I'm immensely grateful to you for giving me my start. I wouldn't have wanted to spend the last two decades anywhere else."

This is true, but Harold's smile has turned to horror. "What brought this on? It's quite a shock, I'll admit."

It's a shock to me, too, she wants to tell him. But he doesn't need to know the intricacies of everything that led to her decision. That's family business. And her family, Dom especially, just wants her to be happy.

"Life," is all she gives him. "What I've had so far has been wonderful and I believe a change of gears is necessary to keep it that way."

So many euphemisms when what they mean is simple: it's time for her to quit.

"Who's wooing you?" Harold steps from behind his desk and sits in the chair beside her. "Tell me what they're offering, and I'll do everything I can to match it."

"It's not money, Harold," she laughs, the first moment of levity she's felt all day. "It's time. I've got two years left with my son before he leaves for college. There are only so many hours in the day. And the window left in my life to try something new is shrinking. I don't want to miss any of it."

Harold's face lights. "Why not a leave of absence? We can arrange that. How much time do you need? Three months? Six?"

She stops him. "This isn't a negotiation. Making this decision has been grueling, but it's made. The time has come to leave."

Though she didn't realize it at the time, the day she paid her unannounced visit to Carolina was the turning point. Describing her heartache, Andi had said, "I'm worried that no matter what I decide to do, it'll feel wrong."

With time, she grew to recognize that she was looking at a complex dilemma as a bilateral choice—work or family. And it's not. What she wants is to soak up her last two years with Cameron. To be the mother she expects of herself while she still can. No excuses. Just genuine dedication to her kid. What she doesn't want is to give up the ICSW work for a return to "normal." Her partner-track career at the firm was a wonderful, challenging journey for which she has lost her desire to continue. If she were to go back, she would likely still work too much, alongside an unbending guilt of never being able to do enough. She also knows she'd be unhappy after doing what she loved for ICSW.

Her career does not have to end because she takes time off. In two years, she can reach out to international connections. Maybe she'll find a new position with a nonprofit or intergovernmental organization. Perhaps even, if in the next two years she finds it too difficult not to practice at all, she'll put feelers out for a contract or two.

Financially, she and Dom will feel a difference, but it will hardly be painful. Dom is a partner at his firm, and if their small family of three can't survive on his salary, they need to further examine their priorities.

After breaking the news to Harold, Andi returns to her office and calls Connie Trujillo, the social worker she took out to lunch to learn more about compassion fatigue. "Remember when you told me it sounded as if I was assuming a lot of personal responsibility for other people's choices? Well, today, I decided to quit."

It's a pun. She did quit her job. But she also quit placing others' priorities above her own. Like her mom has always warned, days go by fast. Andi has decided to make the most of them.

Emma

Deposits for the florist, chapel, reception venue, bridal gown, and caterer have all been paid, but such a rapid outflow of cash necessitates a phone call to Devin. Emma promises herself she won't surrender to the tiny devil who performs a running commentary in her ear every time they speak.

"When is Greta due?"

"October. About a month after the wedding."

"Fabulous." Emma thinks that maybe if they stand close to each other in the wedding photos, Greta will make her look twenty pounds lighter.

As if reading her mind, Devin adds, "Greta's assured me she doesn't feel strongly about being in the pictures. And if it makes a difference, the ones she does join, we can make sure she's facing forward, not to the side."

It's a very thoughtful gesture and Emma suddenly feels like a prude. "Thank you," she says. While her inner devil adds, *Maybe Devin ought to try acting the prude before his spermicidal misadventures spawn a third family.*

Speaking of prudes, Emma is as confused as ever about Ben. After the run-in with Carlton cast a foul gray haze over their otherwise lovely dinner, Ben invited her to his favorite place in the city Saturday night to make up for it. Emma was going to be in San Francisco anyway, going over a list of final wedding details.

"I should say no." She and Portia are at Lyle's dining room table stuffing swag bags for the out-of-town guests. "I have too much going on right now to wonder where this friendship may or may not be going."

"Mother." Recently, every time Emma broaches the topic of Benjamin Guy with skepticism or doubt, Portia answers it with singular exasperation.

"What? I'm trying to practice self-care. Boundaries are important."

Just yesterday, she'd established a new boundary, placing a week's worth of poop-filled bags into an empty box of La-Croix Pamplemousse sparkling water, and then leaving it on Kent's front step.

Kent left the box there for nearly thirty-six hours. Emma doubted she'd ever be able to drink Pamplemousses again.

This week, she was considering emptying the contents of said doggy bags into a new box before delivering it. Maybe seeing and smelling his dog's shit would finally put a fire under Kent's butt to do something about it.

Portia sighs. "It's not self-care if you're saying no to something you actually enjoy. That's not setting boundaries, that's avoiding what you want." Portia stands to retrieve a fresh box of lavender sachets. They're meant to help guests sleep, and the room smells like a dreamscape.

"I don't know if I actually do enjoy dating. It's stressful, all the second-guessing one does around a practical stranger."

"Mother. *Please.*"

Ultimately, she does decide to meet Ben for dinner, if for no other reason than she's practically starving by the time they finish with the bags.

Ben picks her up at Lyle's apartment in a very un-Ben-looking older-model Toyota sedan. "This place is a tiny little gem. And by tiny, I mean crowded. But by gem, I mean they make the best cioppino in the city."

There's nothing wrong with driving an older car. Even better, Emma has been told, than buying a new hybrid since mining the rare minerals required for electric batteries causes so much environmental harm on its own.

"Uh-oh." Ben shoots a glance at her from behind the wheel. "I didn't ask if you like seafood. Do you? We could go somewhere else."

"Um—" Was this the same car Devin bought for Portia when she got her driver's license? What a strange feeling to be sitting in someone else's car, a part of their inner world. It's almost like getting an unexpected peek at their underwear. "I like seafood just fine."

"Just fine?" Ben isn't convinced. "That's not exactly a resounding endorsement. How about Italian? I can show you another favorite place."

Emma would eat the strap off her purse right now, and there won't be a resounding endorsement of anything until she gets some food into her stomach. Her brain is clearly on meltdown.

"Which one? Seafood or Italian? Or how about Mexican?" Ben spots a car pulling away from the curb and slams on the brakes, blocking traffic until the space is open for him to park.

"Are we here?" Emma sees only a T-Mobile store and a juice bar.

"No. I just thought it was easier to stop the car until we decide."

She really is fine with the seafood place. But her blood sugar has crashed so hard that the neural pathways in her brain have gone rogue, and instead she says, "Did you borrow this car from someone?"

"What?" Ben is confused for only a second. Apparently, his brain is not malfunctioning, and he chuckles as he answers. "No. This is my 'life in the city' car. I used to buy a new BMW every couple of years, but you can't park anywhere without getting your doors dinged or your bumper smashed in. I kid you not. One time I was walking to my car, and I saw a bike messenger clip it with his handlebars as he rode past. Scratched the driver's side from back to front."

"Ouch." Bicyclists made her anxious everywhere, forever popping around corners or into her lane of traffic.

"I got sick of paying for repairs. And what do I care? A car this old is probably less likely to get stolen, anyway. That happened to me once, too."

Emma hears the words he's saying, at least enough to make sense of them. But what she's really doing is watching Ben's facial expressions. He can look serious without appearing angry better than almost anyone she knows.

"I do love seafood," she says, "and I'm starving."

He greets her confession like she'd just pulled a cheese board and bottle of chilled champagne out of her purse.

"Fan*tas*tic."

Ben predictably has ordered the house specialty, cioppino. Emma orders the ceviche. Cioppino is delicious, but all that plucking clams from their shells…she'd have broth dripping into her elbows.

When the entrées arrive, she looks down to find that the kitchen hasn't prepared hers correctly.

Ben notices her staring at her food rather than eating it. "Something wrong?"

She waives his concern away with a fork. "It's nothing."

"Seriously. What?" He's tipped over the table now, examining her plate. "Didn't you ask for no cilantro?"

"I did. But it's probably premade, no customizations allowed." She pastes a smile across her face and shrugs. "I'll eat around it."

"Emma—" He's not smiling, he's flabbergasted. "You have the right to ask the chef to remake it."

She wishes he'd stop looking at her. Not once has she ever sent a dish back to the kitchen. She'd been tempted, but the one time she tried, Devin called it "passive-aggressive." Recently, she ordered an iced coffee with oat milk and, knowing how many times she'd been charged extra for oat milk she did not receive, asked the barista to double-check her order.

"It's oat milk. I've been reading since I was five," he'd said. To her face. Then turned around and called her a "Karen" to one of his coworkers.

"Ben, it's nothing." If she excused herself to the restroom right now, maybe he'd send the dish back for her and they could skirt this entire confrontation.

"You told me cilantro tastes like soap. That's not your fault, you know. It's genetic."

She's beginning to sweat again, but now in all the wrong places. "It doesn't matter. I only see a little bit in there."

"Maybe the cilantro doesn't matter, but you do, Emma." He sucks in a breath as if trying to inhale the sentiment along with it, erasing his accidental show of vulnerability from the stratosphere. "What I mean is—you matter to me."

Now it's Emma squeezing the air out of the room.

A woman sitting across from her at the next table catches Emma's eye and smiles—she's overheard their conversation. The restaurant is tiny, just as Ben described it.

"You're freaking out. I can see it." Ben either isn't aware of their audience or doesn't care. His words come with neither force nor constraint.

And in the spirit of contradiction that is their evolving friendship, Emma both loves and hates that he can read her so well. She gulps her wine. "I worry I'm not ready for another serious relationship, Ben."

One of them had to say it. Humans are natural organizers, and labels bring clarity. One may subdivide categories as narrowly as necessary—blue, indigo, sky, navy—but only names bestow meaning, and it finally registers to Emma that she is only confused by this *thing* of theirs because it refuses to show its ilk.

"Devin was the larger of the two of us—bigger career, bigger demands, a bigger need to be seen. And I accommodated his needs for nearly twenty-five years, happy to shrink myself to the size of his shadow.

"Before him, I almost married a man who spun his immense ego into cash. Now he's got so much of it there's nothing left to do but try to buy his way into the government."

His eyes go wide as he connects the dots. "You were engaged to Carlton Willis?"

"I'm sorry if I misrepresented our history. It's complicated."

He bestows his forgiveness by not saying a word.

"Before I got married, I used to think that my perpetual relationship confusion was because of my youth and inexperience. As soon as I matured enough to meet the right guy, the 'where are we going' question plaguing my dating life would disappear. When I knew, I would know, you know?"

Even as she speaks, she's not entirely clear where she's going with this.

"My cratering marriage woke me up to the fallacy of that belief. And I can't help but wish someone had spent the last twenty years developing a GPS for relationships." She laughs. "I'm not having a midlife crisis; this is a geographical one. I need a map."

Ben pauses before opening his mouth to speak. "Are you asking me where *this* is headed? Us?" He draws a finger in the space between them.

"No." The word comes out before she realizes it's true. "I'm drawing a map that I think will work for me." If only this were one of those old-school restaurants where the waiter wrote his name and the day's specials in crayon on the paper tablecloth. She etches a line into the fabric with her fingernail, instead. "We are here. Let's call it a prelude to dating, because when we talk, we talk about real things. Stuff that matters."

He doesn't argue, studying what she's attempting to draw.

"Ben, why didn't you contact me when you returned from South Africa?" Her stomach is rumbling, the ceviche debate unresolved and her dinner untouched. Maybe her hunger triggered her survival instinct—she has now asked several brave questions in a row. Emma is speaking up and taking charge.

He takes a beat before answering. "The first night we had dinner together, you reminded me a lot of myself after my divorce. Skittish and unsure, but also curious. You didn't seem to know what you wanted, and I didn't want to push. When I was newly single, my brain felt like a scene from a National Geographic special."

Emma raises an eyebrow.

He laughs. "No, not sex. I felt like that one animal in the herd who doesn't know where to turn. Running every which way willy-nilly."

"That guy usually gets eaten by a lion."

"That period of time felt pretty close to it."

"How long did it take to figure things out?" Over the months, she and Ben have ventured deep into some sensitive territory, but she's never directly asked for post-divorce advice. Until now.

"It takes as long as it takes." He shrugs. "Just stay away from the lions and you'll do okay."

Emma digs her fingernail into the tablecloth, a half inch or so to the right of their "prelude to dating" stage. "I like hearing from you. It made me sad when I didn't."

"Can I admit to something?" Ben slides his cioppino out of the way. "I made it sound as if it wouldn't be possible to communicate with you while I was in South Africa. And that was true, sort of—I expected to be working insane hours, and that proved correct. But I have an international phone plan. I'm reachable practically anywhere. I just wasn't sure you'd want to hear from me."

She extends her hand, palm up. "Give it to me."

"Why?" The Bradley Cooper grin is back, though he doesn't wait for an explanation before complying.

"Hey, Siri," she says, "set a reminder to text Emma every day at 8:00 p.m."

"Got it," Siri answers. "I'll remind you every evening at eight to text Emma. Anything else?"

"Yes." Emma slides her ceviche to the far corner of the table. "Navigate to the best burger joint in San Francisco."

Ben raises his hand. "Check, please!"

That Afternoon in the Apartment

From *Smart Girls Say Yes* by Fern McAllister

As the final essay in a book of Yeses, I want to tell one story about the power of No. Saying no too often should be no one's goal. We all deserve a full, happy life, and that requires jumping in with both feet. But sometimes, *no* is the word, a single syllable that might just save your life.

At least, it did ours. Here's the story…

The day Emma came home to find Ted switching out the contents of her underwear drawer, she called off the wedding. It wasn't that he wanted the lingerie for himself. He'd replaced it all with Chantelle bras and panties.

"This was supposed to be a surprise." He wasn't embarrassed to have been discovered. He was angry she'd come home earlier than expected. "You look better in these. And your old stuff was from Target."

Emma didn't care where she bought her underwear. She

wanted to choose it herself. This was the last straw in a relationship full of chaff.

Carolina, Andi, and I didn't learn about the breakup/panty raid until several days later. Over the past several months, thanks to book club and a mutual desire to make the most of our San Francisco lives, we'd grown tight. We made a lunch date, grabbed salads from Au Bon Pain, and ate them on the Embarcadero facing the Bay Bridge.

A newspaper peeked out of Emma's shoulder bag. It was open to the For Rent page. Carolina swiped it. "What in the fresh hell is this?"

Emma fessed up. She also told us that she would be the one moving out of the apartment she and Ted shared.

"Isn't the lease in your name?" Carolina asked.

Emma avoided the question. "It wasn't his idea to break up, so why should he have to leave?"

Carolina threw her hands in the air, exasperated. "He was throwing away your underwear!"

Emma ripped the newspaper back from Carolina's grasp. "Honestly, it's better just not to have to deal with him anymore."

"You'll at least change the lease, right?" I asked. "If it's in your name, you're liable for anything he does there."

Emma hedged. "Maybe."

"What do you mean *maybe*?" said Carolina. "He could stop paying rent, trash the place, squat there until he gets kicked out, and leave you with all the back rent and repair costs."

"It's not that easy." Emma looked to Andi for confirmation.

Andi nodded. "San Francisco rental laws make it difficult to kick someone out."

"Apparently, squatters have more rights in this city than landlords," Emma added.

I didn't buy it. "Who told you that?"

"Ted."

Carolina slapped the bench where we sat. "Of course, he's going to say that. He's the squatter!"

It took a few months, but thanks to Andi's free legal advice, Emma kept her apartment. The landlord was hesitant to evict Ted at first. But then Emma asked if he'd at least be willing to exercise his right as owner to enter the property and retrieve her clothing, which Ted refused to give back. He took one look at the ill-fitting hand-me-downs she'd borrowed from friends and said, "That guy's a real piece of work, isn't he?"

Ultimately, Emma got notification that the landlord had canceled the original lease and rewritten a new one. It started April 1st. Carolina's name was on it, too. When the day came at last, they unlocked the door and Emma stepped into their apartment like a woman seeing it for the first time. "I never want to live in a house without bay windows again."

There are as many reasons to love San Francisco as there are people in it. I think Emma loved it because it made her feel as if she were living in a picture book, all brightly painted homes and gingerbread Victorians. There are flower stands every few blocks and old-fashioned hardware stores with wooden floors. You get the feeling Mr. Hooper from *Sesame Street* ought to be standing behind the counter singing a song about "the people in your neighborhood."

She was back in the same apartment on the same street she'd lived with Ted, and yet everything was different. Everything was better. Ted took all the good furniture with him, and Carolina threw out the rest. Then she bought one of those gorgeous Pottery Barn couches with the white slipcover that Andi and I, the Anxiety Twins, could hardly bring ourselves to sit on. Spills, and all that.

We lived three blocks apart, in our twenties, in the heart of San Francisco, in the middle of the dot-com boom. And then one day, Emma found a man standing in her bedroom.

We'd just returned home from running with the brides. She was soaking wet and dressed in her wedding gown.

Carolina was pulling her dress over her head when she heard Emma yell in the next room.

"I know," she hollered back. "It's that damn bag of rice Ted left on the pantry floor. I put traps down this morning."

Ted had given them mice who left poop pellets everywhere and once at a party a big fatty ran across my foot while I was wearing open-toed sandals. The landlord had sent an exterminator who said they ought to put out poison. But then the mice would crawl into the wall, die, and stink up the place. Emma and Carolina decided they would just deal. Anything was better than Ted.

We'd been up since before dawn, but the plan was to change clothes and head out for dinner. Chandler had made reservations at a new Italian place. Andi and I were already on our way to pick Carolina and Emma up.

Carolina turned the corner to Emma's room, joking about holding her dress while she peed. The door was ajar, so she pushed it with her shoulder. It opened a few inches and stopped.

That's when she heard Ted's voice. "Emma, you left me no choice."

"Please go. Or we'll call the police."

Carolina considered that a most excellent idea and turned for the kitchen counter where the phone and answering machine sat. Only, the cordless handset wasn't in its cradle. One of them had neglected to put it back on the charger.

"Let me show you what I'm willing to offer," Ted said. Carolina could either hunt for the phone or listen to what he said next.

She stayed where she was.

Neither Ted nor Emma spoke for a moment. There was a rustling she couldn't identify. Then Emma's voice went cold.

"You took pictures of me in the shower?"

"You're a beautiful woman. And we were engaged. I'd say it was my right to admire my fiancée's body."

"I would never have given you permission to take those." Emma's voice was now growling with fury.

Ted didn't care. "That's what makes them all the more scintillating."

It was at this moment that Carolina realized she might have something just as useful as a phone. She reached into her bike shorts and pulled out Chandler's video camera. It was slightly damp from the rain, but her layers of clothing had prevented damage. She opened the screen and pressed record.

"Give them to me!" Sounds of a brief tussle quickly gave way to Ted laughing.

"You haven't even heard my offer yet," he said.

Carolina gently leaned her shoulder into the door, hoping to move whatever was blocking it just enough to slip the camera inside. Audio evidence of whatever was about to go down was good, but video was better.

It worked.

With an additional three inches of gap, she was able to slide her arm into the room and look inside via the viewfinder screen. It took some adjusting—the bed blocked much of her line of sight—but if she stood and leaned just right, she could keep both Ted and Emma in the shot.

That night, I asked her, "Weren't you worried he'd notice you?"

"I've never prayed so hard in my life. My Catholic mother would be proud."

Ted was holding a black square that Carolina quickly discerned to be his laptop. He opened the lid and turned the screen toward Emma.

"You didn't!" She tried to grab it, but he swept the laptop over his head out of reach, all of it happening too quickly for Carolina to understand.

"Not yet, I haven't," Ted said. "The website isn't live yet. So here's my offer: agree to come back and give our relationship the attention it deserves, and I'll destroy these photos."

"And if I say no?" Emma sounded as if she already knew the answer. Perhaps she wanted to hear Ted say it for himself.

C'mon. Carolina mumbled under her breath. *Say it on video, dummy.*

Ted was all too willing to oblige. "If you say no, then I'll press the button to launch the site. Doesn't take more than a second. I could do it right now, if you want—"

"No!" Emma lunged again, and again Ted dodged her.

"Then come back. I'm having dinner with my mother tonight. It's perfect timing. We'll tell her you just got cold feet."

"You're such an asshole," growled Emma.

"Is that a no?" Ted stretched his fingers across the keyboard as if ready to press the magic launch button.

"Don't!" Carolina could hear the tears bunching in Emma's throat. "Let me think."

Carolina wanted to know just what the hell there was to think about. The man was threatening to put nude pictures of her online. Revenge porn wasn't a cultural phenomenon back in 1999 before social media was a thing. But everyone in that apartment knew that releasing those photos could change Emma's life for months, years, maybe even decades to come. Just look at what happened to Pamela Anderson.

The longer Emma stood there considering her options, the more Carolina wondered what she was supposed to do next. She had Ted's blackmail attempt on video, but so what? All he had to do was smash the camera to make it go away. She and Emma were strong, but Ted was rageful.

What did happen next, Carolina and I may never agree about. She says Andi, Chandler, and I saved the day. I say the lady upstairs answered her prayers. We do, however, agree on this—Carolina had forgotten to lock the front door, so we let ourselves right in.

"Emma! Carolina!" I remember hollering their names while clutching my stomach with laughter. Chandler had just told us that his mother wanted to set him up with a friend of the family he'd grown up with. She was a nearly a foot taller than him and used to beat him up during recess. "Wait till you hear Chandler's news!"

Their apartment was a railroad style, a long rectangle with a view from the front door all the way to the kitchen. Carolina was at Emma's bedroom door, waving us forward.

"What?" we asked.

We knew the answer when Emma's door opened, and Ted stepped through.

"You guys! He was in here waiting for me." Emma tried to run past him. Ted grabbed the silk of her skirt, lurching her back.

"Hey, easy there!" Chandler held up his hands as if trying to calm a bucking horse. "No need to get physical."

Andi said, "Where's the phone? I'm calling the police."

"Actually," said Ted, "Emma was just about to change. We're meeting my mother for dinner."

"I am not." She kicked at his hand, trying to free herself.

Carolina saw her opportunity. "Afraid she's right, Ted. I've got it all on tape." She held up the video camera.

Chandler said, "Hey, that's mine."

"It is. How 'bout you come get it." Carolina held it out to him, but he didn't reach her before Ted lunged.

"Ungh!" Emma kicked again, this time landing a square shot to his kidney. He doubled over, still clutching the laptop to his chest. Emma tried to wrench it from his hands. *"Give it to me."*

Ted not only hung on, but he used her own aggression against her, shoving her backward to the floor.

"HEY!" Everyone was on alert. No one wanted violence. And Ted was just volatile enough that we knew the best strategy was to stay out of his face.

No one moved for a full minute. The apartment had become the O.K. Corral.

"I'll tell you what," Ted said at last. "I believe there's an opportunity for us all to be happy. On the count of three, you delete that video and I'll delete the website. Emma can keep the prints."

The four of us looked to Emma for guidance. This was her decision to make. In the moment, I hoped she'd say yes. In hindsight, I realize how naive that was. If he'd already uploaded the photos to the website, he had physical copies of them that could be replicated to his malicious heart's content.

"NO." Emma eased her way to all fours, then stood, meeting him eye to eye. "You leave here now. Keep your laptop, keep the prints. I'm not worried. Because if you ever make them public, I'll do exactly the same with the tape." She grinned a wide-eyed grizzly bear smile. "I think it'd be worse for you, in fact. My face is partially obscured behind the shower glass. But we've got your face and your voice—the whole Ted package."

That single syllable ended our adventures with Ted. He left the apartment fuming and swearing, knowing all the while that he'd been bested. Emma stood up for herself, and Carolina had her back.

In revisiting my memories for this book, a question I'd never asked occurred to me. "How did you know Carolina had Ted's face on video? He'd been all the way across the room."

Emma looked at me with the brassy tenacity I hadn't seen in years. "I didn't. But neither did he. And in the end, believing in myself was enough."

Take note of what she said, my young readers. *In the end, believing in ourselves is enough.*

September

Fern

It's midnight, sixteen hours before Portia is due to walk down the aisle. Fern is with Carolina and Andi in Emma's living room; they're staying the night to lend moral support.

The three of them were on setup duty at the wedding venue, a small former monastery turned winery a few miles from the house, while Emma attended the rehearsal dinner at a restaurant in town. They set hurricane candles on each of the tables, hung fairy lights from the roof of the veranda, and wove streams of jasmine and grapevine up and down the aisle.

Now Carolina and Andi are toasting the day's success. Emma is in the kitchen reviewing her to-do list for the umpteenth time. Fern sits in the corner not having any fun.

"If I go to prison, I'm going to…" Andi raises her glass and a splosh of champagne lands on her pants. This is a game they created after watching *Orange Is the New Black* and declaring Natasha Lyonne Queen Goddess of the Universe. "I'm going to get a tattoo of a rose."

"Boooringgg!" Carolina gives her a thumbs-down and a *thbbft!* "You have to get something more exciting than a rose."

"Like?"

"Like a Buddha on your butt cheek. That makes you a Buddh-ass." Carolina crumples in on herself with laughter.

"That doesn't even make any sense."

"Buddh-ass," cackles Carolina.

Fern tries to resist snickering but fails. "It is kinda funny, actually."

"I don't get it!" Andi's intelligence often impedes her ability to see the humor in things. "Seriously! Are you trying to say badass?"

Carolina slides to the floor, clutching her stomach while protecting her knee. "Don't make me pee!"

Fern's glad she's not drunk enough to land on the floor beside her. "How does one get a tattoo in prison, anyway?" She can't imagine the bureau of prisons allows for needles and tattoo guns.

"Ballpoint pens." Andi, their resident prison expert, holds up her index finger and pretends to cut it off at the first knuckle. "They take out the ink cartridge, cut it into a sharp point, and *drive* it into the skin." She shoves her nubby finger in Fern's face.

"Easy there, cowgirl. Just curious, is all."

Fern is staying sober tonight because she's worried about what she might say under the influence of alcohol. Now that *Smart Girls* is in production, an even fatter check than the first has landed in her bank account. It's enough to pay for Maisy's first year at Amherst and the fact that she can't share her good news with her best friends has her itching in all the worst places.

Even more, Dakota's production company publicly released news of the deal on Tuesday. She doubts her friends read the industry rags, but they could have seen the news anywhere, heard it from anyone. Meaning, the truth is out there, floating about over her head like Pigpen's dirt cloud.

She's got to tell them first, to get ahead of it, before they find out on their own.

"Hey, you guys?" Like Mack told her months ago, she's just

going to have to rip off the Band-Aid. Take her bruises, make her apologies, and hope forgiveness comes swiftly.

At the moment, however, Andi and Carolina are engrossed in the idea of toilet wine and whether either of them would be desperate enough to make it.

"But if you're using the toilet to ferment the fruit cocktail," Carolina asks, "where do you *go*?"

"In the corner," answers prison expert Andi. "In the showers. Over a drain in the floor. You can claim you're having your period and wear a pad to pee in."

"You guys!" What Fern has to say is far more important.

They turn to her.

"I need to tell you something."

And that's when Emma screams from the other room. "WHAT THE FU—"

Fern and Andi leap to their feet. "Help me up!" Carolina cries.

Emma comes in waving what looks like one of Portia's wedding invitations. "What the hell is he trying to do?"

Fern, the most sober and therefore the quickest, grabs the paper from her hand. It is Portia's invitation. At the bottom is a handwritten note.

Can't wait! Carlton

Fern's voice comes out sounding as incredulous as she feels. "You invited Carlton?"

"You did?" Andi and Carolina echo.

"Of course not!" Emma snatches the invitation back. "I don't have any idea how he managed to get his hands on this."

Andi blows out a deep breath, presumably trying to sober up quick. "It's just a scare tactic. He's snot—" She stops.

Carolina snort laughs.

Emma shoots her the look of death.

Andi starts again. "He's *not* going to show up because he knows he'd be trespassing. You could have him thrown out in front of two hundred guests. The video would go viral in minutes."

"He'd also ruin the wedding. Which is what he wants." Emma clenches her fists and roars. "WHY THE HELL IS HE DOING THIS TO ME?"

"Because he's an ass," Fern answers. "And because he can. He knows a lot of your friends, knows your family. He probably paid some cousin a thousand bucks for their invitation and their silence."

Andi steps forward and gently takes Emma's arm. "It's a million-to-one odds he'll show up tomorrow. Carlton Willis is a bully who's only gotten worse with age. You haven't given him the assurance that he wants, so this is his response."

"I have a thumb drive with a copy of the video in the safe-deposit box at my bank." Carolina's eyes light up, excited by the potential of sending Carlton to the bottom of the swamp from which he came. "Want Queenie to get it and bring it along tomorrow? Then if he shows up, we can play it on the big screen. Put an end to Carlton forever."

Devin had done something sweet and put together a slide show of Portia from the day she was born to the day she and Lyle got engaged. The DJ was scheduled to play it during dinner.

"He can't." Emma's face falls. "Tomorrow is Saturday. The bank will be closed."

"No, I'm sure it's open part of the day." Carolina pulls out her phone and searches the location's hours. "Crap. The drive-though is open until noon but the lobby is closed."

Fern immediately hates herself for it, but she closes her eyes and allows a wave of relief to crash over her. With everyone on high alert for Carlton Willis tomorrow, she doesn't have to say a word about what she's done.

Emma

Get Portia married. The words loop in Emma's head as she slides into her pumps. *Get Portia married.* If she just keeps saying it, everything she can't control—and oh, how much there is—will melt like the last winter snow.

Today, she's walking her daughter down the aisle. Accepting the love and congratulations of her dearest family and friends. Soaking up the light that flashes in Lyle's eyes every time he sees his soon-to-be wife.

She says, "I'm gushing like a Hallmark card."

"What?" Carolina calls from the other side of the bathroom door. She's supposed to help Emma get dressed, but with her bum knee, she's more of a cheerleader than a gopher.

Emma is due at the venue for pictures in ten minutes. She steps out of the bathroom.

Carolina is sitting in a wing chair dragged into the hallway. Upon seeing Emma, she exclaims, "Oh, *Marie.*" She's holding a bag of peanut M&Ms just like Sally did in their favorite, iconic *WHMS* scene.

Tears threaten to ruin Emma's still-wet mascara. "I'm supposed to be wearing a bridal gown when you say that."

Carolina hands over the M&Ms and edges forward to give her squeeze. "Close enough, my precious friend."

The first thing Emma notices when she arrives is Doris gesticulating at a trio of groomsmen like an airport marshal working the tarmac. They've shed their tuxedo jackets and, presumably at Doris's direction, hoisted a marble baptismal font off its footings.

Emma knows what she's doing. The font sits alongside the entrance to where Doris insisted the center aisle begin, and she's been petitioning to have it relocated since their first meeting with the wedding planner.

She'd said, "Can't we just move that thing?" As if it were an appliance cluttering her countertop.

The planner patiently explained that no, its placement is ceremonial and intentional. "The monks brought it over from Italy in 1909."

Emma is tempted to stop the groomsmen before they're discovered and blamed for Doris's actions. But frankly, she has no mental capacity for worrying about Doris Fluke today. She has an ex-fiancé threatening to crash the party and her sanity, an ex-husband whose pregnant girlfriend looks as if she has the Rock of Gibraltar protruding from her belly, and a daughter who deserves one beautiful day to believe that everything will fall into place.

As if she'd summoned him with her thoughts, Devin walks outside and says, "Hey! You seen our girl?"

Emma can't take her eyes off Greta. She's six feet of radiance in a full-length black dress with spaghetti straps that somehow further highlight her amazing boobs and perfectly toned arms. It makes her so angry she wants to spit.

"What?"

"Portia," Devin repeats. "Have you seen her?"

Greta's belly is encased in chiffon. She's very pregnant. A human gift bag puffing over with tissue-paper fun.

She forces herself to look away. "Um—I was just going to peek into the bridal suite now."

Devin moves to follow her, but she has the presence of mind to stop him. "No boys allowed." Every mother deserves one special moment with her child on a day like this.

She turns down the colonnade and makes her way to the room where Portia and her bridesmaids are getting ready. As she retreats, she can hear Doris changing her mind about the baptismal font. "No, I don't think it works there. Move it about a foot to the left."

A moment later, Emma finds Portia, beaming, laughing, and surrounded by her three best friends.

"Mom!" From the shoulders up, she is all bride. The salon swept her hair into an elaborate knot, giving perch to the veil that she and Emma chose, its organza airy as meringue.

The rest of her looks like a lumberjack in a button-down flannel and jeans. For now.

"Hello, ladies. I stopped by to see if you need anything."

Portia checks the clock. "Ooh! I lost track of time. I'd better get into my dress."

The gown is hanging along the wall, steamed and ready.

"You look great, Mom."

Emma couldn't decide on a "mother of the bride" dress, so she bought two. Last night, she tried them both on for Andi, Carolina, and Fern. They voted unanimously for the champagne A-line with the illusion top. "Thank you. I'll return the other one while I'm out returning all the stuff I bought for your Sacramento shower." She winks.

Portia giggles, then mouths, *Thank you.*

Her bridesmaids have pulled the gown from the hanger and unzipped it. One is pooling the skirt on the floor, creating a hole into which Portia can simply step through. She's down to her strapless bra and pantyhose when an explosive *crash!* echoes through the vineyard.

"Dammit, Doris," Emma mumbles. That woman will never learn.

It takes several minutes for the janitorial crew to clean up the mess from the destroyed baptismal font, delaying photographs. By the time the bridal party steps in front of the camera, Doris has sputtered so long and so angrily at the wedding planner that her mascara is running.

"Did I not WARN you?" Doris is so angry her hairdo is shaking. "Did I not SAY the bowl was to be moved?"

"That's it!" The wedding planner throws her hands in the air and walks away. "Portia. Lyle. I wish you every happiness on your big day. But I quit."

Portia gasps. Lyle runs after her. "I'm sure we can work something out."

They can't. The woman is gone. The bridal party, assembled in a line beneath a veranda strung with twinkle lights and flowering jasmine, gapes at her disappearing shape, saying nothing.

"Well, I never—" Doris straightens her back and puffs her wilting hair.

"Mother." Lyle's voice is sharp. "Behave yourself. This is our day."

"But I—"

He walks directly up to her and puts a finger on her lips. "I don't want to hear another word out of you unless it's *congratulations, I love you,* or *Portia is the most beautiful bride I've ever seen.*"

Emma loves her son-in-law so much she could kiss him on the lips, but there's already been enough chaos.

"Glass of champagne for the nerves?" When pictures wrap up, Fern sidles up to Emma holding a glistening crystal flute.

"I love you." Emma takes a long sip. The bubbles tickle her nose and send her belly aflutter. "Where are Andi and Carolina?"

"Out front. On Carlton watch."

Emma had almost, for a brief moment, forgotten him. The champagne suddenly turns sour in her throat.

"Don't worry, though. None of us think he's going to show. Oh, also—" Fern's eyes go wide with good news. "Carolina remembered this morning that Chandler also kept a digital copy of the video. You know, a backup, in case we lost the original. She called him and he agreed to bring it."

"I didn't know he had a copy."

Fern shrugs. "I didn't, either. But if that video was our insurance against blackmail, I guess it makes sense."

Emma supposes it does.

"Excuse me." One of Portia's bridesmaids gingerly interrupts their conversation. "But are you Fern McAllister?"

"I am."

Emma looks at her friend. Does she know this woman somehow?

"I just wanted to tell you that I am such a fan of *Smart Girls Say Yes*. I made my book club read it. We just couldn't get enough." She stops suddenly and looks at Emma. "Oh, my God. Are you *Emma* Emma?"

She inwardly groans but keeps her face placid. This is hardly the first time she's been identified, but it is the first of Portia's friends to make the connection. "That's me."

The bridesmaid squeals. "I loved you! That story at the end. You know, with the revenge porn? What ever happened to that guy?"

Emma and Fern exchange knowing glances. *Funny you should ask*, she wants to say.

"He's history," Fern answers.

"Oh, and congratulations!" She does a little hop and taps her bouquet against Fern's chest. "I saw the announcement in *Variety*. I can't believe Dakota Winters is making it into a movie!"

Did Emma just hear that correctly? "Fern?" She studies her friend's face for clues.

The bridesmaid, however, just keeps talking. "I mean, she's exactly who I'd choose to make it. Is she going to star in it, too? Ooh, have you met her? What's she like? Gorgeous, I bet. And so smart."

"Fern?" Emma can't tolerate one more second without an answer. "Did you sign the deal with Dakota Winters?"

Fern opens her mouth, but nothing comes out.

"She did," squeals Portia's friend. "The announcement said it's in early production, so it won't come out for at least a year but probably two. Is that right?" She directs the question at Fern, whose face is so red the whites of her eyes glow.

"It is," Fern says slowly. Then she looks at Emma. "I'm so sorry I didn't tell you. I was going to and then all the stuff with Carlton—"

Emma stops her. She doesn't want to hear excuses and she sure as hell doesn't want to hear Carlton's name.

Out of the corner of her eye, she sees Doris crossing the veranda toward the colonnade. It gives her a brilliant idea.

"Doris?" She calls while waving her hand. "Doris!"

Doris turns and makes her way over. She's about to speak when Emma interrupts her.

"I know how upset you must be about the whole fiasco with the wedding planner. I explained it all to my friend Fern, here, and she's volunteered to step in for the day."

Emma turns to Fern with a grin that says, *Don't even try to fight me.*

She continues, "Fern is excellent at this sort of thing, so whatever you need, just ask. Absolutely nothing is out-of-bounds." Or perhaps that's too much of a stretch. "At least, nothing that Lyle and Portia agree to, of course."

Fern looks as if she may vomit. The bridesmaid takes her leave. Doris doesn't even stop to thank Emma for coordinating a solution.

"For the amount of money they're charging us here, you'd think they'd be more willing to meet our needs." Doris takes Fern by the elbow and leads her away. Before they moved out of earshot, Emma hears, "I need you to clean a footprint off the aisle runner. If I hadn't unrolled it for inspection, we'd never have known."

There is no preparing for life's milestones. Before becoming pregnant, it's impossible to imagine the sensation of a human life growing in your belly. Nor is it later possible to imagine shoving that same life out of a hole in your nethers the size of a lipstick tube.

Nothing can describe the desperate hope and love and helplessness that is parenthood.

Had anyone tried to tell Emma what it would be like to feel Portia gently take her elbow at the end of the wedding aisle, she wouldn't have believed them. To say she looks beautiful is as insufficient as calling the Grand Canyon "grand," or the sunset over the Pacific "inspiring." She'd once heard a doctor explain that memory is stored in the body more than the brain, and in this moment, Emma understands. She aches with love and joy for this child, this daughter who made her a mother.

Devin is on Portia's other arm, and Emma realizes that nothing he's ever said or done would make her want to strip him of this moment. He is Portia's father as much as she is her mother. They are both better, more complete human beings because of her.

The music begins to play. The wedding is running a half hour behind. Emma doesn't even want to imagine how much that marble font is going to cost Doris and Sylvester. But she doesn't have to. It's not her problem.

"Ready?" Portia whispers.

Devin answers, "Let's roll, Princess."

Emma can't speak. She can barely walk. Her feet have left the ground.

Fern

She is pinned between the wall and an imitation ficus tree. Doris is furious that the floral arrangements on the head table are twenty-four inches tall rather than eighteen, per her instructions.

"You'll have to ask the janitors for a pair of shears," she'd said. "Cut six inches off each of the stems. But be discreet about it! We don't want our guests thinking this was a DIY wedding."

Fern has no intention of asking the janitorial team for anything, not even a hammer to beat Doris over the head with.

"Imagine meeting you here." Mack approaches with a shit-eating grin on his face and a beer in his hand. "Regretting keeping your announcement secret yet?"

"I regretted it from the beginning." She reaches for his beer and takes a long sip. "But I'm taking my punishment. I deserve it."

"Taking your punishment by hiding from Doris?"

Fern scowls at him. He doesn't need to rub it in. "I'm on break. Every worker is mandated to have a break after a certain number of hours. It's the law."

Mack's grin softens, his sympathetic side reemerging. "Need anything to eat? I can bring you a basket of rolls."

"Yes, please." She honestly doesn't know what she'd do without Mack. "And promise you'll check on me before you leave tonight. My invitation to the after-party at Emma's has probably been rescinded."

Carolina

"*Psst*. Wanna see what I got in my pocket?"

"That wasn't funny the first time you said it, Chandler." She laughs, anyway. He's in rare form tonight, acting like a historically underrated knight in shining armor who can't believe his turn of luck. His beautiful loyal wife, Harriet, is sitting next to him, and he's got a thumb drive in his pocket that contains all the video evidence they need to send Carlton Willis running for cover.

Thankfully, they haven't needed it. The friends presented a confident and united front for Emma last night, but Carolina is suddenly so relieved that Carlton hasn't spoiled the wedding that she drops her head onto Queenie's shoulder for support.

"You okay?" he asks, drawing the hair from her eyes.

"More than," she answers. "And thanks."

"For what?"

"Everything." She smiles to herself, listening to his heart beating deeply in his chest. "But also, for the hair." She points to the spot where he cleared away the rogue strands.

He kisses the crown of her head. "I figured it might bug you."

"It was in my eyes." She draws her face up to look at him. "Only now, I can see you."

Andi

She's washing her hands in the women's restroom when Emma steps out of a stall.

Andi's heart swells at the sight of her. Her friend looks like a woman who's having a wonderful evening.

"You having fun? Everything seems to be going beautifully, early hitches aside." She'd heard about the font fiasco, and if that was the worst thing that happened, this wedding would be one for the history books. The kind with happy endings.

"It's a dream," Emma replies. "Portia is smiling and that's what matters, right?"

Andi closes in for a hug. "Think of everything you've managed to overcome since the engagement. Doris Fluke's unattainable standards. Devin's surprise second act. And we won't even mention the guy who didn't have the nerve to show his face."

"No, we won't." Emma leans against the counter, wiggling her toes and momentarily relieving the pressure in her feet. "But you're right. I shouldn't have been worried. Deep down, he's nothing but a coward."

"Bullies don't like it when people stand up to them."

"Or when people have collateral on them."

"That, too."

Emma slides her feet back into her pumps. "Okay, can I have one minute to be petty?"

Andi laughs. "I'll give you two."

"Devin and his need to constantly touch Greta, am I right? It's like, if he's not touching her, he's worried she may not be real."

Andi had noticed the PDA, especially the kissing. She wasn't going to bring it up to Emma in case she hadn't noticed, but everyone at their table found it obnoxious. Dom said he looked like a dog marking his territory. Queenie and Carolina speculated it was just the opposite, not dominance but a sign of submission.

"Maybe she demands it," Queenie offered.

Carolina smirked. "She's probably in charge in bed, too."

Chandler just wanted to know what it was about Devin that Greta found attractive. "He's not rich enough to land a woman like her."

Harriet rolled her eyes. "I didn't know you were rich before I fell in love with you."

"Yeah, but—" Chandler flexed his jelly bean of a bicep. "I had all this to offer."

While the rest of them laughed, Andi explained, "Harriet fell in love with you, Chandler, because thanks to us, she could see how loyal you are. That's hard to find and, once you do, you hang on tight."

Dom took her hand and squeezed it. She loved her man, every big asset and tiny quirk. All of him. He was the one she had been waiting for all those years ago, and he found her.

A drop of water hits her in the face, jolting her from her thoughts.

"You with me?" Emma laughs, wiping her hands.

"Sorry." She blinks twice, clearing her head. "Anyway, Devin. I agree with you, and so does our entire table."

"Oh, well. At least he's not my problem anymore."

"Speaking of—" Andi wiggles an eyebrow. "When are you going to introduce us to Benjamin?"

Emma swats her on the arm. "Not until you promise not to do that when you meet him."

"But it's going well?" Andi prompts. Emma deserves happiness. She shouldn't have to be alone if she doesn't want to be.

"It's good." Emma flashes her a smile. "Not 'kissing him in front of two hundred guests' good yet, but good."

Andi winks. "I love that for you."

Emma winks back. "Thanks, Alexis."

"We need to plan a *Schitt's Creek* super-marathon. Nothing but junk food, good wine, and small-town Canada for two days."

"I'll say yes," Emma grins.

"I love this for us!"

Emma turns as she hears the DJ begin his set. "I'd better get back out there."

"Right behind you."

Emma reaches for the door.

"Oh, my God, Ems. What did you do?"

She gasps. *"What?"*

Andi reaches for her friend's skirt and tugs at it. It takes a bit of force, but she draws the fabric loose. "You were about to walk out with your dress tucked into your SPANX."

Emma

The dancing is about to begin, and, thanks to Andi, Emma isn't about to hit the floor with her underwear waving hello to a roomful of guests. How mortifying that would have been.

The DJ announces the bride and groom's first dance. Portia and Lyle have been taking lessons and they glide across the parquet to Sinatra's "Fly Me to the Moon." She can see Lyle counting out the foxtrot beat as they go—*slow, slow, quick, quick.*

When the song ends, the DJ invites everyone onto the floor. Emma thought there would be a song for the bride to dance with her parents and the groom to dance with his. Then she remembers that Portia felt anxious about Emma and Devin being in such close proximity to each other, and Lyle's father, Sylvester, claims the only way anyone will catch him on the dance floor is if he's dead.

What a strange man. How did Lyle come from these people?

Benjamin stands and crosses the floor to offer her his hand. It's the first time she's seen him at the wedding, though she's felt his presence the entire time. "May I have this dance?"

She accepts. "Do you remember the dances held in the school lunchroom? We generated so much heat all crowded in there that I'd come out drenched to my underwear."

Ben wraps an arm around her waist and pulls her close.

Her first instinct is to pull back. People are watching.

Then she sees Devin plant a deep sensuous kiss on Greta's lips and decides that she no longer cares. She and Ben have probably danced wrapped up in each other far more times than she ever did with Devin. When they were married, Devin claimed he had "two left feet and an ego that was easily bruised." Now that man appears nowhere to be found.

She leans in, letting her cheek brush against Benjamin's chest. He smells of Irish Spring.

"You are the loveliest woman here tonight," he whispers. "Besides Portia, of course."

Emma raises her head to look at his face. The boy she once knew is still there, a bit wrinkled, but fundamentally the same. Eyes that flicker when he smiles, lips that purse when he thinks. And his chin—square and chiseled like a statue she could have found in their art history textbook.

This is a good man. She knows because it's her body telling her so. Not the sexual parts of her body, though they could certainly use some attention. But the core of her. The part that tells her to run when she's afraid, and to worry when she can't make sense of the world. Right now, its message rings loud and clear.

Stand still. Do not run. Do not worry. You are exactly where you are meant to be.

"Ben?" She doesn't and won't take her eyes off his face.

"Yes?" His eyes are laughing. He's happy to be here.

"What do you say we do this *thang*?" She sounds like a middle-aged woman who's forgotten she's no longer sixteen.

"This *thang*?" he mimics. "Tell me what this *thang* is."

"You and me," she says simply. "The two of us and no one else."

His dimples appear as he smiles.

She smiles back. "I'll say yes if you say yes."

He answers her with a kiss.

★ ★ ★

The evening could have ended at that moment, and she would have been happy. She'd fought the idea of Benjamin for so long. But to move more quickly would have been wrong, and if she had, they might not be here tonight, peaceful in each other's arms.

They're still on the dance floor when he squeezes her hand. "Glass of water?" he offers.

"Yes, please." They've been dancing so long she's lost track of time. And if she's not mistaken, her underwear is sticking to her butt, just like old times.

Benjamin turns for the bar just as Devin plants yet another kiss on Greta the Magnificent. For heaven's sake. What does he think he's proving?

Like Ben, Devin, too, makes his way toward the bar. Greta, now alone, moves off to the side and plants herself against the wall.

Emma scans the tables for her friends. She's hardly spoken to them all evening. Maybe she ought to take a minute to say hi.

"You!" A woman's voice echoes above the noise of the music. "Who do you think you are kissing my son like that?"

It's Devin's mother. Emma would recognize that voice even if she were dead and buried six feet underground.

She sees her then, driving her walker across the room with the determination of Daisy Duke trying to outrun Sheriff Rosco P. Coltrane.

"He is a married man. Have you no shame?"

Faces are turning now. People notice the ruckus and start to whisper among themselves. Where is Devin? It's impossible that every guest except for him can hear what's going on.

Greta leans down to speak with the older woman, who is now shaking a finger in her face.

"You are NOT having his baby!" shouts Emma's former in-law. "At least not if I have anything to do with it!"

She was always a demanding woman, but this is outrageous even by her standards. Dementia has made her mean.

"WHORE!" She begins to pound the wheels of her walker against the floor. "WHORE! WHORE! WHORE!"

Emma can't take any more of this. "Mother May!" She bridges the twenty-foot gap in about two seconds flat. "Leave Greta alone. This is Devin's girlfriend." It's the first time those words come out of her mouth without being tailed by vomit.

"No, Emma, YOU are his wife. What are you doing letting Devin run around with such a Jezebel?"

She has to bite her tongue to keep from shouting back, "You're the one who raised him!"

Instead, Emma extends an open palm to Greta, taking her hand. "Devin and I aren't married anymore. He's with Greta now. She's about to give you another granddaughter."

The word stops her, short-circuits Mother May's tirade. She straightens and says proudly, "I have a beautiful granddaughter named Portia. She's graduating from high school soon. On the honor roll!"

"Yes, she is." Emma lets go of Greta and guides Mother May gently away. "You bought her a lovely dress to wear to graduation. Blue with mother-of-pearl buttons."

"Devin was his class valedictorian." This was a fact Emma has heard exactly ten thousand and twenty-eight times. "He went on to law school. If the president is a smart man, he'll nominate Devin to the Supreme Court."

"Now—" Emma can see Devin sprinting from across the room "—wouldn't that be something?"

The guests have mostly gone home, all but a table or two, which includes one with Portia and her bridesmaids. They're exchanging last hugs, trading final toasts.

"To the most beautiful bride ever!" they cheer. "Until next month," one adds, "when Morgan gets married!"

Cheers!

"Hey, Mrs. May, er, Emma." The bridesmaid who broke the news about Fern motions her over. "We were talking about your amazing group of friends. We just hope we're always as close as you all are."

Emma smiles. "It's pretty incredible, isn't it?" The sentiment sends a jolt of adrenaline up her spine. *Fern.* "Excuse me, ladies. There's someone I need to speak to."

She finds her at the valet stand with Mack.

"Please don't go home," Emma says. "I'm still mad at you, but I can't torture you anymore."

"I drove to Walgreens to buy foot powder for Doris's shoes." Fern shakes her head. "That woman is—"

"Something else, I know," Emma finishes.

Fern's face fills with clouds. "I'm so sorry, Ems. I was such a coward."

"Maybe," she concedes. "Though I think I probably have to account for a few of my own choices. I don't know that I ever gave you a fair shot."

The car arrives. Mack gives Fern a quizzical look.

"Go ahead," she says. "It's girlfriend night."

When they return to Portia and her friends, Andi and Carolina are at the table, and they have the women in stitches.

"What are you telling them?" Emma sounds as if she's scolding, which maybe she is. Just a little bit. She still doesn't love the idea of everyone in the world knowing the things she did during that (in)famous year in San Francisco.

"They asked what's our secret to staying friends," explains Andi.

Carolina nods. "And I said a true friend will put up with you even when you're acting like your messiest, most pitiful self."

Andi chimes in, "Then she told them you almost walked out of the restroom with your skirt tucked into your underwear."

"I did!" Emma may as well just embrace the truth. "I'm plenty messy and pitiful."

"And I'm a coward," adds Fern. "They didn't know about the film deal until you broke the news today."

She nods toward the offending bridesmaid who covers her squeal with her palm. "Oh, my God, I'm so sorry."

"Not your fault," Fern protests. "I should have fessed up months ago."

Emma laughs. "So I punished her by putting her on Doris duty all day."

"Deserved it." Fern raises her hand.

As if summoned, Doris appears from around the corner. "Oh, there you are!"

Emma stops her. "Doris, I hope you had a wonderful day. But I'm sorry to say that Fern is officially off duty."

"I only need—"

"I know." Emma takes her by the shoulder and gently turns her around. "Seems like there's always too much to do and never enough time to do it, am I right?"

Portia waits until Doris sputters away and says, "I heard what happened with Grandma. I'm so sorry you had to deal with that."

The apology pokes Emma in the heart like a pin. "Portia." She takes her daughter by the face. "This day was about you and Lyle becoming a family. You don't have to apologize for a thing."

"But you had to play nice with Greta."

"I did it for you. I'd do anything for you, Love Bug."

They stay in their private bubble as long as the moment allows. When it ends, Emma adds one last note.

"Remember, ladies. We all need rescuing from time to time, so don't turn your back on the people who need you."

The drive back to Emma's house is quiet. Benjamin introduced himself to her friends by offering them a ride.

"I won't stay. But at least I can save you the cost of an Uber."

Once he's gone, the gushing begins.

"Him!" declares Carolina. "Keep him."

"Ditto," says Fern.

To which Andi replies, "You're a writer, for crying out loud. Why do you always say 'ditto'?"

Carolina hobbles to the kitchen for the bottle of champagne chilling in the fridge.

Andi opens her gigantic tote and pulls out four pairs of matching Girlfriend Collective lounge pants. "I just figured we'd need them at some point this weekend."

Emma doesn't hesitate to kick off her shoes. "Throw me a pair." Her belly sighs with relief as she unzips her skirt.

The friends each do the same.

Andi didn't buy sweatshirts along with the loungers, so the four of them sit in the wingbacks and on the couch, wide-leg sweats on the bottom, silk blouses up top.

"What's that saying?" Fern asks. "Business in front, party in the back?"

"That's a mullet," says Carolina. "We're business on the top, party on the bottom."

"Ah. Right."

Carolina pops the cork.

Andi clears her throat. "Fern, let's just get this out of the way. That was a shitty thing you did not trusting us enough to tell us you'd signed the film deal."

Fern sighs. "I know. It ruined all the excitement for me. Which, I admit, this isn't about me, but I say that so you know I've been punishing myself and learned my lesson."

"I forgive you," Andi says. "And to be honest, I'm glad you signed."

"Excuse me?"

"Yeah. Those stories are ours. We lived them, and they made us who we are. What do we have to hide?"

"Oh, my God." Fern points at her. "Say that again."

"Which part? The stories made us who we are?"

"No. That we lived them." Fern springs to her feet and snaps

GRETCHEN ANTHONY

her fingers. "This whole time I've been rationalizing my choice by talking about how badly I wanted to see my book brought to life. But that already happened. Like Andi just said, we *lived* those stories. They are us as much as we are them. Dakota Winters can work her magic to make an incredible movie, but it may as well be a work of fiction. Only *we* were there."

"And Chandler," Carolina adds. "He gets pissy when we forget him."

"And Chandler," Fern admits.

Emma watches her friends laugh and quibble together as they've done so many times before. "Okay," she says finally. "I'm in. Go make this thing, Fern. Wake the world up to what a great time we've had."

"Thank God," Carolina says. "I'm way too curious about who they're going to cast to play me."

Andi laughs. "Meg Ryan no longer looks like I did when I was twenty-nine, so I don't want anyone to play me if she can't."

"You never looked like Meg Ryan," says Fern. "You have red hair and freckles."

"I don't care. She's my favorite. That's who I'd want."

Carolina scowls. "No. You're more of a Carrie Fisher. She'd have been perfect to play you."

"In her thirties," said Andi. "God rest her soul."

"God rest Carrie," they all say.

They hold a moment of silence. Until Carolina says, "Ho. Ly. Shit."

She's reading her phone and the friends holler at her until she reads whatever is so astounding aloud.

"'Tech entrepreneur Carlton Willis dropped his bid to win the California US Senate race this evening, citing a desire to, quote, "protect my family from further harm as a result of recent unfounded and scurrilous accusations."'"

"Oh, my God," says Andi.

"No wonder he didn't show," Fern adds.

Emma rolls her eyes. "What an ass." She has known he's

been an ass for twenty-five years, but somehow he continues to prove himself.

Fern sits up. "What else does the article say? Anything new?"

"No," says Carolina. "Just the same old BS about him being shocked and horrified since he's such a big supporter of women."

Emma shoots out of her chair. She's so thrilled by Carlton's news she can no longer sit still. "Let's celebrate. I'll go get the lighter."

As she hustles toward the kitchen, Carolina asks what she needs a lighter for. "Are you hoarding a secret stash of fireworks or something?"

"Better," she says. "Put your shoes on."

The women follow her out the front door and across the front yard.

"What are you up to Emma?" Andi says with a giggle.

Emma opens Kent's side gate. The box is full, and exactly where she'd left it more than a week ago.

"C'mon."

Andi is on her heels. "Is this legal, Ems?"

She chuckles. "It sure ought to be."

She places the box at the base of Kent's front steps, far enough from the roof that she won't start a fire, but in perfect view of his doorbell.

"I forgot something. Hang on." As she turns back toward the house, she hears Carolina say, "Why does Emma have an Amazon box full of dog poop?"

She returns seconds later with a can of lighter fluid. "Back up!" She throws her arms open, clearing a wide circle, then opens the can and squirts a hefty helping of fuel onto the cardboard.

"Tell me you're not planning to do what it looks like," says Andi.

"I think you should go for it," says Fern.

Carolina smirks. "Glad I brought the champagne."

Before clicking the lighter, Emma decides this moment deserves to be memorialized. "Four months ago, my neighbor, Kent's dog began pooping in my yard. I was patient about it at first, but I'd soon had enough. So, I politely asked Kent to fix the hole in the fence through which the dog escapes. I even dropped off the number for my handyman. But did Kent heed my pleas?"

She looks to her friends for a response. "Well, did he?"

"No!" cries Carolina.

"And when I collected enough doggy bags to fill a LaCroix sparkling water box that I then left on his front porch, did Kent do anything to stop the madness?"

"Hell no!" cried Carolina.

"So tonight, Kent, I'm afraid you leave me no choice but to demand your attention."

She raises the lighter above her head and clicks. An orange flame lights the night sky.

"May this small flame light a gigantic fire under your lazy ass."

The lighter falls into the box. The fire explodes, sending red and yellow sparks of fireworks shooting into the blackness.

"'My country 'tis of thee—'" Fern sings.

Carolina takes a swig of the champagne and passes the bottle.

"This is insane," says Andi, taking it.

"I love you guys," says Emma. "I really, really do."

★ ★ ★ ★ ★

Acknowledgments

Let's begin with a riddle.

You have me today, and tomorrow you'll have more; As your time passes, I'm not easy to store; I don't take up space, but I'm only in one place; I am what you saw, but not what you see. What am I?

Well, this is embarrassing. I forgot the answer. Somebody let me know if you figure it out. The point is, I'm a middle-aged woman with too much noise in my brain to remember things like garbage day is Thursday, and it's a left turn to the dentist, but a right turn to the gynecologist. (Boy, did I scare that hygienist.)

And yet! The years and people that inspired this book are carved into my soul. Andi, Carolina, Mack, Dom, Queenie, and Chandler, you know who you are. Thanks for the back then and the now. Double thanks for letting me twist your real persons into the fictional expressions on these pages. All the best parts are yours. The bad stuff, I made up.

Thank you to the many writer and book friends who support and inspire me, even when I act like a whiney child. Josh

Moehling, Laska Nygaard, J. Ryan Stradal, Mindy Mejia, Lorna Landvik, Kathleen West, Nicole Kronzer, Helen Ellis, Pamela Klinger-Horn, Mary O'Malley, Maxwell Gregory, Judith Kissner, Gretchen West, Jennifer Jubenville, Annie and Matthew and the team at Magers & Quinn, and all the people that I'm forgetting here because I do that. A lot.

Holly Root of Root Literary, my agent extraordinaire. Thanks for seeing my potential, especially when I can't.

Laura Brown and Nicole Luongo, the impossibly unstoppable dynamic editing duo. It took two of you to finally pull this book out of me. Frankly, I was scared. That phone call (you know the one) made all the difference. How strong you are! I'm so very grateful to have you.

To all the crew at HarperCollins and Park Row Books… In Minnesota, we have a term for people like you: Super Duper!

Hey, Mom, I did it again.

Thanks to my brother, Andy, who supplied me with horror stories from the dozens of weddings he's performed and loosely inspired the nuptial chaos in this book.

Chad, Connor, Carsten, and J. I love you guys. I really, really do.

Gretchen Anthony
September 2023